THE FAIRY GARDEN

Peter Stipe

Lavender Press
an imprint of Blue Fortune Enterprises, LLC

THE FAIRY GARDEN
Copyright © 2020 by Peter Stipe

This book is a work of fiction. Names, characters, businesses, organizations, places, events and incidents either are the product of the author's imagination or are used fictitiously. Any resemblance to actual persons, living or dead, events, or locales is entirely coincidental.

For information contact :
Blue Fortune Enterprises, LLC
Lavender Press
P.O. Box 554
Yorktown, VA 23690
http://blue-fortune.com

Cover design by Wesley Miller, WAMCreate, hi@wamcreate.co

ISBN: 978-1-948979-41-2
First Edition: September 2020

Dedication

For Elliott, Ginny, and Miles
And for all those who believe in fairies

1
Elizabeth - Birth

ELIZABETH SQUEEZED HER EYES TIGHT to shut out the light. It was dark where she came from. It was quiet. She floated, embraced on all sides by her mother's pink presence. Suddenly, the water left her, and she was thrust out of warm comfort into a cold, bright, awful place. Her head ached, pounding from the pressure of the birth.

She flailed her arms and kicked her legs, newfound freedom, no longer contained, but frightening her with the possibility of falling. She breathed in and screamed in terror. Enormous hands cupped her body and head, supporting her in the midst of cold space. A sudden sharp pull at her belly and the cord was cut, severing her from the life she had always known. There was no pain. The finality of the cut made her cry out again. She was alone in the world now.

A warm cloth slid softly over her body, new wetness, removing the old, familiar coat. She was wrapped in heated fabric, her arms and legs confined. It felt good to be swathed, but it was not her home, not the warm, quiet place where she had always lived. She cried again, a despairing wail lost in the emptiness of this new space.

They floated above her, tiny lights amid the terrifying brightness. "She is beautiful," they chimed. "She is lovely. She is like we are. We must tell the others she is here." No one heard them but the newborn baby.

"It will be all right, little one," the fairies sang, comforting her. "You will be happy in your new life. Your family loves you. They will care for you."

In her mind she sang a reply. "I want to go back. It was good. I was warm. I was never hungry. I was content inside my mother. I have to go back."

"You cannot," they told her. "You are here now. We will watch over you."

Overcome with exhaustion from her journey, Elizabeth fell asleep.

2
Elizabeth – Age Thirty

ELIZABETH SAT AT THE BLACK wrought-iron table on the brick-paved terrace, holding a glass of red wine by its thin stem. It was cool in the shade of the oak and crepe myrtle that guarded the garden. She pushed her auburn hair back from her face and peered out into the dark foliage, watching for her daughter Livvy, playing on the paths that wound through the garden. She couldn't see her little girl, but she heard her singing.

The house and the garden were hers now, bequeathed to her in grandfather Papa's will. He also left a sealed letter for her. Her brother Michael had handed her an envelope. "The will says you get the house. Mom and Dad get half of Papa's investments. I get the other half. I'm sorry there's no money for you. Only Papa's house. You'll be okay, right?" Michael rested a reassuring hand on her shoulder for a moment, sincerely concerned for his younger sister.

"I'm fine. Everything is fine," she answered grimly.

No, it wasn't fine. It wouldn't be now with Papa gone. But Michael didn't understand, nor did her parents. There had been so much loss in the past months. The house was all she had from Papa, but it was enough. She thought of Papa's letter.

Dear Elizabeth,

I know how much you have loved my house and my garden. Even when you were a little girl, it was your special place. It is yours now. I understand money would have been nice for you to have, but if I had left the house to anyone else in the family, they would have sold it. There's so much here. It's more than just a house and a garden. It's worth more than money. You need to be the one to keep it. And with your job, and Lucas' legal and political career, you are set for money. Take care of our house. I hope you make it yours and enjoy many years sharing the garden with our little girl Olivia.
Love, Papa.

Papa must have written the letter months ago. He didn't know Lucas would leave her. Elizabeth hadn't seen that coming, either.

Elizabeth looked back at the house behind her, at the French doors from the terrace which led into the living room, at the white columns supporting the roof that sheltered the half of the terrace closest to the house. It was a wonderful house, a brick colonial with more white-painted columns in the front. But it was the backyard, the garden Elizabeth loved. Papa's backyard wasn't really a yard at all. It was a long, formal English garden, stretching behind the house, bound on all sides by moss and ivy-covered weathered brick walls. The walls were high, too high for a child to see over, too tall for even an adult to climb easily. Oak, magnolia and crepe myrtle trees hung over the whole garden. Brick-lined walks made of crushed white oyster shells separated beds of myrtle and pachysandra.

Spaced throughout the garden were three circular brick-paved junctions of the paths, rimmed with boxwood. Two, on either side of the garden, were banked with wrought-iron benches and dominated by statues of dancing children on brick pedestals; a boy at one end and a girl on the other. Real children weren't allowed to play in the garden—they might crush the flowers. Elizabeth remembered her childhood here, being permitted only to walk along the paths. She had the same rule in place now for Livvy, but Livvy, like her mother when she was young, darted off the paths once she was out of the sight of grown-ups. The third circle, the largest, was in the center of the garden. A bronze armillary, mounted on the top of a short column, consumed the middle of the circle. Verdigris stained rings, marking the cycles of the seasons and the time of day, formed a hollow globe. The metal rings were pierced by a narrow bronze shaft, tipped with a polished brass arrowhead, pointing due north.

Livvy danced into view on one of the paths. The tiny girl pirouetted around the armillary with her arms stretched above her head. She was five and had the innocence of a child; every day was a new adventure. Livvy threw her arms wide and spun with her eyes closed, her face turned up into the springtime sunshine. Her long sundress, her choice of dress-up clothes for Papa's funeral, twirled around her body. Inside the wide-flung dress, her narrow torso was as lithe as a sapling. She sang a song, her voice melodious though the words were hard for Elizabeth to make out. Dizzy from spinning, Livvy fell and sat, giggling on the grassy plot next to the white seashell path. When her balance returned, she stood. She leaned down and peered into the flowerbeds, holding her white-blonde curls back from her face. She began talking to herself, hovering over the blossoms. Then she straightened and walked deeper into the garden, still talking quietly, her child's voice sing-song.

Elizabeth was concerned when she lost sight of her daughter. She worried what could happen to her baby unattended out there in the vastness of the formal garden. What if she fell and was hurt? What dangers lurked out there? No! Be logical, Elizabeth reminded herself. It will be all right. The garden is walled in. It's private and safe. Except for the fairies.

She relaxed for a moment. Still, she had lost so much this past year. First, her husband Lucas, then her Papa, her grandfather. Both losses were unexpected. Don't troubles come in threes? She couldn't bear to lose Livvy, too.

Elizabeth held up her glass, catching the sun. The wine was deep burgundy, tinted pink, orange, lavender and purple where it washed the edge of the sparkling crystal glass. She swirled it, sniffed and took a sip. *This moment should be perfect*, she thought, *with the sunshine, the warmth, the wine, and Livvy dancing in the garden. It would have been wonderful to share this time with Lucas or Papa, or both.* But aside from Livvy, she felt abandoned and alone now. Lucas had left her and now Papa was gone. A fresh wave of the despair washed over her. She willed herself not to allow tears. She reminded herself as she had done all day, and at the funeral, "Livvy needs me to be strong, now more than ever.

There was a stir of motion on the garden path, Livvy running up the path laughing. "Mommy, guess what?" She jumped up the brick steps from the garden one at a time and climbed, wriggling onto her mother's lap.

Elizabeth set her wine on the table, being careful not to spill. "What, Honey Bunny?"

"There's fairies in the garden!"

Elizabeth hugged her daughter. She had been just about Livvy's age when she first discovered the fairies. It had made her feel special to talk with the fairies, to dream about them at night. Maybe she had clung to her belief in them too long. Maybe, she wondered, that belief had blinded her to the hard realities of life with Lucas. Elizabeth had always counted on her fairy friends to save her from dangers and hard times. There was no way to turn back the clock, no way to bring back either Lucas or Papa.

Elizabeth turned to her little girl. "Really? Fairies? Tell me about them."

"There's all kinds of fairies. And you wanna know a secret?"

"Sure. What's the secret?"

Livvy squirmed closer, cupped her hand and whispered in her mommy's ear, her moist breath tickling. "One of them is named Olivia. Just like me. And she's my own special fairy."

"Really." Elizabeth said the word as a statement, not a question, her tone flat, emotionless. She looked across the white-painted railing into the garden. The garden was beautiful in the spring sunshine with the early flowers. It was filled with sounds and never-ending motion. She heard the hum of the bees and other insects. Birds sang, flying from tree to tree and hopping from branch to branch. There were butterflies and dragonflies. She saw no fairies. For years the fairies were there for her but now they were gone. For that she was glad. She'd had enough of them.

"Yes, Mommy. Really. There's Olivia and the Queen and a grumpy man-fairy called Thomas. They're the only ones I've met but I think there's more."

"Oh, I expect there are more. Do you like seeing the fairies out there?"

"Yes."

"Well, go play. See if there are more fairies. See if they live in a castle."

"Okay." Livvy slid off Elizabeth's lap. Then she paused and leaned to her mommy, burying her face in Elizabeth's lap. "I miss Daddy," she mumbled.

"And Papa, too. But I want Daddy to come home."

"I know, sweetheart. But Daddy's gone to live somewhere else. And Papa passed away. You know they both love you. Papa's looking down from heaven right now, watching you."

"I know." Her voice betrayed her sadness.

Livvy was a child with a child's resilience. She recovered quickly, pulled away and brightened. "Can I go play now? Do you think there are unicorns in the garden too?"

"I don't know. Why don't you go and see?"

Little Livvy hopped down the steps, one at a time, reaching her hand up on the stair railing. Then she ran back into the garden, her white sandals flying along the path. Elizabeth sat alone again, watching Livvy play. Seeing her imagine the fairies brought it all back to her. She had believed the fairies were real for years. Papa played along, making her believe he also saw them. Maybe he did believe in them; maybe he didn't. It didn't matter now he was gone.

True, the fairies had given her support she never could get from her parents. But where did believing in fairies get her? Anger crept in as she reminisced. If they were real, what had they done to bring her to this point in her life? Should she tell Livvy the fairies weren't real? After her experiences with the fairies, she didn't want her daughter growing up depending on them the way she had.

Out in the garden, Livvy leaned to the flowers again and began talking to the blossoms. The breeze brought her child's voice clearly up to Elizabeth. "Hello again, little fairy," Livvy said. "Where is the Queen?"

3
Elizabeth – Age Six

TODAY WAS SUPPOSED TO BE her special day at Papa's house, her birthday, but Elizabeth was restless. She sat at the table on the terrace, head down, chin tucked, listening to Papa and Daddy talk about baseball. Their beer mugs dripped with condensation. Elizabeth didn't care about baseball. She looked hopefully to Momma, but Momma was sitting quietly with her thin-stemmed glass of white wine. Occasionally she chimed in with her own thoughts. There were glasses of lemonade on ice for Elizabeth and her brother. Elizabeth gulped hers. Michael sipped more slowly, mostly leaving his glass on the coaster. His shoulders hunched, his eyes were focused on a video game, his thumbs darting. She fidgeted. In the garden, cicadas chirped.

Elizabeth sucked on her paper straw, slurping the last of her lemonade and rattling the ice cubes, craving the grownups' attention. Papa leaned back in his chair, a twinkle in his eye. "Elizabeth, do you think there are fairies living in the garden? I'll bet there are. Why don't you go take a look? Be very quiet so they won't hear you coming. Then come back and tell us if you find any."

At last! Something to do, somewhere to go, she thought. She hadn't gotten any presents yet. *Maybe they hid my birthday presents in the garden!* Elizabeth slid off her chair cushion and tiptoed without a word down the brick steps into the garden. She started like a tightrope walker, arms out, balancing on the bricks that edged the white crushed-shell walk, but she kept stumbling. She shifted to the middle of the path, picking her feet up high and placing each step carefully so the broken shells wouldn't make a sound. Papa had said noise would scare away any fairies. Elizabeth paused and looked back. Behind her on the brick terrace Papa and her family sat at the black iron table watching her, smiling. *They're laughing,* she thought. *They don't believe I'll find any fairies. But I know I will!*

Once Elizabeth was out of earshot, Papa confided to her parents with a quiet chuckle, his voice soft so Elizabeth wouldn't hear. "I made a tiny fairy figure for her. I shaped it out of white polymer, grinding it and polishing it the way I did back when I was a dentist, working with crowns and bridges. Then I painted it. Only one fairy is finished so far. But I have another one in my shop, ready to paint. They're no bigger than this." He held up his index finger. "They're little dancing fairies with tinted glass wings I glued on their backs. They're mounted on steel wires so they won't fall over when I stick them in the dirt. I put the one I finished out there in the flowers. She'll like it when she finds it."

Elizabeth wasn't usually allowed to roam in the garden at Papa's house without a grownup beside her. There were flower beds, and Elizabeth knew the rules. She wasn't to go into them. On the rare moments she was allowed into the garden, she was ordered to stay on the white shell walks. But where could she go, what could she do without straying from them? Elizabeth moped along the path thinking, *Momma and Daddy worry I'll run in the flowers, breaking the blossoms. It isn't any fun.*

She moved along the white walkway slowly, quietly, a step at a time. Early summer Virginia sun baked through the trees. Elizabeth squeezed her eyes shut and tipped her head up, seeing red as the sun beat down on her eyelids. She peered into the foliage again, blinking, and slipped farther into the garden, under the trees. It was cooler in the shade among the greenery of the garden than it was on the terrace. Butterflies and dragonflies flashed, dancing in the sunlight filtering through the leaves above her. Sunbeams shone, caught in the mist that rose from puddles, remnants of an earlier shower. Bees hummed.

She stopped. At the edge of the path, among the flowers and the myrtle plants, beneath a rose bush, she saw the fairy. It stood perfectly still, one leg reaching out with toes pointed in a position Elizabeth had learned in her Tiny Dancer beginners' ballet class. The fairy figure wore a short pastel pink and blue gown, cinched at the waist with a thin yellow belt. Blonde hair fell in waves around a miniature face, the locks held back by a garland crown of little flowers. Lightly colored wings like those on the dragonflies spread from the fairy's back.

Elizabeth squatted for a closer look, her smocked birthday party dress tenting out around her knees. The little fairy posed unmoving, frozen in its dance step position. "Hello, little fairy. What's your name?" Elizabeth asked.

A second fairy appeared from beneath a low-spreading boxwood and stood next to the dancing fairy figure with her arms clasped behind her back. They were dressed alike; the second fairy also wearing a short light-blue tunic, bound around the waist with a saffron thread that might have been drawn from inside a flower blossom. This fairy's hair was dark auburn, exactly the same color as Elizabeth's, falling in curls, held back from her face by another tiny garland. This fairy had no wings.

"I am Olivia," said the second fairy. Elizabeth didn't hear a voice. She heard only a tinkling sound like a faraway wind chime, but she understood what the music meant and knew what the second fairy said. "What is your name?" continued the second fairy.

"I'm Elizabeth."

"Elizabeth! What a beautiful name. Are you named for your queen?"

"My queen? That's silly! We don't have a queen. We have a president. And he's a man."

The fairy gave a short laugh, the sound of a small bird. "Oh, how foolish of me. Of course you do not have a queen. That was years ago. Long before you were born. Back at a time when we first came to this place, hiding on your sailing ships. I forget sometimes how long it has been and how few years you humans live."

"Are you a fairy queen? Or a princess?" whispered Elizabeth so quietly only the fairy could hear her. Intuitively, Elizabeth knew this moment and this fairy were not for her parents, or Michael, or maybe not even for Papa, though this was his garden. Her family wouldn't understand. They'd tease her.

"No, I am just Olivia. I am nothing but a small, ordinary fairy. I am nobody special. But I know the Queen of the Fairies. Sometimes I play with the Princess but she has to stay inside the palace. It is her place until she becomes the queen. The princess is still very small."

"Is this the princess?" Elizabeth touched the hard, plastic head of the dancing fairy.

"No, that is only a statue your grandfather made. It is pretty. And it is the same size as a real fairy. But it is not really a fairy. Real fairies are real. We do not have wings. Our dresses are not hard like this statue. They are made from the spun silk of spider webs and are dyed with the colors of flowers."

Elizabeth wasn't disappointed the statue wasn't real. It was pretty, shiny, and dancing. But she had a real fairy next to it talking with her. "Are there other fairies? Where are the rest of the fairies?" she asked.

"Yes, we are many. Most of the fairies do not like to be seen by humans. It has not always been pleasant when humans and fairies meet. We choose to remain unseen. It is safer that way. But you are a little girl. We know about you. We have been watching you since the moment you were born. You are special, not like most humans. You talk with the statue of a fairy. I imagine it will be safe for me to be seen by you and to talk with you. You mean us no harm."

"Does Papa know you live here?"

"Not really. He has seen us in his dreams in the middle of the night. He imagines what we are like. That is how he could make this figurine look so much like we are. But we have never let him see us."

"My Papa is nice. He plays with me. He wouldn't hurt you."

"We have to be careful. We have lived here in this garden for a long time. This has been our home far longer than he has lived here. We cannot know if we are safe with him."

"Where are the rest of the fairies?" Elizabeth asked again.

"They are all around you, watching you right now," Olivia said. "Our houses are everywhere in the garden. Our palace is near the brick wall on the farthest edge of the garden. You can neither see the rest of the fairies nor our houses. Not yet. The other fairies are watching you to decide if you are safe to be with. The Queen warned me not to allow myself to be seen, but I believe you are acceptable and will not harm me or the other fairies. I will likely be reproached when you leave."

"What is reproached?"

"Chastised. Scolded. I will get in trouble for having done this without the Queen's permission."

"But I won't hurt you. I won't hurt the fairies. I like fairies."

"I believe you. It will take time for the rest of the fairies to trust you. You must wait."

Elizabeth turned and looked back to the terrace. Momma was calling her. "Elizabeth, come on back now. Garden time is up. We're almost ready for dinner."

Elizabeth stood, smoothing her dress, brushing off bits of bark mulch. "Coming, Momma," she shouted.

She turned back to the tiny fairy. "It's been nice to meet you, Olivia," she said politely. "Can I see you again?"

"Of course, Elizabeth. I will watch for you. Whenever you enter the garden, I will be here. I will find you. You will find me."

Elizabeth clapped her hands and giggled. "Cool," she said. "See you later, Olivia." She waved to her new friend and ran back up the path to Papa, Daddy and Momma, and Michael. It was time for dinner. And then there would be cake and presents.

"Cool? What is cool," puzzled Olivia as she walked back to her palace. "It is the springtime. The air is warm."

4
Elizabeth – Age Thirty

IT STARTS SO INNOCENTLY, **ELIZABETH** thought, looking into the shallow remains of her wine glass, thinking of her daughter. *It always does. Livvy has no idea what lies ahead of her if she believes in the fairies, if she becomes friends with them, if she relies on them. She's young and I remember how much fun they were when I was her age. She'll outgrow them. My problem was, I never did.*

Elizabeth swished the last of the wine and sipped it, holding it in her mouth, enjoying the way the flavors shifted before she swallowed. The once cool wine had become warm. *Everything changes if you give it time,* Elizabeth mused. *If wine ages too long it becomes sour. People die. Romance and love, too. Maybe I should let Livvy go. I could look the other way, play along and let my baby Livvy enjoy the moment while she's still a child. But then she'll grow up. She can't avoid that; we all get older. Wiser, too. We know what's real and what isn't. When Livvy grows up, she'll forget the fairies.*

Livvy danced again, hopping from foot to foot, waving her arms as she looked at the flowers. *It's been a terrible day,* Elizabeth thought. *Papa's funeral. My family was there with me. I felt no support from them, but I never did when I had troubles earlier in my life. And there was Livvy, right by my side, holding my hand. She's only five years old, but what a little trooper! We pulled each other through today. We can count on each other.*

But where was Lucas? I'd told him about Papa's passing. One would have thought he'd have had the dignity and respect to come join us for the funeral. But no. Not Lucas. I shouldn't be surprised. He was probably at work up in Richmond. Maybe he's enjoying his evening after work right now with that woman. Livvy doesn't need to know all the details, the whole sad, sorry story of what he did to me, to her, to both of us. He's gone. Livvy and I will move on together. We're strong. We're resilient. We have no choice.

5

Elizabeth – Age Six

ELIZABETH BURST UP THE STAIRS from the garden, charged across the brick-paved terrace and in the French doors to the chill of the air-conditioned living room. She was flushed, sweating and grinning all over.

Papa beamed at her. "Did you see any fairies out there in the garden?"

"Yes! Two!" Elizabeth exclaimed. "But only one of them was real."

Daddy and Momma smiled. Papa laughed. "Did you? That's wonderful! What was the fairy's name?"

"Olivia. And I'll call the plastic one Ariel like in The Little Mermaid."

"You're so dumb," Michael said. "There's no such thing as fairies. Papa just made one for you. They don't have names."

"Do so. She told me her name is Olivia. But you can't see her. None of you can. She only lets me see her."

"There's no such thing as fairies," Michael repeated. "When you grow up, you'll know. Fairies are for babies."

"Michael! It's Elizabeth's birthday. Be nice." Momma scolded, but Elizabeth saw Momma smile. For a moment, Elizabeth became angry watching her family laugh about it.

None of them believe me. There's a real fairy in the garden. That's fine if they don't know. Olivia is only for me. The rest of my family will never see the fairies.

~~~~~

Dinner was done. The candles on the cake were blown out and the cake had been served. Elizabeth opened her gifts; a doll princess from a Disney movie from Michael and new summer clothes from her parents. Momma and Daddy put her into the high, four-posted bed in her special room at Papa's house. The room was small, with windows looking out into the garden. They kissed her goodnight and tucked her in with her bear, Jefferson. Michael was also in bed in his room down the hall. Now it was Papa's turn to come in to see her.

"Did you have a good birthday, little one?" he asked.

"Yes."

"What was your favorite present?"

"Meeting Olivia out in the garden."

"Olivia? Oh yes, your fairy. I'm glad you like it."

"No! Oh. Yes. I like the little fairy statue too. But I mean Olivia. The real fairy."

Papa smiled and kissed her good night. "Of course. Olivia, your fairy."

When Papa left and the door to the bedroom was closed, Elizabeth slid from the big bed, tiptoed soundlessly to the window, and pushed back the ruffled curtains. She sat in a chair and looked down into the garden. Somewhere out there were fairies. Lots of them. And fairy houses and a palace; Olivia had said so. Now Elizabeth saw only the garden in the moonlight, the crepe myrtle branches swaying slowly in a breeze. Fireflies floated through the darkness. Elizabeth sat by the window watching, waiting for her parents and Papa to go to bed.

She dozed, her head on her arms on the window sill. She woke when she heard her parents and Papa coming up the stairs. Elizabeth waited until their bedroom doors closed. Then, quietly, she cracked open her door and was out. The hall light was off; the house was dark and still. Elizabeth slipped silently down the dark hall, down the stairs, unlocked the terrace doors and tiptoed onto the terrace. She walked gingerly along the path into the garden. The shells beneath her bare feet were sharp and she had to tread carefully.

Elizabeth came to the spot where Papa had set the tiny statue of the fairy. She sat down cross-legged on the path in her white cotton nightgown. In little more than a whisper, she called out sing-song into the nighttime.
~~~~~

"Olivia? Where are you?"

Far on the other side of the garden, among the branches of an oak tree, she saw a dot of light, no more than another firefly. The light floated toward her, glowing and growing larger. It hovered above her. Olivia appeared out of the light.

"You can fly!" Elizabeth said. "But you don't have any wings."

Olivia drifted down through the shadows and landed on her tiptoes on the garden path. Then she too settled cross-legged, sitting in front of Elizabeth. "We do not need wings to fly. Wings are for birds and insects."

Elizabeth nodded, absorbing this first tidbit of knowledge about real fairies. "I told my Momma and Daddy about meeting you. And Papa and my brother too. I hope that's okay. They laughed at me. They don't believe fairies are real."

"Of course they do not. Humans lose the magic when they grow older. I am surprised about Michael, your brother. He is not too old to know. And your grandfather, your Papa too. He is older but he should know better. The garden and his house are filled with fairies. Even if he cannot see us, he should be aware of our presence. He dreams about us whenever we are near to him while he sleeps. He shares this awareness with you."

"Will I stop seeing you when I grow up?"

"I do not know. Perhaps. If you are a friend of the fairies maybe you will not stop seeing me."

"I'm only visiting at Papa's house. My parents will make me go home tomorrow. I don't know when I can come for another visit."

"Whenever you come to your Papa's house, come out to the garden. I will always be here."

"But what do I do until I come to Papa's again?"

"You will have to wait."

"I don't want to. Can you come visit me in Richmond?"

"No, I cannot. All the fairies must travel together. That is the way it is with fairies. Each of us is a part of the whole community. If I were to visit you, all of the fairies would have to leave the garden to come with me. We have our homes here. The Queen lives here and decides where we may go. She has decreed we must stay in the garden."

"But I don't know when I'll come back. I'll miss you."

"I have seen you other times when you visited your grandfather. We will see each other again this summer."

"I know. But I'll still miss you. You're the best thing I got for my birthday."

"That is very nice. But you are tired. I can see your eyes closing. You must sleep. Go back to the house. Come into the garden again before you leave tomorrow. I will see you then."

The fairy light faded and blinked out. Olivia was gone. Dejected, Elizabeth stood and returned to the house, locking the door to the terrace behind her. She climbed the wide stairs, went to her bedroom and fell onto the bed. In an instant, she was asleep.

She dreamed of fairies.

~~~~~

Elizabeth ran to the garden as soon as she finished her cereal in the morning. "Olivia?" she called. "Where are you?"

Only the hum of insects answered. She ran down the path, no longer concerned about the noise of her footsteps. She turned a corner of the path and was hidden behind boxwoods, deep in the garden.

"Olivia!" Elizabeth called again, demanding. Her fists were clenched on her hips. She stamped her little foot. "Come out and see me. I want to see you. I want to talk to you again before I have to go home."

"I am here," chimed the fairy voice. "Do not make such noise. You will frighten the other fairies."

Elizabeth turned and found Olivia sitting among the low myrtle, her ankles crossed, her knees tucked up in front of her. "The council is meeting with the Queen," Olivia said. "They know I let myself be seen by you. They are displeased."

"But why? I won't hurt you."

"I know. But they do not. There is mistrust. The Queen will decide what is best for us."

A second fairy appeared. At first, he was a blurred image, like a memory. Then the colors of his clothing deepened and his face became clear. He was tiny too, hardly bigger than Olivia. The new fairy wore a white tunic and cream-colored leggings. Short boots made of some sort of light leather covered his feet. A dark red cloak hung in folds over his shoulders, draping behind him almost to his ankles. His helmet might once have been an acorn
~~~~~

shell before it was sculpted to fit his head. He was clean-shaven except for a dark goatee, trimmed neatly, pointing from his chin, and he held a tall, thin staff in his right hand.

"Go, Olivia," he commanded, pointing with the long staff to the farthest side of the garden. "The council met last night but the Queen has not yet made her decision. Now go. You must not be seen here, talking to this girl."

Without a word, Olivia slipped through the myrtle, then up into the tree branches, suddenly flying in the direction she had been told to go.

The new fairy turned to Elizabeth. "Olivia was wrong to let herself be seen by you. And now you know of our presence. We cannot erase that memory from your mind. You too must go. If the Queen decides it is permitted, you will be able to see Olivia again when you next visit our garden. If she decides otherwise, you will never see any of us again."

"I told Olivia I won't hurt you. I like fairies."

"Yes. That is true. We are aware. You are a special child, Elizabeth. We understand your nature. It is the reason the Queen is deliberating about this matter. There is hope for you."

"What is your name?" She was puzzled by his word 'deliberating'. She was tempted to ask this new fairy about the word, but she needed to know his name first.

"I am Thomas, an emissary for the Queen. Now go. Your family is waiting."

Thomas vanished, fading into mist. Elizabeth was alone again in the hot garden. "What is deliberating? And what is an emissary?" she wondered.

Back on the patio, Momma called, "Elizabeth! It's time to go."

She trotted to the house along the white shell path. As she passed the center of the garden, she noticed a wide ring of mushrooms had sprouted overnight on the small lawn next to the walkway. She imagined she saw a faint, narrow path tramped into the grass leading into the circle. There was a clear spot in the middle packed down by tiny feet.

Momma hustled her out to the driveway in front of the house. When she was strapped into her car seat, Papa handed her the little statue of the dancing fairy. A thin metal rod protruded from the toe of one of the dancing fairy feet, still caked with traces of black dirt from the garden. "Here you go, little one. You almost forgot Olivia. Go out in your garden with your daddy when you get home. Find a nice spot up there in Richmond to put her. Then you can play with the fairies every day when you go outside"

"Thank you, Papa." She took the plastic fairy and held it tightly. It was hard and unmoving, nothing more than a toy. It wasn't really Olivia, not a real fairy. She called this plastic fairy Ariel. But it was all she had; a tangible connection between her and Olivia and Thomas and the other real fairies.

6

Elizabeth – Age Thirty

RULES? THE FAIRIES HAVE THEIR rules and there are rules for humans too. Elizabeth sat on the terrace remembering all that had gone wrong. *There are laws and Lucas should have known better. He's a lawyer after all, now on the staff of a representative in the Statehouse in Richmond. But he has so little respect for the laws, the rules. And our vows. It doesn't matter anymore. It's too late to complain about it now. He's left me.*

Elizabeth stopped her anxious, angry thoughts and watched as Livvy walked slowly back from the garden. Her daughter's face was red, her body sticky with sweat. Pale blonde hair clung to her face in wet tendrils. She grinned. "Mommy, my new fairy friend Olivia says to tell you hello. She misses you. She says it's okay and she understands. What does she understand?"

"She thinks I don't believe in fairies anymore. That's what she understands."

"Do you believe in fairies?"

"No, Honey Bunny, not anymore. I did when I was a little girl like you. But I'm a grownup now."

"But you do believe in fairies, don't you, Mommy? You say you don't, but you do. You have to." Livvy was insistent. "You can't say you don't believe in fairies if you know about Olivia. You do believe in Olivia. Right, Mommy?"

The child's logic was undeniable. In spite of herself, Elizabeth smiled. "Of course I believe in fairies. I knew Olivia and the Queen and Thomas when I was little. They were my friends."

The child begged, "Do you want to come down in the garden and play with me and Olivia, my fairy?"

Elizabeth felt tempted. The fairies might offer her comfort now, the way they always did when she was a child. She was hurting today after Papa's funeral, and she needed someone to comfort her, to give her a hug, even just to sit and talk with her about how she felt. Whenever there were boyfriend troubles, in the beginning with Lucas or earlier with her other boyfriends, Olivia and the fairies were there for her, always her refuge. But Elizabeth shook her head. "No. I need to get supper ready. Do you want to help me?"

"Okay." Livvy paused, looked back at the garden, and trudged reluctantly through the door from the terrace and into the kitchen with her mother.

It was late summer. The air cooled quickly after sunset and it was too chilly to eat outside in the evening. Elizabeth and Livvy prepared salads with sliced chicken. They ate together inside at the dining room table, looking through the paned picture window to the garden. The house was quiet. They were alone. They didn't talk, each lost in her thoughts. But while they ate, they both stole looks at the garden outside, watching for fairies.

Then it was bedtime. They had decided Livvy would sleep in the room that had always been Elizabeth's when she was a child. Elizabeth had concluded she could no longer sleep in that room or any of the rooms above the garden with its fairies. Fairies were her friends when she was a child, but that time was in the past.

She couldn't bring herself to sleep in Papa's room, either. She couldn't imagine sleeping in his bed, a bed he had left for the hospital only a few days ago. She planned to sleep in the room across the hall her parents always used when they visited. It was in the front of the house, away from the garden, looking down on the front lawn and into the street.

In her old room, Elizabeth tucked Livvy into the big bed and sat on the edge beside her.

"Mommy, I like having fairies for friends. It's cool. They tell me they'll always watch over me and make me safe."

"Yes, they'll always be with you when you're in the garden. Sometimes when you're not here at Papa's house, when you're other places, if there are gardens, other fairies will be watching you in those places, too. But you can't count on them to protect you all the time. Sometimes you'll still need people to take care of you, and sometimes you'll need to take care of yourself."

"You take care of me too, Mommy."

"Yes, I do, and I always will, Honey Bunny." Elizabeth hugged her little girl, brushing a white wisp of hair off her forehead.

"Did Olivia and the fairies take care of you when you were little?"

"Yes."

"Did Daddy know about the fairies? Did the fairies take care of Daddy too?"

"I told Daddy about the fairies, but I don't think he could see them. I don't think he really believed in them."

"Did they take care of Daddy?" Livvy persisted with a question that seemed so obvious to her, if not to her mother.

If the fairies took care of Lucas, why would he have abandoned her and Livvy? It was a path Elizabeth didn't want to follow with her child.

"No, I don't think so," Elizabeth answered. "They left him alone and let him do whatever he wanted. Now go to sleep, Olivia. Sleep tight." Elizabeth gave her a last hug and a kiss. She tucked Hamilton, Livvy's stuffed bear, in with her and stood. As she was about to turn out the light at the door, she stopped for a moment and looked back. Livvy seemed so small in the big four-poster bed. She was smiling, the bedspread tucked up to her chin, snug in her little fists. Her body was a tiny hump under the covers. Hamilton peeked out beside her.

"Good night Mommy. I love you."

"Good night. Sleep tight. I love you too." Elizabeth closed the door and started down the stairs. Behind the door, she heard Livvy stirring. *She's sneaking out of bed*, Elizabeth thought, *going over to the window to look out at the garden to see if there are fairies. I hope they don't come and fly her out to the garden tonight. And I know I can't even keep her safe by locking the window. If they want her, they'll fly right through the walls and take her. She needs to sleep. It's been a hard day for her.*

Elizabeth went downstairs and prepared a mug of green tea. It had become her drink in the evening now with Lucas gone. When the tea was ready, she stirred in some honey and took the steaming cup to her favorite place, the big, winged armchair by a living room window facing the garden. She turned the lights off, seeking the serenity she always found best in the dark.

She selected music on her iPod and put in her earbuds. Elizabeth had been raised on classical music, playing the violin for several years when she was young. She listened to many types of music when she was growing up and still enjoyed most of them, but she came back to the complexities of classical to relax. She chose a collection of Schubert piano impromptus and left the volume low. The music soothed her. She closed her eyes, but only for a moment.

Startled, Elizabeth woke, attentive, watching the garden. There was motion in the darkness outside. Trees swayed slowly. Seeing none of the twinkling fairy lights she remembered from her childhood, she began to relax. Then she spied a dark form moving through the high branches. It stopped.

What is it, she wondered? *An owl? Olivia warned me about owls when I was little. What was it she said? I can't remember. Whatever is out there in the trees is too big to be a fairy; it certainly can't be a fairy. I won't let it be. How could I have clung to my belief in fairies for so many years, till I was grown and married? But what is it, that big dark being moving through the treetops?*

Elizabeth had learned many lessons from the fairies. There was good and evil. The world was filled with dangers. Fairies sheltered her when she was a child. They insulated her from anything they perceived as dangerous. But the older she got, the more they seemed to guard her from lessons she needed to learn on her own. Maybe, she mused, that was why she was so blind to what Lucas did. Why was she so stupid, so foolish, and so trusting?

Maybe the fairies helped her when her parents hadn't. Momma and Dad always had their plans for her. She was supposed to grow up to be successful and rich, maybe a doctor. Nothing could stop their daughter, her parents thought. She shouldn't let anything get in her way. She wasn't supposed to let boys distract her. She should be like Michael, living out their dreams, achieving everything they had planned for her. Then she and Michael both disappointed them. Michael settled down with Eve and abandoned his high-tech career aspirations. Now he sold antiques. And Elizabeth? She married Lucas, a man they believed worthy, a lawyer with money, coming from a well-connected family. But she became a nurse instead of a doctor.

And Lucas? Now Elizabeth and her parents knew what he was truly like. *He's a bastard*, Elizabeth thought. Still, she was happy with the choices she made with her life even if Lucas had left her.

I'm strong, she mused. *I'm going to be okay. I must stay strong for Livvy.*

Elizabeth took another sip of the warm, sweet tea and stared again into the garden. The dark shape high in the branches was still there, not moving, watching the garden and the house. Elizabeth kept her eyes on the lurking, sinister animal in the treetop. Her tea was cooling and the music was nearing the end.

She continued to reflect on the directions her life had taken. Elizabeth now realized her parents had allowed her to follow her own path. That was good, but it was less about them giving her freedom to do what she wanted with her life and more about them being too involved with their own lives to be involved with hers. *When I was little*, she thought, *Papa and the fairies were the only ones other than my friends who seemed to care. The fairies all helped me. They protected me even when I was too foolish to take care of myself.*

Sometimes the fairies were too protective. Sometimes they pushed me in directions I didn't want to go. Papa might have given me room to make mistakes but he was always there to pick me up. And now, finally, I can accept the fairies aren't real.

If they were real, Elizabeth believed, they would have done something for her these past few months. They should have warned her about Lucas. They could have told her what he was doing. They might even have done something to help her keep Lucas. And they certainly wouldn't have let Papa die. Where were they when she really needed them?

Lucas' betrayal and Papa's death were out of her control. She knew that. It wasn't her fault, but she worried maybe she had allowed herself to be too busy to visit Papa as often as she should have these past few years. She worked in a nursing home in Williamsburg, not far from his house. Perhaps she could have dropped by after work. But she always rushed home to Richmond to pick up Livvy from child care and fix dinner for Lucas. And then Lucas would come home late anyway. She could have made the time to stop by and see Papa, but she didn't. And when she did come to Papa's house, always bringing Livvy, sometimes coming with Lucas, she made sure she steered clear of the garden. She no longer needed or wanted the fairies meddling in her life. She walled them out. Now it was too late. Now they were gone, and she was alone with her little Livvy.

Elizabeth recalled the awful telephone call that came only a few days ago. She had been at work. It was from Dad; Dad, who never called just to chat. She knew if he was calling it was bad news.

"Elizabeth, it's your grandfather. We got a call from one of his neighbors. Papa called them to say he needed their help because he wasn't feeling well. He's had a heart attack, and they've taken him to the hospital in Williamsburg. Your mom and I are heading there right now. Michael is taking time from his antiques to come all the way from Staunton, too. Can you get over to the hospital to see him?"

Elizabeth left work and was in the hospital at his bedside minutes later.

"Oh Papa. Hold on. Don't die. What will I do if you die?"

In her mind she heard an answer. "You'll be fine. You are a strong woman. You have your little girl, Olivia."

Then he was gone.

Despair engulfed Elizabeth again, remembering that awful moment. "Oh, God!" she said. Then she sat in silence, numb.

A nurse had come to her at Papa's bedside and led Elizabeth down the hall to a quiet waiting room, set out with tables, sofas and chairs. Her parents found her there, sitting among other anxious strangers, all of them waiting for news about critically ill loved ones. Dad put a hand on her shoulder, comforting. "Elizabeth? Are you okay? It's hard for all of us. What can I do? What can I say?"

Elizabeth composed herself. She couldn't cry, not now with her parents. She had to do something, say something, but what? Her voice choked. "Yes, I'm okay. Of course I'm okay. At least I was with him when he passed. What do you need? How can I help you, Daddy?"

"There's nothing for you to do. I'll take care of the arrangements. Just be here with the family."

Elizabeth's immediate concern was Livvy. She was still in Richmond, in the child care center where Elizabeth had left her that morning. She needed to be picked up in an hour. Lucas would have to do it. But when Elizabeth called him and explained what had happened, he said he was sorry for her loss, but he was busy at the State House and couldn't get to Livvy till later in the evening. No compassion, no sympathy, no offers to help. Elizabeth kissed her parents and left for Richmond.

The next morning, Livvy and she were back in Williamsburg. When they met her family at Papa's house, Dad was all business. "I've got things started with Papa's church and with the funeral home. All the arrangements are coming together. I've talked with his lawyer. We'll go over the will here at the house, right after the service."

It was Dad's way of handling his emotions. Elizabeth had seen it before. Her dad would concentrate on planning, on working, on business. It was how he dealt with stress. Stay busy. Think. Don't allow time for feelings.

Mom took a different approach. She sat quietly with her hands folded, not looking at anyone. She sealed herself off from everything. Papa was Dad's father anyway, she seemed to think. Let Dad handle it. She never really felt Papa was a part of her family. She could cope best if she remained aloof.

With her parents grieving in their own ways, Elizabeth felt abandoned and alone again. She held Olivia and waited for Michael and Eve to arrive. Together they would get through this time.

After the service, they returned to Papa's house and Dad dug right in. "Let's make quick work of the will," he said. "It's very straightforward. Here, I've made two copies; one for you Michael and one for you, too, Elizabeth." He handed each of them a stapled, letter-sized document, so thick it could barely be folded. Then he gave two sealed envelopes to Michael. "Aside from all the legal language, the important parts of the will are only a few pages long," Dad continued. "I'll take care of all the legal and financial business. I expect Papa explained everything about your inheritance in your letters. Michael, I should be able to get you some of your money by the end of the week. Elizabeth, you get the house. You can sell it if you wish. But we know how you are with the garden here. You've loved the garden ever since you were a little girl."

Michael looked at the two envelopes. "Here," he said, handing a letter to Elizabeth. "One is to you. The other is for me." He ripped his open. Eve rested a hand on his shoulder as he read it. *That's Eve*, Elizabeth thought. *Always there for Michael. Not like me and my Lucas.*

Elizabeth clutched her envelope. *Why didn't Dad give it to me? Is it because Michael is older? Because he's a man?*

She asked Michael, "What did Papa say in your letter?"

"He says he loves me, and I should put my inheritance to good use. He says maybe I should use some of the money to expand our antique business."

He looked at Eve. "We can do a lot with this. We need to talk about it." Then he looked at Elizabeth. "Aren't you going to open yours?"

"Later. There's time. No reason to rush." Livvy snuggled closer, needing to be comforted and offering her own solace to her mother.

Dad and Mom stood. "It's been a long day," Dad said. "We really need to head back to Richmond. I've got to work first thing tomorrow morning."

Mom had been unusually quiet all day. But she came to Elizabeth as they were leaving. "Oh Elizabeth. Are you going to be okay? First this awful business with Lucas and now Papa passing away. You've got the house but he left you no money. You could always sell the house if money is tight."

"I'm fine," Elizabeth answered. "Let me think about what to do next. Maybe Livvy and I will move in here. There's really no reason for us to stay in Richmond with Lucas gone. And my job is here in Williamsburg. Why would I want to sell the house? We could live here."

"Oh honey. Are you sure? The house is worth a lot. That beautiful garden really enhances its value."

"I'll think about it."

Then Mom and Dad, Michael and Eve all left, and Elizabeth was alone with Livvy. Elizabeth opened Papa's letter. She couldn't forget the words.

There's so much here. It's more than just a house and a garden. You know that. It's worth more than money. You need to be the one to keep my house.

Papa's letter made her certain keeping the house was the right decision. Mom and Dad saw it only as money. Elizabeth knew its true value. Livvy and she would live there.

Elizabeth sat quietly in Papa's house. Now it was hers. It was dark and still inside. She looked out the window again and puzzled over what to do next. The last shallow bit of tea in her cup had become cold. She reminisced about some of the good times with her family and Papa, sitting right here at the window and outside in the garden with the fairies. She recalled the Fourth of July soon after she first met her tiny fairy friend Olivia.

7

ELIZABETH – AGE SIX

THEY ARRIVED AT PAPA'S LATE in the evening, and Elizabeth was sleepy, so it was straight to bed. Tomorrow was the Fourth of July and there would be parades in the morning and fireworks at night.

After Momma turned out the light and closed the door, Elizabeth, tired as she was, slipped from the bed and ran to the window to look out at the garden. There was a new moon; no light. The garden was terribly dark, and she had been afraid of the dark ever since she was born. The only things visible were the faint shadows of the oak and crepe myrtle swaying gently in the summer breeze. She went back to bed, hoping to wake early in the morning and sneak out to the garden before anyone else got up.

Instead, she awoke in the middle of the night. A light glowed in her room; Olivia sat on the foot of the bed smiling, beaming with happiness. "Welcome back, Elizabeth."

"Olivia!" Elizabeth whispered, grinning, thrilled. She kept her voice quiet so she wouldn't wake her parents.

"The council and the Queen have decided. You are accepted. Not your family. Not even your grandfather. But you can see me again. Other fairies will decide, each for themselves, when they will allow you to see them."

"I've already seen Thomas. When he came to send you away."

"Yes, Thomas. He can be very hard, very rigid in his actions. He only does what the Queen decrees."

Elizabeth nodded, pretending to understand. "What does 'decrees' mean?" she whispered.

"Orders. The Queen tells us what to do and what not to do. Most of us abide by her decrees, her orders. Thomas always does her bidding."

"So that's why you got in trouble for seeing me? The Queen told you not to see me?"

"Yes. But now she has assented."

"How did you get into the house? How did you get into my bedroom?"

"Walls are only walls. We can enter by windows or doors too, just like humans, but walls of human dwellings are not real for fairies any more than our houses are real for humans. Humans walk through our houses all the time and don't even know it. Your walls are not barriers for us. We live in a different world."

"I don't understand," whispered Elizabeth.

"Think about mirrors," Olivia explained. "You see yourself and you see other people in a mirror, but you and they are not really there. What you see are images, reflections on a piece of glass. And their right hand is like your left hand. Everything is reversed. Images in mirrors are not real any more than the little fairy your Papa made is a real fairy. It is only a reflection of our world. Our world is real to us, and it is difficult for us to see your world. The human world is real too, but only for humans. Most humans are not at all aware of the world of the fairies. Both are real, but rarely are they visible to each other."

"I took the little fairy Papa made for me home with me. Daddy and I stuck it in our garden. I like to look at it because it reminds me of you. I called it Ariel at first, but now it's Olivia too."

"I know. There are other fairies where you live with your family. They told us what you did with the little statue. The message traveled to us through our fairy network. It is part of the reason the Queen decided you are acceptable. She understands you are different, that you are a friend of the fairies."

"I'm happy I get to see you again."

"I am happy too. You are able to move between our two worlds. It is a rare honor. Now you need to go back to sleep. Come see me tomorrow in the garden when you wake up."

Olivia floated to the wall and hesitated for a moment. She looked back at Elizabeth and smiled. Then she flew through the wall. As soon as she vanished, Elizabeth fell asleep.

~~~~~

Elizabeth was out of the house, into the garden at sunrise. Other than her, the only one of her family who was awake was Michael, sprawled on the couch watching a *Star Wars* re-run on television. He didn't look up as she left.

She raced down the path, searching in the foliage for fairies until she saw one, posing under a pruned boxwood. It stood stock still, its arms thrown out, poised on one toe, one leg bent at the knee, the other leg pointing back. From her dance classes, she knew this position was an arabesque. It took Elizabeth only a moment to see it was another one of Papa's little plastic statues, shiny and painted. This one had a dark, pointed beard and a long red cape. Elizabeth ran farther down the path, leaving the little plastic fairy behind.

Olivia stood in the middle of the path, grinning. "Come on, Elizabeth," she said. "This is a big moment for all of us and for you. Today is the first day you are here in the garden since the Queen welcomed you into her kingdom."

"Will I meet the Queen today?" asked Elizabeth.

"I do not know. Probably not. She is inside the palace. But you might see the palace. And I think some other fairies will allow you to see them. Come!"

Olivia led Elizabeth farther away from Papa's house, almost to the mossy brick wall at the end of the garden. She stopped and held up a tiny hand. "Watch." She waved her hand. "This is our home."

When she swept her arm, the boxwood hedges in front of the garden wall began to fade, then the wall itself and the spreading ivy shifted, dots of light transitioning point by point, till the bricks and ivy were gone. In place of the rough garden wall, a smooth, turreted wall appeared, the top serrated with battlements. In the middle of the fortified wall was a gate with a heavy double wooden door. Behind the gate was a wide, cobblestone courtyard leading to a palace with cone-roofed towers. The palace was barely higher than the garden wall itself as though it and the wall were really the
~~~~~

same. Small pennants waved from the top of every tower. A bigger flag hung above the gate in the fortified outer wall. The Queen was in residence.

Houses and small buildings appeared among the myrtle and pachysandra. Narrow roads followed the garden paths. At the center of the garden where the armillary stood nestled a marketplace with canopied shop carts and booths. Among the carts, vendors sold little vegetables and other wares. Slowly, as she watched, tiny fairies began to appear, walking along the village lanes, carrying bundles through the market and standing next to the vending carts. They seemed to sparkle. Some glowed the way Olivia sometimes did. These fairies tended to their business and ignored Elizabeth, only glancing at her for a moment, then looking away. They watched her warily but with interest and maybe a touch of fear.

Elizabeth stood amazed, a hand at her mouth. Olivia watched her.

"Oh, it's wonderful," Elizabeth said. "How did it all get here?"

"It has always been here," answered her fairy friend. "We have been here ever since your human people built the garden."

"But I never saw it before. I never knew."

"You see the trees and bushes and the other plants in the garden. We have used the wood from the plants and the mud from the garden to build our houses. The walls of the palace are built with pebbles that are small for you but like boulders to us. You see only the plants, not what we have built using them. That is the way we want it to be with most humans."

Elizabeth looked again at the fairy town and the palace. For a moment, the hedges and the gardens came back into focus and the world of the fairies was gone. Then the garden vanished again, fading back into the fairy village. Both worlds were real.

"I see the fairies in the marketplace," she whispered.

"That is because they are letting you see them. There are probably some you still don't see. Many of the fairies are allowing you to see them because they believe it is what the Queen wants. Others are still reluctant. They are afraid. We have lived for centuries with fear and mistrust of humans. Some of the fairies don't know with certainty that you are different. They have been told it is so by the Queen and Thomas but they do not believe it."

Elizabeth's brother came running down the path toward her, scattering the little fairies on the roads and in the marketplace, sending them tumbling and flying.

"Michael! Be careful. You're scaring the fairies."

He laughed, scoffing at his little sister. "There's no such thing as fairies. Grow up, Elizabeth. Come on. Momma and Dad want to finish breakfast and then we're going to see the parade."

Elizabeth watched as the village, the palace and all the fairies in the market vanished, fading into nothingness like a clearing fog. When they were gone, the garden became just a garden again.

"There are too fairies!" she asserted, pushing Michael as they walked back to Papa's house. "They were all around you. They have a whole town right in the middle of the garden."

"There's no such thing as fairies," Michael repeated.

"You believe in your stupid Star Wars movie. Why not believe in fairies too?"

"Star Wars is just a movie. It's not real. There are no Ewoks or Jedi Knights here in Williamsburg. And no fairies."

"There are too fairies."

Momma scolded them as they came up to the terrace. "Stop fighting, you two. Help me set the table for breakfast out here in the shade. It's a nice morning to have breakfast outside."

"Momma, Michael doesn't believe in fairies."

"Michael, be nice to your sister. If she likes fairies, it's okay. Now we've got to get moving. There's the Fourth of July parade in Colonial Williamsburg. We've got to hurry and get down there. Fifes and drums! Soldiers will be marching with their muskets!"

"Cool!" Michael sat at the table and began eating his bowl of cereal with strawberries.

"You believe in soldiers marching with fifes and drums and muskets," Elizabeth taunted. "But not in Jedi Knights or fairies."

Daddy sat down with the family and sipped his coffee. "In a galaxy far, far away," he quoted, smiling. "Anything is possible."

"That's right," Momma said. "Star Wars, fairies, the continental army. Everything is possible. Believe in anything you want to believe in."

Papa turned to Elizabeth. "You went out in the garden really early. Did you find another fairy?"

"Oh yes. Thank you for making another one, Papa. He looks just like Thomas so I'll call this one Thomas. But I don't think the real Thomas dances. He's too serious and only does what the Queen wants him to do."

"He can dance if you want him to."

"I don't think so, Papa. Thomas doesn't dance. And there's a whole town out there. Lots of fairies, and a palace."

"Of course. You can play out in the garden with the fairies any time you visit me."

Daddy leaned over and hugged Elizabeth. "We'll take your second fairy Thomas home with us and put him in our garden in Richmond, next to Olivia."

"Thanks, Daddy. And thank you Papa for making another fairy for me."

"You're welcome, little one."

Momma repeated, "You can believe in anything you want to, Elizabeth."

Michael finished his breakfast and dropped his spoon clattering into his bowl. "Fairies are dumb. They're not real. Star Wars is dumb too. Let's go see the parade. The soldiers are real in the parade."

~~~~~

Later that evening, as Momma tucked Elizabeth into her bed at Papa's house, she saw Elizabeth's bear lying on the floor. She leaned over to pick it up.

"Here you go." Momma tucked the bear in next to Elizabeth. "You dropped Jefferson on the floor. He might be sad having to sleep on the floor by himself."

"Jefferson's just a stuffed bear, Momma. He's not real."

"Of course he is." Momma patted the bear, noticing as she had for the past few months how the soft plush had been worn down to fabric on one side of his head. Jefferson's face was pushed sideways too from Elizabeth's nightly hugging. "You always hold Jefferson while you fall asleep. Poor Jefferson. See how sad he looks with you leaving him on the floor. He needs you to take care of him." Momma turned Jefferson's face downward, squeezing his head to make his face look sad, the eyes frowning.

"Momma! He's just a stuffed animal. I'm a big girl. I can go to sleep without a stuffed animal."

"All right." Momma tucked the bear in the bed next to Elizabeth anyway.
~~~~~

She kissed Elizabeth goodnight, patted Jefferson, and left the room quietly. As soon as she was gone, Elizabeth threw Jefferson back on the floor.

Papa came in. "How's my little one? Did you enjoy the parades? And the fireworks?" He picked up the bear, leaving it on the edge of the bed.

"Yes. I love the fireworks. They used to scare me, but not anymore."

"You're getting to be all grown up."

"Yes. And now I'm a big girl, I don't need a toy bear with me to fall asleep anymore. Momma thinks Jefferson is real. But he's not a real bear. I don't know why Momma thinks he's real."

"Your Momma believes in Jefferson because she thinks you believe he's a real bear. Sometimes she still likes to think of you as her little girl."

"That's silly."

"Not for her."

"Then why doesn't she believe in fairies? You do. You know they're everywhere in your garden. You know the fairies are real."

"Of course. That's why I made Olivia and Thomas for you to have in your garden up in Richmond. Now go to sleep, little one. You've had a long day."

"Goodnight, Papa."

~~~~~

Olivia's light filled the bedroom as she woke Elizabeth in the middle of the night. "Come with me," she said.

Elizabeth stumbled from the bed and stood on the rug. Olivia reached over and touched her on the shoulder. It was the first time the little fairy had touched Elizabeth. It felt soft, like a down feather. Suddenly, Elizabeth floated up, off the bedroom floor, held by Olivia's touch.

"Come," Olivia commanded. They drifted to the window and out, through the glass into the chill summer-night air above the garden. For a brief moment, Elizabeth was afraid of falling. Olivia nodded to her, sliding her hand from her shoulder down her arm to hold her hand. "I will keep you safe."

They flew down together and landed in the center of the garden at the armillary, in the middle of the fairy marketplace. All the shop carts were closed, small awnings folded, thin canvas tarpaulins covering the tops of the carts. There were no fairies in the marketplace this night. Tonight was
~~~~~

special. No business would be conducted because the Queen planned to come out of the palace.

Across the garden, the shimmering light of the palace shone on the surrounding walls, lighting the courtyard and beaming through every window. Faint music played.

"Oh," Elizabeth exclaimed. "It's so beautiful. And I hear the music."

"Yes. There was a celebration tonight in your honor at the palace. Do you like the music? I think it is so much nicer than that shrill flute music the humans played in your parades today. All that drumming. Even here in the garden, far from your parades, we could hear that awful noise. And there will be no fireworks like human people do. Fairies do not celebrate by blowing things up."

"I like fireworks."

"They are noisy. They are dangerous. Fairies do not play with fireworks."

"I can't go in the palace. I'm too big."

"The celebration will proceed out of the palace now you are here."

As Elizabeth watched, the palace doors swung wide. Then the doors in the gate at the front of the protecting outer walls opened. The music became louder.

"Won't Papa and Momma and Daddy and Michael hear the music? What if they wake up?" Elizabeth asked.

"No. They do not believe in fairies. They cannot hear the music. They will sleep."

"But Papa believes."

"Possibly. If he really believed in us, he could see us all the time the way you do. Then he could hear the music too. He knows of us only from his dreams. He may dream he hears the music."

Fairies appeared in the doorway to the palace and began to march in columns across the pebbled courtyard to the gate. The first ones to emerge from the palace were fairy soldiers, no taller than the length of Elizabeth's hand, leading the procession. When they reached the narrow road outside the fortress gate, they fanned out, lining the sides of the path from the palace through the fairy village to the marketplace. The soldiers stood guard, protecting the others in the procession. Their miniature armor was made of seashells and beach glass. They held long, impossibly thin spears, barely as thick as blades of grass. They seemed to be so tiny they would be powerless. But Elizabeth understood the fairy soldiers' magical power protected the path, the marketplace, the village, and even the magnificent palace.

Throngs of tiny fairies emerged from the green growth and flower beds in the garden. They crowded along the path to watch the parade. They chirped to each other in excited, high-pitched fairy voices as they waited for the parade to approach. "The Queen is coming! Tonight we see the Queen!"

Musicians followed the soldiers from the castle, leading a long procession of brightly clothed royal fairies into the marketplace. Many of the fairies danced along the path. The music was high pitched, chiming, humming, and celestial. Elizabeth tried to count all the fairies, but there were too many. Finally, a brilliantly glowing coach came from the palace, pulled by pure white mice. It crossed the courtyard, passed through the castle gate and followed the throngs of fairies to the center of the marketplace. It was surrounded by more of the soldier fairies, the biggest of the tiny warriors.

The coach circled the marketplace once and stopped. The fairy crowds became silent. The usual, nightly hum of insects had also quieted.

After several moments, the coach door opened. The Queen emerged slowly. She was dressed in a long spreading gown made of a shining fabric. It was as though light itself had been woven and fashioned for the Queen. She appeared to be taller than the other fairies, though, to Elizabeth, she was still very small. She surveyed her subjects sternly, without smiling. Then she turned to Elizabeth and beamed, the smile bringing even more radiance to the nighttime garden than all the light emanating from the palace and the multitude of fairies combined.

"Welcome, Elizabeth!" said the Queen. Her voice, like Olivia's, was a musical tinkling that Elizabeth understood. "Welcome to my kingdom. You are the only human we have welcomed since we left England many long years ago."

"Thank you, Your Highness," said Elizabeth, bowing. It was the first time she had ever met royalty, and she didn't know what to say, but "Your Highness" seemed proper.

The Queen spoke again. "You are special. We have known about you since the moment you were born. You are different. You are not like most humans."

"I feel special."

"Yes. You are honored to be able to see us. Treat us well and we will allow you to remain as though you are a citizen of my kingdom. It is rare for fairies anywhere ever to allow a human this honor."

"What do I have to do now that I'm a citizen of the fairy kingdom? Can I be a princess?"

"No. You have no duties. All the fairies have tasks to serve me. They all know what they must do. But you are human. All you need to do is be kind to us and not tell other humans about us. Our lives here in the garden must be kept secret. Humans cannot know of us. Only you. Can you keep our kingdom a secret?"

"Yes, Your Highness."

"Very good. If you ever betray my trust in you, or the trust of all the fairies, you will lose all contact with us and you will forget forever almost everything about my kingdom. Be good, Elizabeth. Treat us well. Do not talk of us with other humans."

"I'll be good to you. I'll keep the fairies a secret. I won't tell anyone. Not even Papa."

"I trust you will do as I command."

The Queen turned from Elizabeth and climbed back into the coach. The impossibly beautiful fairy music began again. The coach rolled around the fairy marketplace and the armillary and began its journey back to the palace, drawn by the trotting mice. The long procession of fairies followed. One last little fairy got to the gate late, lagging, distracted by a small bug on the path. Then he ran in, through the gateway, across the courtyard and darted in the palace door. The gates quietly closed, and the palace door slammed shut, echoing. The music faded. Only Olivia remained with Elizabeth. As Elizabeth watched, the lights on the castle walls and in the windows suddenly blinked out, and the garden was dark again.

Olivia spoke. "Now you have seen the Queen and all of her subjects. Now you know all about us. You must remember what the Queen has commanded. Heed her words. Keep us to yourself. Other humans cannot know about us."

"Not even Papa? Papa lives here. You said he dreams about fairies."

"Not even him. If he seems to believe in fairies, you may talk some with him about us. But you cannot tell him everything. You cannot tell him about the palace, or the marketplace, or that so many of us live here. And anytime you talk with anyone, anywhere, the Queen will hear you. Thomas will be watching you, and he will know. The Queen's powers reach far beyond these walls. Do not trifle with her power."

"Trifle?"

"You need to take her seriously. She is powerful. She can be dangerous. If you do not obey her, it will be terrifyingly bad for you."

~~~~~

Elizabeth woke up late the next morning, exhausted from her nighttime adventure in the garden. Momma sat on the bed, nudging her shoulder to wake her. "Elizabeth. Baby. It's time to get up and have breakfast. We're going home in a little while."

"I'm sleepy, Momma. I was out in the garden late last night with the fairies. They had a parade."

"Of course, dear. Just like the Fourth of July parade in Williamsburg with the fifes and drums."

"No. It was different. And they made me a citizen of the fairy kingdom, too."

"Of course they did. Now it's time to get up. Hurry along."

Momma left. But before Elizabeth was out of the bed, Thomas appeared, standing on the bed, his feet spread, firmly placed on Elizabeth's pillow, his hand on his staff. "Did not the Queen instruct you never to talk about our kingdom?"

"Yes," Elizabeth confessed, flushing and feeling guilty, already afraid the Queen might exclude her from the kingdom of the fairies, making her like all other humans.

"And did you not tell your mother about our celebration last night?"

"Yes. But she didn't really believe me."

"No, she did not believe you. But you must never talk about us again. Do you understand?"

"Yes."

"This is a warning to you from the Queen. Be advised you must heed her warning."

"Yes."

With a small popping sound, Thomas vanished.

At breakfast, she found the little plastic statue of Thomas lying next to her
~~~~~

cereal bowl. She poured milk into the cereal and picked up the little fairy. It startled her to see, as she took a close look, that the statue really looked exactly like Thomas. It was the same way the first toy fairy looked so much like Olivia. But, of course, Thomas was too important to dance like the little plastic statue.

"I went out to the garden this morning to get the fairy for you," Papa said. "I didn't want you to forget it. I want you to have it for your garden back home in Richmond."

"Thank you, Papa. It's really nice. It looks like Thomas. But I told you Thomas doesn't dance. He's too serious. He's an emissary for The Queen of The Fairies."

"Emissary," said Daddy. "That's a big word. Where did you learn it?"

"From the fairies." As soon as Elizabeth said it, she realized it was a mistake. She covered her mouth with her hand. But she continued. "I don't know what it means though. I think it means he works for the Queen. But that's only make-believe. This Thomas is the real fairy Thomas. Fairies aren't really real. I know that."

Her parents and Papa smiled and nodded. Michael laughed and said, "Finally. You're starting to talk like a grown up."

She didn't see Thomas, but she heard him. "That is better, dear Elizabeth. Keep telling them you do not believe in fairies."

8

Elizabeth – Age Six

IT WAS ALMOST THE END of summer. There was time for one last visit to Papa's house before school began. As soon as she arrived with her family she walked quickly into the garden, leaving her family with Papa on the terrace. When she was out of sight of her family, hidden behind the hedges, she ran to the back of the garden.

"Olivia?" she called quietly, her voice barely above a whisper. "Are you here?"

"Of course, Elizabeth. I knew you were coming. I have been waiting for you." Olivia appeared, stepping out from beneath a fallen yellow leaf, a sign of impending autumn.

"I'm going to start school on Monday. I'm going to be in first grade."

"Yes, we know. We have heard this."

"When school starts, I won't be able to come see you as much as I have this summer. I'll be in school all the time."

"That is all right, Elizabeth. There are fairies in Richmond. They will be watching over you, and they will tell us about you. They will keep you safe."

"Can I see those fairies? Can I see their palace and their village?"

"No. Only we share this honor with you, only here in your grandfather's garden."

"But I won't be able to come see you. I'll miss you."

"We will wait for you. We will be here whenever you visit your grandfather."

"He always comes to our house for Thanksgiving. But we come here at Christmas."

"What is Thanksgiving? Is it the time when you say thank you to people?"

"It's polite to always tell people thank you. Thanksgiving is a holiday. It's about when the pilgrims celebrated a harvest, I think."

"Do you have parades and fireworks like you did at that celebration in the summertime?"

"We have parades. There is one we watch on television, but it's in New York. No fireworks."

"Good. No fireworks. And Christmas? What is Christmas? I have heard of your holidays. But fairies don't celebrate these days. I know so little about these human festivities."

"It's when the baby Jesus was born. Santa Claus comes down the chimney and puts toys in our stockings. And we give each other gifts."

"I think I would like Christmas. Gifts are good. And you will come here at Christmas?"

"Yes. We come and stay lots of days at Christmas. It's cold. Will you still be here when it gets cold?"

"Of course. We are always here."

"What if it snows?"

"If it snows, it snows. We are always here."

"Then I'll see you at Christmas. Say 'hi' to the Queen for me."

"High?"

"Yes, tell her 'hi'."

Olivia frowned, puzzled by Elizabeth's request. "If you ask me to do so, I will tell the Queen you say 'high'."

"I've got to go now," Elizabeth said. "Momma and Daddy and Michael are going out. I have to go with them to buy school clothes."

When Elizabeth left, Olivia turned toward the palace walking slowly, not flying. "Elizabeth has asked me to do such an odd thing," she pondered. "But I must do what she asks. I must tell the Queen Elizabeth says 'high'."

~~~~~

Christmas music played in Merchants Square on the edge of Colonial Williamsburg. There were wreaths in the shop windows, garlands and
~~~~~

decorations on light posts. A tall Christmas tree was decked with lights and shiny ribbons and balls. Carolers clustered in a semi-circle, singing. Elizabeth sat on a bench next to Papa, clasping a paper cup of hot chocolate between mittened hands. Papa sipped a cup of coffee, steam masking his face for a moment. Crowds of tourists and shoppers strolled along the brick-paved square. There was a thin dusting of snow, not even an inch deep, worn to bare bricks by all the footsteps. The sun was bright, and where the brick paving was exposed in the sunlight, it was wet.

Elizabeth remembered when she had slipped out of the house earlier that morning for a quick visit to Papa's garden. The thin snow, shallow for humans, had been deep for the little fairies, almost up to their knees. Fairy workers had been hard at work clearing the fairy marketplace with small shovels. Moles, tethered to carts, were taking away load after load of the snow, removing it to a distant corner of the garden. Magic doesn't work against acts of nature, Elizabeth realized. She wondered if grownup humans would notice the dusting of snow had been cleared from the garden paths.

Elizabeth puzzled over everything about her secret fairies. She knew she shouldn't talk about the fairies with humans. She wanted to share her special secret with Papa, but she was afraid. She knew she ought to keep it a secret, but it was too wonderful to keep just to herself. Now she was with Papa and they weren't in the garden at his house. Fairies lived in gardens. Maybe it would be safe to talk about the fairies with Papa there in brick-paved Merchant Square, far from his house.

"Do you believe in fairies, Papa?" Elizabeth asked.

"Of course, little one. Don't you?"

"Yes. But have you ever seen them in your garden?"

"I think so. Sometimes I imagine what they would look like. I dream about fairies sometimes at night. It's odd. As an adult, I never dreamed about fairies until I moved into my house here with my garden. That was twenty years ago. But I always dreamed about fairies when I was little, when I was your age."

"Can I tell you something, Papa?"

"Of course."

"I'm not supposed to tell, but your garden has real fairies living in it. There's a whole town with little houses. And lots of fairies. And the Queen lives there too, in a big palace."

As soon as she said it, she realized it might have been a mistake. She sucked in her breath, covered her mouth with her mittened hand and looked around to see if there were any fairies listening. She saw none. It felt good for Elizabeth to share her wonderful secret with Papa. But she worried. Would Thomas know? What if he finds out? What will the Queen do? Elizabeth remembered when Olivia had told her the fairies can't leave the garden without the Queen. But hadn't the Queen told her there were fairies everywhere watching? Were there fairy spies in Merchants Square watching her, listening to what she said? Was it safe to talk with Papa here?

"Papa? You can't tell anyone we talked about the fairies. The Queen will be angry. And we can only talk about the fairies outside, away from your house. They want me to keep them a secret."

Papa smiled. "Of course, little one. We'll keep the fairies a secret, just for you and me. And we'll only talk about them when we aren't at my house."

"That's right. Those are the rules. And we can't talk about them when we're at my house in Richmond, either. There are fairies in our garden too. I can't see them, but I think they will tell the fairies here in Williamsburg if we talk about them when we're at my house in Richmond."

"Okay. Let me know when it's safe to talk about the fairies. We'll keep it our special secret. Don't you worry, little one."

"Okay Papa. It's our special secret. You do believe in them, don't you?"

"Of course I do. You know what else? I used to be a dentist before I retired. Remember? And you know about the tooth fairy who leaves money under your pillow when you lose a baby tooth? You just lost your first tooth and did the tooth fairy come?"

Elizabeth smiled. "Yes! He left me a dollar. Does the tooth fairy live in your garden?"

"I don't know. Maybe. Maybe all dentists have tooth fairies living in their gardens."

Elizabeth gave her gap-toothed grin, thinking about this new bit of fairy lore. "Cool," she said. She stuck her tongue into the gap in her mouth. Then she wiggled another loose tooth with her tongue.

Santa Claus walked up to Elizabeth and Papa. He wore a long red coat trimmed with white fur and a matching red and white hat. A garland of greenery, red apples, and berries was tucked in his white hair. His white beard rolled down over his chest.

"Ho, ho!" he bellowed. "Who do we have here?"

"I'm Elizabeth."

"Ho, I knew that. And have you been a good girl this year, Elizabeth?" He was full of cheer, beaming, red in the face.

"Of course I have. Didn't you know that too?"

"Of course. And what do you want for Christmas, Elizabeth?"

"You're supposed to know, Santa. You're supposed to know everything. When I'm sleeping, when I'm awake."

"I do. I do. I just want to know for sure. I'm just checking." Santa handed her a lollipop.

"I want a puppy or a kitten. Maybe a pony too? Except my Daddy says I can't have a pony. And a pink fairy palace I can set up in my bedroom."

"Okay. So it's a no for the pony. We'll have to see about the puppy and the palace. You be good till Christmas, Elizabeth. Be sure to eat your vegetables. Ho, ho!"

Santa walked away. Papa wrapped his arm around Elizabeth's shoulder. "Well he's a jolly old elf," he said.

"I don't think he's the real Santa Claus. I don't think he's an elf, either."

"Why not, little one?"

"He's too big to fit down the chimney. I think he's a pretend Santa here to make little kids believe in Santa. Some of my friends say Santa's not real."

"What do you think?" asked Papa.

"He's real. Fairies are real too. But some of my friends don't believe in fairies either. They don't know because they've never seen real fairies."

Papa smiled and hugged his granddaughter. "They're real. We know because we've seen them."

<center>~~~~~</center>

After the stockings were opened on Christmas morning, Elizabeth snuck from the house into the chill of the winter garden. No one saw her leaving, running down the path in her robe and fuzzy slippers. Momma and Daddy were working with Papa in the kitchen preparing a special Christmas-morning breakfast. Michael had a new video game connected to the television. He was busy blowing up invaders from outer space.

Olivia appeared as soon as Elizabeth stepped off the terrace. Elizabeth's special little fairy wore a coat made of tan mouse fur, a peaked fur cap, and knee-high leather boots. "A good morning to you, Elizabeth. And what is it you humans say? Merry Christmas?" She walked with Elizabeth to the garden center at the armillary.

"Yes. Merry Christmas to you too, Olivia."

"Have you received gifts? You told me that gifts are given on Christmas day."

"Yes. We get to open the real presents later, but Santa Claus came. I had all sorts of stuff in my stocking. Candy and barrettes with ribbons for my hair and a little toy pony. I wanted a real pony, but I guess Santa brought me a toy pony instead as a joke."

"Is it not uncomfortable having toys and candy stuffed into your stockings?"

"No, Olivia. That's silly. We hang a big sock on the fireplace. We call it our stocking. But it's not a real stocking. It's a sock, just a big sock we hang up for Santa to put things in. Mine is almost as big as I am and it has my name on it in glitter."

"You have told me that this Santa Claus comes down the chimney. He brings you gifts, and he comes down the chimney? I do not understand."

"Yes. He parks his sleigh on the roof and he comes down the chimney."

"His sleigh? He parks on the roof? How does he get the sleigh up to the roof?"

Elizabeth giggled. "Don't you know? His eight tiny reindeer can fly. They pull his sleigh. That's how they get on the roof. You're a fairy. I thought you would know about that if anyone would."

Olivia shook her little head. "What you are telling me is impossible," she said in her tinkling voice. "I do not understand about tiny rain deer. I know about deer. They are everywhere. Sometimes the deer get into our garden. They jump over the wall. But I do not understand about these rain deer. Everyone knows that deer can't jump as high as the top of a house. They can jump but they cannot fly."

"Santa's reindeer can." As she said it, Elizabeth started to have doubts. If a smart fairy like Olivia didn't believe in Santa's reindeer, maybe Santa wasn't real either.

Elizabeth tried again to explain it to Olivia, searching for a logical answer.

"People say Santa's supposed to be a jolly old elf. He's magic. So his reindeer can fly. And that's how he comes down the chimney."

It sounded so sensible when Elizabeth said it, but Olivia's small face turned pale. "He is an elf? Oh, this is not good. There was an elf here last night? Right here in the garden and up on the roof of your grandfather's house? Oh my, the Queen needs to know. Elves are dangerous. They are not as bad as gnomes, of course. But they are evil creatures. And do not ask me about trolls, those horrible creatures from the north. Or goblins. Elves are enough trouble. I must tell the Queen immediately." Olivia stood and started to fly back to the palace.

Elizabeth was startled by Olivia's reaction to the news that Santa was an elf. But again she tried to explain, catching the little fairy by her furry sleeve before she could fly to the Queen. "No," she explained, persisting. "Santa's a good elf. He brings presents and candy to good boys and girls. He's always watching us to know who's bad or good."

Olivia settled back on the cold bench next to Elizabeth. "Oh yes! I expect he is always watching. That is what elves do. What does he do to the bad boys and girls?"

"I don't know. I'm a good girl."

"Then what does this elf Santa do to your brother Michael?"

"He brings him toys, too. Michael's a pain, but he's okay. He's good, I guess. He doesn't believe Santa's real anymore, anyway. And he doesn't believe in fairies."

"He is a pain?"

"He's annoying sometimes. But he's okay."

Olivia contemplated the concept of Santa Claus. Then she stopped and turned to Elizabeth. "Ah. I think I understand. If this Santa Claus really was an elf, he would have magic. He could go straight through walls the way fairies do. He would not have to go down a chimney. And he could fly. So he would not need a sleigh with flying rain deer. This Santa story is preposterous."

"Preposterous?"

"Preposterous. Ridiculous. Nonsense. I think the whole story is making believe. I do not think your Santa Claus story is real. It is a story made by grown-up humans to entertain their children."

Elizabeth sat in shock. She understood some of her friends might not believe in Santa anymore. But Olivia? If anyone might know the truth about Santa, it would be Olivia.

"You don't believe in Santa Claus? But who put the candy and the pony in my stocking?"

"I do not know. Your parents or Papa maybe? Use logic. You need to think logically to know the difference between making believe and reality."

"If you say so. But I still want to believe in Santa."

"If you enjoy that belief, it is acceptable. I am relieved this Santa tale is nothing more than a human story made up for children. Elves would be a real problem if they were truly here in our garden."

"Could I ask you something else, Olivia?"

"Of course. You can ask me anything."

"You said the elves are always watching us. Is that true for fairies, too?"

"It is not quite the same with fairies as with elves. Elves are evil creatures who are everywhere. They are invisible. But they are always there, watching you, stealing things, causing mischief. Did you ever find something was missing, and you cannot understand where it went? Elves took it. Fairies do not do that. We are always good. We do not cause mischief like that."

"Are you always watching me?"

"Whenever you are here at your grandfather's house or in his garden, we are here. We watch over you to make sure you are safe. Other fairies are in other gardens, many gardens. They are in your garden at your house in Richmond too. There are no fairies in most places because those other places are dangerous for fairies. Elves are part of the problem. There are also animals and some humans that concern us."

"So you are with me here in Papa's garden, but not other places?"

"That is correct. Be aware, we cannot protect you anywhere but here. I must go now. The Queen has summoned me." Olivia vanished.

Elizabeth walked quickly back to the house. She was shivering from the cold. Olivia was her friend, but Olivia had just proven that Santa Claus was not real. Elizabeth was crushed at losing the magic of Christmas and Santa Claus. It all made sense now that her fairy friend had cleared things up. But she was relieved her conversation with Papa in Merchants Square was not heard by the fairies. And there was always the tooth fairy. Papa told her the tooth fairy was real. She clung to that hope.

Absentmindedly, she reached into her mouth and wiggled the loose tooth. She tasted blood, the metallic taste helping her keep a grip on reality. She lived as a special citizen of a magical world. Olivia and the other fairies were among her closest friends. She wanted to assure herself of that reality. She banged through the French doors from the terrace and went to Papa in the kitchen.

"Hold me," she begged him, hugging him. "I'm cold."

"Of course you are," Momma said. "What were you doing out in the garden in this weather without a coat?"

Papa smiled and gave Elizabeth a hug, rubbing her back. "It's okay, little one. You will always be welcomed in my garden."

Elizabeth looked at Papa and grinned her gap-toothed grin. "The fairies wished us Merry Christmas," she whispered to him. "And they didn't watch us in Merchants Square. They can't."

In the garden, a cardinal landed in the sweeping branches of a bare crepe myrtle tree. A fur-clad fairy watched the bird from beneath the frozen plants nearby.

"I bring a message for your sovereign ruler, the Queen," chirped the cardinal. "It is from your fairy clan stationed in Merchants Square." It dropped a twig from its beak to the ground. The fairy darted out from the pachysandra and picked it up.

The fairy clutched the twig, noting the miniscule runic scratches that covered it end to end. "I will see that Thomas delivers this message to the Queen." He turned toward the palace and vanished into the cold greenery, carrying the twig on his shoulder.

9
ELIZABETH – AGE THIRTY

ELIZABETH SAT ALONE IN THE darkness inside, sorting out her thoughts. The owl, or whatever that dark being in the garden was, had moved, maybe to another part of the garden, but a sensation of evil remained. Everything seemed surreal. Elizabeth felt out of touch with the world since she'd lost Lucas and Papa. She was left feeling nothing but a black void inside.

What is left? I have Papa's house with its special garden. I have my job at the nursing home and I have to go back to work beginning next Monday. There is still the townhouse where Lucas and I lived in Richmond, filled with our old furniture. And I have my little girl, Olivia. I need to get started with the next steps in my life. It's time to make sense of everything and move forward to begin to set things right. I can't stay in this awful, emotional place. I have to do something. But what?

I won't get any help from Lucas. Maybe my friends might offer their support. Possibly even Michael and Mom and Dad will help. But I can't count on advice anymore from the garden fairies. I don't want it from them, anyway. They let me down by their absence when I needed them most; when I was struggling with Lucas and our marriage, and now with Papa's passing too. They no longer existed for me. They failed to help.

And tomorrow? What should I do? Where could I start? I have so little time before I need to be back at work. I have to act quickly.

She was exhausted and knew she needed to go to bed. Elizabeth shifted in the chair, moving her feet from the ottoman to the floor, preparing to stand and head up the stairs. To move at all required a supreme effort. Inertia consumed her. It felt more comfortable to stay where she was. *Maybe I'll spend the night sitting, possibly even sleeping in the chair by the window.* She stayed, slumped in the chair, thinking, sorting out her plans.

I'll make plans to place Livvy in kindergarten here in Williamsburg for the coming fall and possibly find childcare for the remaining weeks of the summer. I'll see about selling the Richmond townhouse. Lucas has already moved in with his girlfriend. There is no reason at all for me to stay in Richmond any longer. Papa's house is already furnished so I could sell most of the furniture in our townhouse. Lucas might complain, but I don't care. He gave me everything in the settlement, the house, the furniture and alimony. He got Loki, the dog... and the girlfriend. The furniture is all old and worn, the same inexpensive chairs and tables we bought together in grad school and more odds and ends from when we were first married. My plan is coming together.

But still she couldn't focus on how to begin. Her thoughts flipped between planning for the days ahead and worrying about the fairies. *There's so much I have to do. So where do I start? What do I do first?*

The music she had been listening to ended. She removed her earbuds, gazed out the window and watched as the dark being in the treetops showed itself again, flapped twice and glided low across the garden, over the wall and away. She still saw no fairies. *That's good*, she thought. *I don't want the fairies to be here. They're useless, now nothing more than a nuisance.*

Maybe they were a fantasy all along, Elizabeth speculated. *Would it be best if Livvy understood too? Maybe I should have a talk with her about them and explain to her they're only make-believe. I want to make sure my little girl doesn't get caught up in that nonsense. It's okay for her to believe in them while she's still a little girl. But in the years ahead it'll only lead to trouble and a broken heart. That's how it had turned out for me and I don't want that disenchantment for Livvy. At what age should I warn Livvy about the fairies? Now or later?*

Elizabeth shook her head, remembering the foolishness that was the world of the fairies when she was a child. *I really did believe in them when I was small. But where did that get me as an adult?*

At the top of the stairs a door opened quietly. Elizabeth sat still and listened. *It's Livvy. Going to the bathroom? Looking for me? What is she doing out of bed this late at night?*

Soft footsteps crept on the dark stairs. Elizabeth stayed hidden, sitting quietly in the shadowed darkness by the window. She saw Livvy's tiny figure in silhouette against faint moonlight, padding barefoot across the living room to the French doors. As Elizabeth watched, Livvy unlatched the door, stepped out, and, closing the door behind her, ran out to the terrace, skipping down the steps into the garden. Her white nightgown blowing in the cool night breeze, Livvy raced down the path to the armillary and stopped. She twirled once, arms out. She leaned forward, her hands cupping around her mouth, calling into the darkness, though Elizabeth, inside the house, couldn't hear her. Livvy spun again, her nightgown flaring away from her slender child's body, moonlight surrounding her with a translucent glow. Then she sat on a bench.

Elizabeth watched, afraid for her daughter to be engaging with the fairies. *It was what I did when I was a child, but what has it done for me? My marriage failed. And now Papa's gone.*

Is that a light in the trees out in the garden? I'm done with the fairies. They couldn't save my marriage and they couldn't save Papa. They're no longer real for me. But what is that twinkling light I see floating through the trees to Livvy? No! It can't be a fairy. Fairies aren't real. I won't let them be. No more!

Elizabeth watched the light stop in front of Livvy, glowing. It horrified Elizabeth to see the fairies were back, even if only for Livvy. And maybe for her too, though she willed them away.

No! Go away! You need to leave us alone, she thought. *You're not real, and even if you were, you can't help us. Where were you when I needed you? Why didn't you do something? If you could have saved Papa for even a few minutes, the EMT's would have saved his life and then I could have cared for him in the nursing home.*

Elizabeth hoped she was imagining the whole scene. Maybe the light wasn't really there. Maybe it was a reflection on the glass window pane. She turned her head, hoping the light would shift in the window. If it was a reflection, it might vanish if she moved, but the light stubbornly stayed, hovering in front of Livvy.

Livvy was in the garden for only a minute. She gestured with her arms, talking to the light. Then she stood up from the bench and walked slowly back to the house. The light in the garden blinked once, drifted to the back of the garden, flared and was gone. Hidden in her chair in the dark, Elizabeth watched her slim daughter dance through the door, latching it silently. Livvy tiptoed back up the stairs to her room, her feet padding softly on the floorboards. The bedroom door closed with a click.

Elizabeth sat in the dark house in silence for a few more minutes. Finally she got up, put the dirty tea mug in the sink, and climbed the stairs. Before she went to her own bedroom, Elizabeth opened Livvy's bedroom door softly and walked in. Livvie slept soundly, clutching Hamilton to her face. Elizabeth tugged the covers to her daughter's chin and patted her softly on her shoulder. Livvy stirred but didn't wake. She might have been dreaming of fairies.

Elizabeth went to her new bedroom on the front of the house and settled into the bed. It had been a long, hard day. Her only relief was she was in a room facing away from the garden, though she knew it offered her no shelter from the fairies if they came for her. She did not dream of fairies. She dreamt of her childhood. She dreamed of her awkward adolescence.

10

ELIZABETH – AGE TWELVE

ELIZABETH SAT UNSMILING, SLUMPED ON a bench in the center of the garden. The round, latticed shadow of the armillary was at her feet. Her shoulders were rolled forward, concealing her small new breasts. As she looked around the garden, she began to see transparent shadows becoming houses. It was good the garden was slowly shifting to what it had once been for her. It was comforting that it hadn't changed while it was hidden. She still missed Olivia, having endured the sentence she received from the Queen as a child.

She remembered that awful Christmas night six years earlier. Eight fairy soldiers had come to her while she slept in her bed at Papa's house. They all placed their hands on her shoulders, lifting her up out of the bed, the covers dragging behind her and falling on the floor. Olivia had flown her from her room like this before, but this was not Olivia taking her. With the soldiers, she felt a sense of foreboding. The soldiers flew her out the window and down to a wide space outside the gate in front of the palace. They stood close to her, surrounding her, confronting her, watching, each with his feet spread, one hand on his hip, the other on his spear. She felt paralyzed, frozen in place. She was surprised she didn't feel cold.

In front of her, the Queen sat on an elaborate golden throne, marked with geometric patterns and undecipherable runic writing. The throne was mounted on a wide, raised platform made of water-washed pebbles. Thomas stood beside the Queen on the platform. Like the soldiers, he stood with his feet set, one hand on his hip, the other on his staff. Ice frosted everything in the winter garden.

The Queen spoke, her voice commanding. "I have been told by my fairy subjects that you talked in detail about my kingdom while you were with your grandfather in a nearby town market square. They told me that you and he decided to share information about my kingdom. I will not even ask you if this is true. I know it to be so."

Elizabeth felt suddenly weak, terrified of what the Queen might do.

"What do you have to say for yourself, Elizabeth?"

Elizabeth was barely able to speak. When she did, her voice was timid, little more than a whisper. "Yes, Papa and I talked about fairies when we were in Merchants Square. But he believes in fairies. He knows you're real. He sees you in his dreams. Olivia said I could talk with him a little about the fairies."

"Olivia is foolish. I ordered you never to talk with anyone about us." The Queen's voice echoed throughout the garden. "Yes, Olivia suggested you could talk with your grandfather a little about us. She was wrong to do so. And yes, your grandfather does believe we might be here. But you were told not to tell even him everything you know about us. And you have done this."

Elizabeth looked fearfully at the angry queen and then at Thomas. Thomas smiled, smirking. She looked around for Olivia but couldn't find her. The only fairies she saw were the Queen, Thomas, and the soldiers. "Where is Olivia?"

"Olivia is not here," the Queen announced with a dismissive wave of her hand. "Do you remember what I said would happen if you spoke about us with other humans?"

"Yes."

"This is what I have decided. You will have no contact with any fairies and you will not see our kingdom for five years. After that I will decide what is to be done with you. You are a special child. You are not like other humans. But I cannot tolerate what you have done."

"Can't I still see Olivia?"

"No. I am done with you. Now go. I will meet with you again after five years has passed, and I will decide then what to do about you."

The Queen vanished, along with the golden throne and the rock cairn, twinkling out till there was only a single, small flash of light. With Thomas watching and directing, the soldiers gathered around Elizabeth again, floating, touching her to lift her off the ground. They flew with her, rushing up across the garden to the house and through the wall to her bedroom. She barely slept, and when she did doze, there were no dreams. She woke in the morning, crying.

Elizabeth ran to the garden before breakfast. Birds scattered, darting away from her in terror. She couldn't see the palace though she knew where it was supposed to be. The fairy village was gone, too. Before the Queen's awful verdict, she hadn't always been able to see the fairy town, but she had always felt its presence. Now even that sensation was gone.

"Olivia?" she called. "Olivia, where are you?"

There was no answer, no sound. A breeze ruffled through the crepe myrtle and the old oak branches, all stripped bare by winter. Otherwise, nothing moved. The garden had become an ordinary garden, formal and still beautiful, even in mid-winter, but with no evidence of fairies. Elizabeth's stomach sank, emptiness at the loss of Olivia and her wonderful fairy kingdom. She counted the years out on her fingers and made a mental note of the date when she might be able to see Olivia again. Slowly she walked back to Papa's house.

Her parents and Michael were preoccupied with breakfast preparations. Nobody noticed her change of mood but Papa. "What's the matter, little one?" he asked, pulling her aside.

"Nothing."

Quietly he took her, an arm around her. "I know you. This isn't like you. What's the matter?"

"They're gone," she whispered to Papa. "The fairies and the palace and the town. The Queen found out we talked about the fairies when we were in Merchants Square and now they're gone. I can't see them again for five years. I'm only six years old. Five years is like forever."

Papa hugged her. "Then we won't talk about them again. We'll know about them though. Both of us. And in five years, when they're back, you can give me a little sign, a wink or something to let me know. And we won't have to talk about them."

Elizabeth had smiled weakly and snuggled closer to her grandfather. He folded her up in his arms.

~~~~~

Elizabeth was approaching her twelfth birthday. It was midsummer, and she had been with her family at Papa's house for a week, ever since school ended. In the garden, the village appeared more and more each day among the flowers and the shrubbery. The week passed with the fairy kingdom appearing slowly as though rising from murky water. At first, the palace was an ephemeral vision against the garden wall, as transparent as thin, wet linen. Bit by bit, more of the fairy kingdom came to light. Each day it became clearer, the colors of the houses more vivid, with small details emerging. The town appeared uninhabited. It seemed the fairies had chosen to remain invisible to her. She had still not seen Olivia.

"Olivia?" she called as she had every day she had been at Papa's house since the five-year sentence ended. "Olivia? Can I see you again?"

Today, like a miracle, Olivia stepped from beneath a rosebush and walked to Elizabeth. For a moment Olivia suppressed a smile, but she gave in, beaming with happiness. "Welcome Elizabeth," she said. "It is good to be seen again. And it is good to see you."

Elizabeth broke into a grin. "Olivia! You're back. I'd hug you if you weren't so tiny."

"But I am still tiny. You have grown much bigger."

"I'm almost twelve."

"Do you still believe in fairies?"

"I'm talking with you, so of course I do. It's not like I'm a child who believes in stupid kid stuff like Santa Claus and the tooth fairy and unicorns. I know what's real. I know fairies are real. I won't ever outgrow that because I know the truth about fairies."

"That is good. I have missed you, Elizabeth. It was hard for me being away, unable to talk with you. Very few fairies have humans for friends."

The little fairy and the young woman looked at each other, thrilled to be renewing their friendship. "This is special for both of us, I expect," Elizabeth said. "Most kids outgrow fairies. I don't play anymore with the plastic fairy
~~~~~

palace I got for Christmas back then. But you're real, not a toy. You're alive. Oh, I'm so glad you're back. It was awful when we couldn't see each other."

"You still need to be careful, Elizabeth. The Queen is still watching you. Don't talk at all with anyone about the fairies. Not even your grandfather."

"I won't. I've learned my lesson. And Papa understands. It'll be fine."

"It has not been easy for me, either," confessed Olivia. "But that time is in the past. The passage of time changes many things, but never friendships."

"We're still friends then?" Elizabeth asked.

"Of course. And there is something else. The Queen would like to meet with you. You are staying at your grandfather's house tonight?"

"Yes. I'll be here for the rest of the weekend."

"I will come for you after everyone is asleep. I will lead you to the Queen like I did years ago."

"Okay."

"Do not tell anyone, not even your grandfather. Not a word. Do you understand?"

"Yes."

"Very good. I will tell the Queen you are ready to meet with her tonight."

Olivia drifted into the rose bushes and was gone. Elizabeth ran laughing back to Papa's house, dodging the fairy houses and the vendor carts in the village square. She found Papa in the living room watching baseball on the television with Daddy and Michael. They all looked up quickly. Then, Dad and Michael turned back to the game. Papa watched her.

Without saying a word, Elizabeth gave him an exaggerated wink and a thumbs-up. Still grinning, she looked out at the garden, then back to Papa. He smiled and returned the thumbs-up. He remembered and knew what she meant. Elizabeth put a finger to her mouth and whispered, "Shh!"

Papa nodded. Still smiling, he turned back to the baseball game. "Two strikes on the batter," he said. "We've got him. Give him the curve ball low and outside."

They all watched for a moment in silence. On the television, they heard a cheer from the crowd in a stadium far away. "That pitch is almost impossible to hit," said the voice of an unseen announcer. "It just seems to vanish for the batter."

"Got him!" shouted Michael.

Dad stood. "Inning's over," he said. "You want another beer, Dad?"

"Sure." Papa looked back grinning at Elizabeth and raised both hands, fists clenched, cheering. "Perfect!" he exulted. "Absolutely perfect!"

Dad and Michael thought he was cheering for the baseball game. Only Elizabeth knew what he really meant.

~~~~~

Elizabeth went to bed and lay awake, excited and anticipating her meeting with the Queen. She was a little afraid, remembering the last time she and the Queen met. But she knew this visit would mean the end to her five-year sentence. In spite of her excitement, she fell asleep.

She dreamt she was back in Richmond in her bedroom with her girlfriends. They were talking with excitement about music, movies, and a school basketball game they had all gone to see. Whatever the subject, they always came back to the topic of boys. Boys in a rock band, boys on television and in the movies, a boy who was a star on the basketball team.

She woke with Olivia's brilliant light filling the bedroom. Olivia didn't speak. As she did the first time, she floated to Elizabeth, lifted her from the bed with a feathery touch and flew her through the window. They drifted above the garden and descended in front of the town square by the armillary.

The Queen was waiting in the garden center, this time sitting on a large toadstool at the center of a ring of mushrooms spread across a patch of grass next to the armillary. Dew sparkled in the moonlight on the blades of grass. Old, white-haired fairies in long silk-brocade robes sat on each of the mushrooms in the circle. Thomas, also dressed in a silk robe, stood beside the old fairies, his face expressionless. Ranks of little fairy soldiers stood in a circle behind the ring of assembled fairy dignitaries. A scattering of other fairies stood behind the soldiers. It was silent. Even the cicadas were quiet.

The Queen stood. The fairy dignitaries seated on the mushrooms stood as well. The soldiers and other fairies knelt.

"Welcome Elizabeth," proclaimed the Queen.

Elizabeth curtsied, a gesture she had learned in ballet class. It seemed like the proper thing to do. "Good evening, Your Highness," she said.

The Queen nodded and spoke, her face stern, but her voice hinting at compassion. "It has been five years since you had contact with my kingdom. Five years without seeing us or knowing anything about us. I have kept my
~~~~~

kingdom obscured from you as I do with all other humans. You made a serious mistake at that time. Have you changed your ways?"

"Yes, Your Highness."

"I have begun to allow you to know of us again over the past few months. You have kept our secret?"

"Yes. I have told no one, not even Papa."

"That is as it should be. And now I have allowed Olivia to meet with you again."

"Yes. Thank you, Your Highness."

"There is a special bond between you and the world of the fairies. That connection has always been there, even when you could not see us. I can withdraw your awareness of us again if I so choose. Do you understand?"

"Yes."

"Keep my trust. Keep our secret, and you may remain in contact with us."

"Thank you, Your Highness."

"Many of the fairies are now afraid of you. It will take more time for you to regain their trust. I will not order them to allow you to see them. It is a thing which each of them may decide in their own time."

"That's okay."

"Go now. Do what I have told you to do. Never do what is prohibited by me and we can enjoy a long existence together." The Queen was stern, definitive even in this moment of forgiveness.

"Yes, Your Highness."

The Queen sat again on her toadstool. The dignitaries in The Queen's council also sat and the soldiers and other fairies got back to their feet. The garden became quiet. Olivia flew up to Elizabeth's shoulder, touched her and began the flight back to her bedroom. When they were inside and Elizabeth had floated back to her bed, Olivia finally spoke.

"You did well, Elizabeth. Can you come meet me in the garden tomorrow?"

"I'll try. In the morning, if Mom and Dad don't make me go someplace with them, I'll come out to see you."

"Good. Now sleep. I will see you tomorrow."

11
ELIZABETH – AGE THIRTY

ELIZABETH DREAMED OF HER AWKWARD life as a twelve-year-old, bringing back memories that were not always pleasant. She woke from her dream in the middle of the night. Yes, there was her first tentative experience with being in love. There was also the age-old torment of adolescence. She remembered the resentment she held for her parents. She had hated her mother for at least a year, believing Mom had no idea what it was like to be a woman. Even when she acknowledged her mother did know, she dismissed her as being out of touch with the way things were for a girl in the present day. Elizabeth had believed Mom was clueless and would never understand what it was like to be in love.

It came to Elizabeth suddenly that, as close as she and Livvy were, a time might come when Livvy, too, would tune her out. What would Livvy be like when she hit adolescence? It was an unsettling thought. *I'll be better with my little girl than Mom was with me*, she vowed. *Right now, it's the two of us against the world. We'll go at life together, side-by-side, shoulder-to-shoulder. By the time she hits adolescence, we'll be so close, we'll know each other so well, we'll avoid all the typical 'I hate my lame mom' business. I won't be her buddy. I'll still be her parent at times. But we'll be friends.* She fell into a restless sleep again.

12
Elizabeth – Age Twelve

EARLY, BEFORE BREAKFAST, ELIZABETH RETURNED to the garden. She walked with her head down and her shoulders rolled forward in the new posture she had adopted to hide her emerging woman's body.

Olivia flew across the garden to her without being summoned. "Good morning!" she chimed cheerily. They sat beside each other on a bench, Elizabeth's long, knobby-kneed legs dangling to the ground, Olivia sitting cross-legged.

"Hey, Olivia. How are you today? What's up?" Elizabeth spoke with little energy in her voice.

"I am well. We really did not have time to talk yesterday when we met and certainly not last night when you met the Queen. Tell me, Elizabeth, how are you? What is happening in your life now? Nearly six years have passed. That is a long time for a human."

"I'm practically an adult. I'll be in seventh grade next year."

"That is good. So, everything is well with you?"

"I guess. It's okay. How about you?"

"Life in the fairy kingdom is always good. But you do not appear sure about yourself. You do not sound like you are happy."

Elizabeth slumped again, her shoulders still tucked forward. She wore a baggy shirt. "I don't know. Everything is good, I guess. Mom told me this is supposed to be a special time in my life. But it sucks."

"It sucks? Who sucks and on what? I do not understand."

"It sucks means it's no fun. I mean, look at me. I'm fat. Sometimes my face breaks out. I don't know. It's just weird. My whole body is weird. Disgusting things are happening to me."

"I do not understand. You look like you have become a lovely young woman while I have been kept away from you."

"Yeah? My body's changed, practically overnight. That's part of it. But I don't feel lovely. I feel disgusting sometimes. And boys. They're so dumb."

"Ah. Is this about your brother, Michael?"

"Yes. No. Michael can act really strange now that he's fourteen. He spends a lot of time in his bedroom with the door closed. Sometimes he smells. But it's the boys in school. They look at me funny and they talk dirty and laugh about stuff. I hate it."

"They are changing too. Wait a while and they will become more pleasing."

"That's what Mom says too. I don't know. Everything is so weird now."

"You and your mother have talked about this?"

"Yeah. We had 'The Talk'. All about 'the birds and the bees', she called it." Elizabeth made quotations signs with her hands as she spoke. "How dumb is that, the birds and the bees. I mean, I know what's going on. I have the internet. I looked it up. And I've talked about it with my friends. But I don't know if everything they told me is true. They think they know everything, but they're probably in the dark as much as I am."

"Wait. You have confused me. What is it about the birds and the bees you do not understand? And what is this inter-net?"

Elizabeth shook her head, exasperated. "The internet is a place you can go on a computer to learn stuff. And the birds and the bees? It's how Mom explained things to me."

"The inter-net? Computers? There is no need for these things. Everything you need to know you can learn from fairies and magic. I do not know of this inter-net. I know of other nets, but not this inter-net."

"Okay. But you know about the birds and the bees, don't you?"

"Of course. I know all about the birds and the bees."

"Could you explain the birds and the bees to me? Maybe you can explain things better than Mom did. Mom got kind of embarrassed."

"I can try. This is what I know." Olivia flew to the lawn and sat cross-legged, facing Elizabeth. Elizabeth also sank to the ground, leaned forward, arms on her knees, and waited to learn the truth about sex.

Olivia began. "Birds and bees both can fly. Let us talk first of the birds. Birds come in many sizes and colors. They are mostly stupid, timid creatures. Except for hawks, eagles, and owls; those are birds that kill. You need to be particularly careful with the owls. They are the smartest of all birds and they can be vindictive. Owls never forget, and they will settle a grudge years after they believe they have been wronged. Crows, starlings, and blue jays are noisy and argumentative. Every day some little thing will set them off and they will go on and on about it. The cardinals? Oh my, those cardinals are something. Always looking for sexual pleasure, particularly at this time of year in the spring and even into the summer. They never stop. But most birds are docile and foolish creatures, afraid of their own shadows. Sparrows are just silly little things. The same is true of the chickadees."

"I think Mom was trying to warn me about the cardinals," Elizabeth said with a mischievous smile. "What do you know about the bees?"

"The bees are a lot like fairies. They are hard-working and obedient. They, too, honor their Queen. Bees are good and they share their honey with the fairies. Other insects are less noble. Hornets are violent beasts who kill without mercy for any reason at all. We do not like the hornets. Flies are dirty. You cannot imagine what they eat and how they breed. Butterflies are very pretty, but the problem is they know it. One day they are a worm, and then just like that they become beautiful. They can be vain, shallow creatures without anything of value to offer the world except their beauty. Moths are like butterflies, but except for the Luna Moth, they are ugly and they, too, know it. Perhaps this is what your mother was talking about. You have suddenly become a beautiful young woman, Lizzie. You are like a monarch butterfly. You need to be aware of how much more there is to you than your beautiful appearance. Do not become vain like a butterfly. You should not become shallow. You are a special being."

"No. I don't think that's what Mom was talking about. She was talking about something else. Eggs and pollen and stuff like that."

"Oh. I like eggs and pollen. I had pollen for my morning meal today.

Fairies also eat small vegetables, some kinds of meat, and honey and nectar of course. On Midsummer Day, fairies gather birds' eggs, robin's eggs, sparrow eggs. Every family enjoys a special holiday feast of a cooked egg. The birds understand. It is their unborn young we are eating, but they allow us to do so. I imagine they see it as an honor for us to feast on their eggs."

"One egg feeds a whole fairy family?"

"Yes. There is always some left over, and we make a special stew for the day after the festival. It is a tradition. Is there anything else you need me to explain about the birds and the bees?"

"Is there anything else for you to tell me?"

"I could tell you about dragonflies. Dragonflies are valuable. They serve as messengers for fairies in the summertime. We must use birds in the winter when the dragonflies die. When you see swarms of dragonflies in the summer you can be sure there is a fairy council, a conclave nearby."

"What's a conclave?"

"A formal gathering, like last night, where the Queen makes decisions about important fairy business. We use several other insects as work animals. Beetles carry things for us, and some ants. Carpenter ants help us a lot. They build things. Cockroaches are awful animals that serve no purpose for us."

"I saw the mice pulling the Queen's carriage and moles working to help fairies remove snow from the marketplace back when I was little."

"Yes. We have a few animals who serve us. Most animals are useless, and we don't even let them know we are here. Squirrels can be a nuisance. They are unpredictable creatures and they are very hard to domesticate. Chipmunks are better, but they can be so involved in raising their young they simply cannot do everything we ask of them. Fairies hate raccoons. They are nasty animals. We do not ever let raccoons see us or our kingdom. Snakes? You will never see a snake in your grandfather's garden. The Queen has banished them. They are afraid to come back over the wall."

"That's good. I hate snakes. What about cats? Papa has a cat. Lucifer. Do you like cats?"

"Lucifer knows we are here, as do all cats. Cats have that special sense of things humans cannot understand. Cats can be unpredictable, but they are not as bad as squirrels. They simply have an independent mind, all their own. We have cast a spell on Lucifer to make him treat us with respect. It is what we must do to be safe. He does not bother us."

"What about dogs?"

"Dogs do not seem to know about fairies. If they do, they do not seem to care. We have no reason to think about dogs. They have no reason to think about us. Have I answered all of your questions about the birds and the bees?"

"No. I mean, I like that I can talk with you again, and I like everything you've explained about the birds and bees. But I think Momma was trying to explain sex to me. And I think she was trying to explain what is happening with my body."

"Oh." Olivia looked puzzled for a moment, a quick frown crossing her face. "You want to know about human reproduction and breeding? I understand it is a very emotional topic for humans. I am afraid I cannot help you much with that. With fairies it is different. We do not breed the way humans do."

"How do you do it?"

"That is for the Queen to say. I would rather not discuss it."

"Can you tell me anything you know about how humans do it?"

"I cannot tell you much. I can only tell you what the fairies know. We usually leave humans alone when they are in their houses. Humans commonly breed indoors, and it is of little interest to us."

"So, you don't know how it works for humans?"

"I understand a little. There was this one time, back when your grandmother was alive. She and your grandfather were out here in the garden alone together in the evening. They were drinking wine and then suddenly they were doing what it is you humans do. It is such a ridiculous thing you do. All of the fairies who were there were laughing and laughing while we watched them. When it was finished, your grandmother said it was magical. That made us laugh even harder. Magical. Really! We couldn't stop laughing."

"That's disgusting. My Papa and Nana? And you watched and laughed?"

Remembering it, Olivia couldn't help laughing again, the sound musical, chiming. "Oh, I know I should not laugh. I know this is important to humans. I imagine you will enjoy it once you do it and get used to it. But what fairies do to breed really is magical. That is all I will say about this subject."

13
Elizabeth - Age Thirty

Elizabeth woke at dawn and lay quietly in bed, lingering, reminiscing about her sex talk with Olivia. It led her to remember her first love, and the other boys who seemed to matter when she was younger.

Love, she mused. *It's a ridiculous concept. That a man and a woman should fall in love and live together happily ever after? Crazy! Everyone is always evolving, their lives changing. What seems to be working one day might not be right after a few years have passed. I was so in love with Lucas when we first met, and I believed he was in love with me too, back then. Maybe he really was in love with me at first. And then it all went to hell. There was also Zach. I was stunned by what I felt with him for the first time. And Derek. He'll always be special to me, even if I discovered over time he was such a loser. None of those relationships turned out to be "the one," but I honestly thought I was in love with each of them.*

Maybe Julia understands how it works. She seemed to have a good grip on how to handle men. I always got good advice from her. She was my best friend for so many years, but we've lost touch. Should I talk with her? I'll give her a call.

But it doesn't always turn out badly. Look at Papa and Nana, happily married for decades. Or Mom and Dad. I think they're happy—it's hard to know with them. At least they're still together. Or even Michael and Eve. I don't understand their relationship, but they seem to be in love. They have some strange connection. They're devoted to each other. Maybe I'm just unlucky with love. Right now, I'm fine without a man in my life. I don't need to have a man to make me happy.

14
Elizabeth – Age Twelve

IT WAS THE END OF the school year, and Elizabeth had gone with her family to visit Papa in Williamsburg. Now, they were getting ready to return to Richmond and Elizabeth was eager to return home to see her friends. Mom took her aside and asked, "When summer vacation starts, would you like to stay with Papa for a few weeks? Michael will be at camp most of the summer, and Dad and I both go to work every day. We don't want you sitting around the house all summer with nothing to do."

Typical, Elizabeth thought. *They don't have any concern for me or for Michael. All they have time for is themselves and their jobs. I don't really matter to them, do I? I might as well be an orphan. I'm basically raising myself. My life is all a mess, a huge tragedy. I guess I have no choice but to make the best of it. I should say yes and act like I agree. They'll make me stay here anyway. But then, Papa and I do have fun together, and there are the fairies to think about.*

"Could I?" Elizabeth feigned eagerness, putting a good face on her sad situation. "Is it okay with Papa?"

"Yes. We've talked with him and he says it'll be fine."

Papa reached out and gave Elizabeth a hug. "Of course you can stay with me this summer. You can go to the pool every day. We'll do things out here in the garden. You'll have a good time."

Elizabeth's face glowed. This was starting to sound like a good idea after all. "Awesome! I can't wait."

"Yeah, that'll be great." Michael gave a short, sarcastic laugh and a dismissive wave of his hand. "Splashing around in a pool every day? Sure, sounds like fun. I'll be at computer tech camp. That's where the real fun is."

"Don't forget I'll have the garden," Elizabeth added.

Papa smiled and gave her shoulder one last squeeze before she left.

~~~~~

Elizabeth had been staying with Papa for more than two weeks. Every morning after breakfast she was off, pedaling her bike through the neighborhood to the pool. She practiced with her age-group swim team for an hour and stayed till lunchtime, hanging out with new friends. Her afternoons were spent at Papa's house. She was inside reading a book if it was hot, out in the garden talking with Olivia when the weather was tolerably cool.

Today was hot until a thunderstorm blew through late in the afternoon. After the storm, it was still humid and Elizabeth remained inside, lying on the living room sofa, reading. She listened to music in her earbuds, her favorite music, a new boy-band comprised of three brothers. She had told Papa they were immensely talented, and she had even made him listen to them once. They were also very cute, except for the sullen one. Their poster hung on her bedroom wall back in Richmond. Papa was interested and had listened, but he was unimpressed by their music. Now he sat across from her, also reading. He couldn't hear her boy-band, only her off-key humming as she sang along with the boys.

The doorbell rang. Elizabeth didn't hear it because of her music. Papa did and he went to open the front door. A tall, thin boy stood there, shifting anxiously from foot to foot, looking distractedly back at the street where he had left a bicycle lying on the lawn. He appeared to be about Elizabeth's age. His long blond hair was faded by pool water and the summer sun. His eyes were a striking green.

"Yes?" asked Papa, though he suspected he knew what this was about.

"Does Elizabeth live here?" the boy asked, his voice husky.

"No, but she's staying here this summer. I'm her grandfather. And you are?"

"I'm Zach. From the swim team. Is she home? Can I see her?"
~~~~~

"Yes. Come on in." Papa held the door for the boy and led him to the living room.

"Elizabeth, you have a visitor."

Elizabeth looked up, saw Zach, and burst into a beaming smile. She dropped her book and pulled out her ear-buds, snapping off the music. Quickly, she caught herself. *Gotta stay cool*, she thought. *It's Zach. Stay calm. I can't let him see I like him.*

She suppressed her smile and stood up.

"Oh, hi Zach. What's up?" She turned from him for a moment, gazing out the window at the garden, hoping to display an overtly casual attitude, a lack of concern he had come to visit her. Papa saw through her actions, aware of her excitement. Zach didn't. But he was grinning too, consumed by her presence, thrilled simply to be visiting her.

"Not much," he said. "I've downloaded the new Flash Frogs music. I thought you might want to listen."

Elizabeth rolled her shoulders in a shrug. Papa had noticed she had been standing straighter lately. She seemed less self-conscious, more confident since she arrived to spend the summer. For a moment she almost reverted to her former slumped posture. She pulled herself taller and smiled at Zach. "Sure. Why not?"

Papa interrupted. "Elizabeth, why don't you take Zach out back in the garden to listen to his music? I'll get started on dinner in the kitchen."

"Sure. C'mon, Zach." She led him out the French doors onto the terrace and down the brick steps into the garden. They sat side-by-side on a bench in the center, at the armillary. Cicadas hummed in the heat. Dragonflies darted, flashes of black, green, gold, and red. Butterflies swarmed through the flowers. The garden was dappled with sunlight and shade.

"What's that thing?" asked Zach, pointing.

Elizabeth was startled, wondering if Zach might have seen a fairy. Then she saw he was gesturing at the armillary. "My Papa calls it an armillary."

"What's it do?"

"I'm not sure. I think it's sort of like a sundial, only more complicated. Something about the sun and the moon and what time it is. I guess the rings and the arrow tell what day it is, what season too."

"Oh. It looks old, all rusted and everything. It must have been out here in the garden forever." Zach thought about it for a moment, not more. He was young, unaware of his own mortality, and for him, the passage of time was irrelevant. The infinity of forever was incomprehensible. "Well, here's my Flash Frogs. Give a listen."

He gave her one earbud, keeping the other for himself. He started the music, and they continued to sit side-by-side in silence, each of them connected by one ear to his device, sharing the songs. Their shoulders almost touched. Olivia sat on top of a flat-topped, pruned boxwood across the garden watching her, smiling.

Elizabeth closed her eyes, for the moment shutting out the fairies, ignoring Olivia, listening, rocking in rhythm with the music. Zach rocked as well, synchronous with Elizabeth, his luminous eyes also closed.

When the music ended, Zach pulled out his earbud. "Pretty cool, huh?" he asked.

"Yeah. I like it. It's awesome."

They sat together, neither knowing where to start, what to say next. Papa pulled them back to his reality, calling from the terrace. "Elizabeth? Dinner's almost ready. Let's go."

"Coming Papa," she called.

"Yeah, I gotta get going too," said Zach. "My mom will have dinner ready."

They stood and ambled back through the garden, up to the terrace and in through the French doors. For a moment, their arms swung in harmony as they walked. They brushed arms and for a bare second, their fingers almost laced together. Then they pulled apart, embarrassed.

Olivia chased after them, running at first, then flying from branch to branch, bouncing with excitement from point to point, to a flowering bough of a magnolia tree, to the terrace wall, and in through the doors behind them. Elizabeth could hear Olivia's tinkling fairy voice. "Elizabeth! He is beautiful. He has green fairy eyes. Oh Elizabeth, I think he likes you!"

They were at the front door. Olivia perched on a narrow hall table and watched. Elizabeth opened the door and Zach stepped through. Elizabeth leaned her shoulder on the doorjamb, holding the doorknob in one hand. Zach was on the threshold. He paused and turned.

"Come on, Elizabeth! Kiss him," urged Olivia. She flew behind Elizabeth and pushed, nudging her back and shoulders. Elizabeth tipped forward, off balance; she couldn't stop herself. Her chest and firm little breasts pressed against Zach's thin chest. She looked up. His face was right there. He leaned down. Then he pulled back.

"Gotta go," he said abruptly. He twisted through the door, leaped down the front steps, and ran across the lawn to his bike.

"Bye, Zach," she called after him.

"Bye. See you at the pool for practice tomorrow," he shouted back. He pedaled away on his bike.

Elizabeth dodged back out to the terrace to wait for dinner. She sat, distracted, not knowing what Papa might be thinking, not knowing what to say to him about her new friend, Zach. Her mind was chaotic, trying to make sense of all that had just happened, scrambling to understand everything she was feeling.

Papa came out carrying a tray. He set out two plates with hamburgers and potato salad. Then he put down two tall glasses of iced tea.

"So," Papa began. "Tell me about this young man. Zach."

"Oh, him." Elizabeth tried to appear nonchalant, dismissive of the enormity of the first time a boy came to visit. "Yeah. Zach. He's from the pool. He's on the swim team with me."

"He seems nice; a polite young gentleman."

"Yeah. Whatever. He's a really good swimmer."

"Okay. Well, you can tell him, he's welcome to visit anytime we're both home."

"Yeah. Okay. I'll tell him tomorrow.

When Elizabeth fell asleep that night, she dreamed of Zach, of his long blond hair and his startling green eyes.

~~~~~

Zach's visits became an everyday event. Elizabeth and he were together at the pool for practice every morning. They swam with their teammates for the first hour. Endless laps, timed sprints, and coaching on new strokes filled part of the morning. The rest of the time until lunch they spent joking with their teammates and eating vending machine snacks while sitting in the white plastic chairs set in the shade near the pool.

Mid-afternoon each day back at Papa's house, the doorbell rang, and Zach would be there on the steps. He stayed till dinner time. Papa was always
~~~~~

nearby, but he left the two of them alone.

Elizabeth and Zach played backgammon at the table on the terrace, laughing and screaming together at the rolls of the dice. They talked about music and movies and books. Olivia sat on the terrace wall, rapt, attentive, watching and smiling. Other fairies flew by from time to time, possibly on errands, though they might have been curious about Elizabeth's new boyfriend. Sometimes the fairies stopped and sat with Olivia, watching Elizabeth and Zach, talking quietly in their chiming fairy language. It annoyed Elizabeth that they were always there, watching her, but she grew accustomed to their presence.

Most days, when it was nearly time for him to leave, Elizabeth walked with Zach into the garden for a few minutes. They sat at the armillary or at the other two circles where there were the statues of dancing children. Sometimes, during these moments when they were alone, they held hands. There was always an awkward moment at the front door as he was leaving. They were both afraid of what the other might think if anything more happened between them.

Most nights, Papa and Elizabeth ate dinner together on the terrace. They sat talking one evening after dinner as dusk was setting in. Throughout the garden, high among the crepe myrtle blossoms, and lower in the ivy and the boxwood, tiny points of light glowed, drifting with the breeze. Papa believed they were fireflies; Elizabeth knew they were mostly fairies.

"So, Elizabeth, would you like to have Zach stay for dinner some evening?"

"No, that's okay. He has to go home for dinner."

"It wouldn't be a problem. Why don't you ask him?"

"He can't. His mom thinks he's too young to have a girlfriend. I mean, that's so dumb. He's fourteen. He's going into ninth grade. He's practically a grown man."

"Ah. Is that why he always comes here? You can't go to his house?"

"Yeah. But it's so stupid," Elizabeth said. Her mood became sullen. "I mean, he's one of the best swimmers on our team. He'll be going out for the swim team in his high school. He's old enough to have a girlfriend."

"So, his parents don't know he's seeing you? They don't know he's here every day?"

"I don't know. I guess not." Elizabeth looked down at the brick paved terrace. She worried Papa would forbid her from spending time with Zach, like his parents had forbidden him from having a girlfriend, just like the Queen had shut her out of the fairy kingdom for those five long years.

"It's okay, Papa. He's a good guy," Elizabeth pleaded.

"Yes, I know he is. I don't want him getting in trouble with his parents though. They should know about you. You need to be thoughtful, Elizabeth. You need to understand his parents' concerns and respect what they think."

"He'll get in trouble."

"You have a swim meet next week. I'm coming to watch, and if I meet his parents there, I'll have to talk with them. I'll let them know he comes to see you and that I think he's a gentleman. I'll tell them he's okay with me and with you."

"No! He'll get grounded, and I won't be able to see him."

"I think it'll be okay. I won't bring it up if you don't want me to. But if it comes up, I won't hide it when I meet his mom and dad."

Elizabeth hung her head. She knew this was a fight she didn't want; a fight she couldn't win. Papa always seemed to understand and know what was best. It aggravated her, but she said nothing, letting her silence convey her displeasure with Papa's plan.

~~~~~

When Elizabeth and Papa went to the swim meet, Zach's parents weren't there. She was safe. After the meet, Papa drove her back to the house. She got out of the car and walked, scuffing her flip-flops, into the living room and threw herself onto the sofa. Now that they'd had the final competition, swim practice was over for the summer. She would be going back to Richmond in a few days. It would be the end of her time with the fairies for a while. And the end of her time with Zach, too.

"How are you doing?" Papa sat in his chair across from her.

"Fine."

"I guess you're relieved Zach's parents weren't there."

"I guess."

"But now the swim team's done for the year."

"Yeah."

"You'll miss Zach. You ought to keep in touch with him."

"Yeah. We have each other's phone numbers and email addresses. We'll
~~~~~

text and everything."

"That's good. Maybe you'll see him next summer."

"Maybe."

Elizabeth stood and walked without a word up to her bedroom. She shut the door and fell face-down onto her bed. *My life is over,* she thought tearfully. *I won't see Zach for weeks, months, maybe forever.*

Olivia appeared, sitting on the pillow next to her. "Do not worry, Elizabeth. It is true love. Zach will wait for you."

15
Elizabeth – Age Thirteen

THE SUMMER ENDED, AND ELIZABETH returned to her family, friends and school in Richmond. She and Zach exchanged emails and text messages for the first few days. They wrote about school, their teachers, music, movies. By Thanksgiving they had almost stopped writing; there was nothing new to share. She stayed in Richmond with her parents and Michael. Zach went with his family to visit relatives in North Carolina.

Elizabeth wrote to Zach the week before Christmas. "I'll be in Williamsburg at Christmas. Want to come over?"

His reply was brief. "Can't. Going to North Carolina again to my mom's parents for Christmas. See you next summer."

Elizabeth was embarrassed. She had told all her girlfriends in Richmond about Zach and wished she could show him off to them. She had hoped maybe she could shoot a picture of them together if he came over at Christmas.

Elizabeth didn't hear from him again. Months passed. She spent time with her Richmond girlfriends and even went to two parties with them, including boys. There was animated dancing, imitating what they all saw on television. One of the boys asked her to go see a movie with him. They went, driven by the boy's father, but there was no excitement, no connection. He wasn't Zach. He asked her to another movie, but she said no. There wasn't a second date.

~~~~~

Then it was summer and Elizabeth came back to stay at Papa's. She was taller and her body was more mature. She had a new racing swimsuit that fit her like a second skin. She was ready for the first day of swim practice, ready to see Zach again and start where they had left off in August.

Papa noted her eagerness for the first practice. He sent her off on her bike and waited for her to return at lunchtime. She came back in the door grinning.

"How was practice, Elizabeth?"

"Good." She was still smiling, her face lighting the room. "What's for lunch?"

"Sandwiches. We can eat outside." They carried their lunches to the table on the terrace.

"Was Zach there?" Papa asked.

"Yeah." She was grinning, looking hard at her sandwich. Her auburn hair hung forward, shielding her face. Papa couldn't see her eyes.

"Do you think he might stop by again?"

"Yeah." She looked up at Papa now, her smile wide, light in her eyes.

"Okay. That's fine. I'll go dust off the backgammon game for you."

Elizabeth giggled. "Thanks, Papa."

The doorbell rang mid-afternoon. Elizabeth ran and opened the door. Zach was there, taller, his hair still long, his eyes still a striking green.

"Hey," he said to Elizabeth, his voice deeper than a year ago. "Hey," he said again as he passed Papa. Papa watched him carefully, conscious of the way he'd grown into a youthful manhood. Elizabeth led him out to the terrace.

They settled back into their old habits. A year had passed in their short lives, but it was as though it had been only a day. Backgammon, music, and laughter dominated the afternoon.

Late the first afternoon, they walked quickly into the garden, eager to be alone, but trailed by an excited Olivia. They held hands for a moment, looking at the flowers, not talking. Neither could think of anything to say; this was not a time for words. They wandered in silence, their minds racing. Then they returned to the terrace. It was like Zach's first visit a year ago.
~~~~~

Olivia flew after them, chirping at Elizabeth. "He's the one, Elizabeth. We both know it. He's come back for you just like a prince in a fairy tale. Oh, maybe this is your moment. Maybe today he'll really kiss you!"

They stopped at the front door as they had every day last summer when she was twelve and he was fourteen. They were a year older now, more aware and mature. Papa was in the kitchen, working on dinner. They were alone. Olivia flew, bouncing excitedly on the hall table, on the door jamb, on the porch light. "Kiss him, Elizabeth. This is it! Kiss him!"

Neither of them said a word, but they leaned toward each other. Zach's arm found its way around her shoulder; hers went around his waist. She looked up. It was only for an instant; their faces touched, then their lips brushed each other's cheeks. Elizabeth felt the soft beginnings of whiskers. And heat. They pulled back, each of them flushed, agitated.

Zach stepped away from her, smiling. "See you tomorrow, Elizabeth." He turned slowly and walked, then jogged to his bike at the curb and rode away without looking back.

She wandered into the kitchen, distracted, unable to concentrate, dreaming. *I kissed him! I think he kissed me too!*

Papa had been in the kitchen the whole time. He busied himself with a platter of fried chicken. They didn't look at each other, but he was aware something special had just happened. Elizabeth was blushing and again suppressing a smile. She wanted to shout, dance, tell Papa all about it. She also wanted to keep it a secret, like the fairies in the garden. This secret was not even for Papa.

"Place mats and silverware are on the counter. Go set up on the terrace. I'll be along with the food in a couple of minutes."

"Okay, Papa."

She took the place settings and floated out to the terrace. She set the places, and sat at the table, restless, staring into the garden. Bees were buzzing. Swarms of dragonflies, below the terrace at the garden entrance, flew off to the center at the armillary and on to the back wall where the palace was. Birds were fluttering, hummingbirds hovering and darting. Olivia was dancing a jig, bouncing on top of the terrace wall.

"Oh, Elizabeth! He kissed you! And you kissed him. Oh, what was it like?" Olivia stopped her dance and sat, cross-legged on the wall, elbows on her knees with her chin in her hands.

"It was okay." Elizabeth's heart was still pounding, remembering the feel of his body, the whiskers, the smell of pool chlorine and the new scent of a man.

"Come on Elizabeth. I know you. Was it not grand?"

"Yeah." Elizabeth couldn't help smiling. She couldn't stop herself, adding, "It was more than okay, more than grand."

Olivia flitted off into the garden. "Oh, this is so wonderful. I must tell the Queen of this."

<div align="center">~~~~~</div>

Late at night, Olivia led Elizabeth floating out of her bedroom and into the garden. She delivered her to the front of the palace where the Queen waited for her.

The Queen spoke, her voice resonant and melodious. Her face glowed with understanding and compassion. "Elizabeth, we should talk about this boy. Zach, you call him. Tell me about him."

"He's on my swim team. He's a friend. That's all." Now Elizabeth was afraid the Queen, unlike Papa, might forbid her from seeing Zach. She could work around whatever her Papa did about Zach, but she knew the Queen's words could be absolute. She remembered the five-year sentence imposed by her; a judgment that ended so recently.

"Does he know of us? Have you spoken with him about the fairies?"

"Of course not. And Olivia is always there when he comes over to see me. And other fairies are always around us. I even see some of them in the bushes when I'm at the pool."

"Yes, we are watching over you, even at the pool. I have a colony of fairies who live there. Be careful with this boy, Elizabeth. He is a good boy, but he is still a boy. Understand why his mother is concerned about what could happen to her son with you."

Elizabeth became petulant. "What could happen? We don't do anything wrong."

"No. But you need to know this. Boys are boys. Humans are not like fairies. Fairies only breed when I decide we must. With humans, the desire to do so is always there."

Elizabeth pouted. "We're not 'breeding' as you put it. He just comes over and we hang out."

"Hang out? What is that? What hangs out?" Olivia interrupted with a trace of alarm in her voice.

"It just means we spend time together. We talk and listen to music and play backgammon on the terrace. That's all."

"Yes." The Queen nodded.

"Fairies don't do it? Fairies don't… you know, have boyfriends, go on dates, all that?"

Olivia chimed in. "Go on dates? I do not understand. Every day has a date."

The Queen spoke, momentarily exasperated. "Olivia, please. Let me discuss this important matter with Elizabeth. Do fairies breed? Rarely. Humans only live a few years. Less than a century for most of you. All creatures have a defined lifespan. Some insects only live a few days. They are born, they breed and they die. Your pets, your dogs and cats live about a dozen years, maybe a few more. That is all. They have litters of their young as soon as they are able. But fairies live a thousand years or longer. Olivia is more than four hundred years old. I, myself, am aged, almost a thousand years old. My daughter, the princess, is the same age as Olivia. She will take my place as Queen when I pass."

Elizabeth nodded, seeking understanding and waiting for more. The Queen continued, her head tilted back, staring intently at Elizabeth.

"Because we live so many years, it is wise we do not spend so much of our lives breeding. There would be too many fairies if we did. The last time I decreed we must breed was more than three hundred years ago. That was to assure us of having enough fairies to colonize more of this new land when we arrived four hundred years ago on your sailing ships. I must partake in the breeding when it is our time to do so. It is part of my duty as the Queen. It is not so with humans."

"Okay. And I'm human. But I don't want to 'breed' as you call it. Not now. The idea of it… I know what we do. I talked about it with my girlfriends back in Richmond. It's gross. It's disgusting. I won't do that. But I don't think I can wait hundreds of years either."

"Of course not. You are a human; your time will come. But remember this. With human boys, all they want to do is breed. Your friend Zach. Right now, he is playing games with you and listening to music. That is good. But he also is a human boy so he will want to breed with you. You must be careful with him. You must be cautious and remain always in control of yourself and of him so he does not make you do things you should not do."

"I won't. I'll be good. He'll be good too. He's a good guy."

"Yes, he is. But he is also a human boy."

Elizabeth answered defiantly. "I want to see him. I'm going to."

Then she considered the immense power of the Queen. "Can I still see him?" she begged.

The Queen looked her in the eyes, pausing. Elizabeth waited, intent on what the Queen would say. At last the Queen spoke, her voice ringing. "Yes. And we will be here to help you if Zach or any other boy tries to do things with you which should not be done."

Was it another of the Queen's threats? Was it a warning? Was it assurance of the fairies' protection? The Queen stood, her glow intensifying. "I must go now," she said. She floated back toward the palace, trailing glittering motes of dust. She drifted through the fortified wall, across the courtyard, into her palace.

"Come now," said Olivia. She touched Elizabeth on the shoulder, flew her to her bedroom, and put her back into her bed. Elizabeth was asleep in a second. She did not dream.

~~~~~

Every morning at swim practice, Zach and Elizabeth were near each other whenever they could be. They swam in different lanes doing different workouts, but when they finished the practice and their teammates gathered in the shade, joking and chattering loudly, Zach and Elizabeth sat quietly at a separate table. Their friends teased them at first. The boys called out to Zach, telling him he was hen-pecked; the girls sang foolish songs about the couple. Zach and Elizabeth laughed and ignored the teasing until it stopped. It was understood at the pool that Zach and Elizabeth were "an item."

Each night, when Elizabeth went to bed, she called her girlfriends back in Richmond and whispered into the phone so Papa wouldn't hear her. "Yes, I kissed him. Yes, he kissed me too. I think he liked it! I don't know if he can come see me in Richmond when we start school, but right now, this is summer and it's really happening." She reveled at the thought of her
~~~~~

girlfriends back home in Richmond sharing her gossip every day.

~~~~~

A swim meet ended the summer. Papa watched as Elizabeth and Zach's team competed against boys and girls on a team from the next town. Elizabeth won a medal in one race and got ribbons in two others. Zach, who swam in an age group older than Elizabeth's, won four races.

After the meet, Elizabeth walked away from her teammates and approached Papa. She wore rubber flip flops and her t-shirt covered her sleek racing swim suit. Her hair was wet and slicked back. Marks from her goggles rimmed her chlorine-reddened eyes.

Nearby, Zach stood with a man and a woman. He had a loose t-shirt and knee-length baggy shorts over his Speedo. He had covered his long hair with a cap while he swam, but his hair was wet and raked away from his face. Four medals on ribbons clanked against his chest.

Papa asked, "Are those Zach's parents? Should we introduce ourselves?"

"No!" Elizabeth tugged at him. But it was too late. Zach, looking embarrassed, followed his parents as they walked toward Elizabeth and Papa. They stopped, smiling at Elizabeth.

"Are you Elizabeth?" Zach's mom asked. "I've heard about you."

Elizabeth couldn't make eye contact. She looked down at the concrete pool deck. "Yes."

"Zach says you're a nice girl and a good swimmer. You did well today."

"Thanks."

"I'm Elizabeth's grandfather," interjected Papa. "She's been staying with me this summer."

Zach's father reached out and shook Papa's hand. "We're Zach's parents, Bill and Sandy. It's nice to meet you. So, Elizabeth doesn't live here in Williamsburg?"

"No, her family's up in Richmond. She'll be going back next week to start school there."

"Ah. Yes, Zach starts school here next week as well," said the father.

Zach's mom spoke up. "Zach tells us you and he have become friends here at the pool. He told us you and he like the same music."

"Yes." Elizabeth was still looking at the wet pool deck. She peeked at Zach and noted that he was also looking away from his parents and Papa,
~~~~~

staring out over the still, glassy surface of the pool. She heard the pool pump humming.

"Well, that's good. It's nice to meet you and your grandfather," concluded Zach's father. "You have a good year in school, Elizabeth."

"Thanks."

They were gone. Elizabeth exhaled. "Thank you, Papa, for not telling them Zach comes over."

"Quite all right. I think it went well. Maybe next year when you're both older, things will be different for him and his parents. A lot can change in a year."

~~~~~

Zach came for a brief visit the morning Elizabeth was to return to Richmond. She quickly introduced him to her parents. Michael looked Zach over and turned away, disinterested though they were the same age. Zach was an athlete; Michael wasn't. They had nothing in common, nothing to talk about.

Elizabeth took Zach out into the garden for a walk while her parents gathered her bags and loaded the car.

"We need to stay in touch when you get back to Richmond," said Zach. "The same as last year."

"We will. I'll text you every day."

"I'll miss you. Maybe I'll see you when you come down at Christmas? We'll be staying home this year."

"I'll miss you too. And I'll let you know when I get here for Christmas."

They stopped. Then they kissed, right on the lips, holding the kiss for several seconds. They stepped back, breathless. Finally, they walked to the house, holding hands till just before they rounded the corner of the hedges and came into sight of the terrace.

As she settled into the car to leave, Elizabeth reached out, took his hand, and gave a brief squeeze. "Bye Zach," she whispered.

She looked back and waved as they drove away. Zach stood, slump-shouldered, his long swimmer's arms hanging by his side. His face showed no emotion. Elizabeth also saw Olivia hovering by the doorstep. She was too far away to be sure, but it looked to Elizabeth like Olivia was crying. It was certainly a sad moment to be leaving Zach until Christmas, but seeing
~~~~~

Olivia moved to tears puzzled Elizabeth.

~~~~

The text messages between them began during her drive back to Richmond. For the first week, they swapped messages all through each day, beginning as soon as they woke up and ending when they went to bed each night. It had been the same a year before, but there were more texts now, and the messages were longer, more intense, and more filled with passion.

When school began, the texts became less frequent because their days were consumed with school work. Boys in her school in Richmond asked her out, but she always said no. Elizabeth remained loyal to Zach. As the weeks passed, they went for days between messages, though they still kept in touch. Elizabeth worried Zach might be forgetting her.

In one exchange, Elizabeth texted, *I miss you soooo much. I can't wait to be with you again at Christmas.*

Zach's response was terse, but intrigued her. *Miss you too. We have a lot to talk about. See you.*

Elizabeth planned her return to Papa's with her family for Christmas. As the holiday approached, all she could think about was Zach. Elizabeth, anxious she could be losing Zach, planned how she would restart their romance. She had sent him a text letting him know when she would arrive. She signed it, boldly adding the word "love," and hit send before she could reconsider. He answered. He would be coming to visit the first afternoon she was back.

Waiting for him to arrive, Elizabeth considered how to get ready. She mulled over her wardrobe. *Ah, how about my scoop-necked red top?* She tried it on; leaving several other garments she had sampled lying on her bed. *Yes, this is it. Maybe I've outgrown it and it's a little tight, but he'll notice my body if I wear this. And here are my perfect-fitting blue jeans. I'll take him for a walk in the garden, of course, so I'll need to wear a coat. But I'll leave it unbuttoned so he can still see my body. I could sneak some of Mom's makeup. No, Mom would notice and say no.*

The doorbell rang. *He's here!* Elizabeth ran and opened the door. Zach came in, lounging and nonchalant. "Hey, Elizabeth," he said.

She wanted desperately to kiss him and knew she couldn't do it till they were alone. She reached out quickly and touched his arm. "Hey, Zach. It's
~~~~

good to see you again. Thanks for coming over."

"Yeah. No problem."

They walked into the living room where Papa, her parents, and Michael were trimming the tree. With a fire burning in the fireplace and Christmas music playing, it was perfect, just like a special Christmas program on television. Her parents looked up and smiled, greeting Zach briefly. Michael ignored his sister and her boyfriend. Papa smiled and came to them, shaking his hand. "It's nice to have you back for a visit, Zach. How's school been this year so far?"

"Fine."

Elizabeth picked up her coat from the couch where she had left it to be ready. "We're going out for a walk in the garden," she announced. They went out the French doors, across the terrace and down to the garden path. Olivia flew up to them eager and excited. She was fur clad and wore her tan leather knee boots. She followed them, hovered, and finally settled on a bare tree branch, watching from a distance.

The garden was cold, the ground frosted in shady spots, but it felt warm to Elizabeth; she was with Zach. As soon as they were alone and out of sight of the house, Elizabeth stopped, turned and pulled Zach to her. "God, I've missed you," she said. He was taller than she remembered. She stretched up to kiss him.

He pulled back.

"Zach? What's the matter?"

"I don't think we should do this."

"What?"

"I don't think we should be seeing each other. I mean, it was great last summer. I really like you. But it's different now."

"What?" she pleaded.

Olivia flew up from her tree branch, floating closer, her face stern. She lit next to them on a frozen boxwood, wary.

"I mean, you're a cool kid, Elizabeth. But, well… I've got a girlfriend here in school. She's on the swim team. I can't be seeing you, what with my girlfriend and all. That's what I came to tell you."

"What?" Elizabeth's voice squeaked and tears started to rise.

"Come on, Liz. I mean, last summer was cool. But you're just a kid. I'll be sixteen next month. I like older women."

Olivia swooped in, grabbed Zach by his long hair, and pulled. His head jerked back, and he looked around the garden, wild-eyed and startled. In a flash, two of the Queen's soldiers appeared, stabbing at his face with their thin spears. He swatted, though he couldn't see them. Elizabeth watched in astonishment, a hand covering her mouth.

"Mosquitoes? This time of year? In the cold? This is crazy!" Zach stumbled and kept swatting, looking around for his tormenters.

"Go," said Elizabeth. "Get out of here. Just go." She sat on the icy bench next to the armillary, shaking, holding in the tears so he wouldn't see her cry. *I can't let him see me cry.*

Zach dashed back to the house. The soldiers chased him, joined by more fairies, swarming through the air, harassing him until he reached the doors. He rushed through the living room without a word, his head down, eyes averted. Papa, Elizabeth's parents, and even Michael watched him till he was out, slamming the front door.

Papa turned away from the Christmas tree and grabbed his coat from the closet. "Let me take care of this," he said. "I'll go see about Elizabeth."

He pulled on the coat and headed out the doors, down the terrace steps into the garden. He found Elizabeth sitting on the cold bench, clutching the front edge. She wasn't crying, but tear tracks marked her red cheeks. Flocks of sparrows and chickadees clustered near her on branches and on the ground. He couldn't see hordes of fairies had also gathered with her, ranks of soldiers, Olivia, the Queen, and Thomas who was holding a spear rather than his usual staff. Papa sat beside his granddaughter and waited in silence for her to speak.

"He's gone?" she finally asked.

"Yes. Are you okay, little one?"

"Yes. He's a bastard. He's got a new girlfriend."

Papa pulled her to him, his arm wrapping her in. "I understand. I'm here for you. So is your family. You're not alone with this. We'll get through it."

"Papa, why did he do this?" Her voice was high-pitched and weak. For a moment she almost cried again. Her shoulders shook.

"I don't know. He's young and foolish? It happens."

"I hate him."

"I know. You'll be okay. He's the one who's losing out. He's lost you."

She snuggled closer to her grandfather. "What do I do? How do I…" She couldn't even think of what she wanted to say.

"It's not easy. It never will be. You'll find a new boyfriend. Maybe he'll break your heart too. Maybe you'll break his. But you'll fall in love again."

"I wasn't in love with him, Papa," she said with a touch of exasperation. "But I don't think there will ever be another boy. Not like Zach."

"There will be. But about being in love. Weren't you? Didn't you think you were?"

Elizabeth shrugged and laughed, her voice still catching as she spoke. "Maybe. I guess I thought I was. But now I know he's a bastard."

Papa laughed as well. "I don't like it when you swear. But he deserves it."

Elizabeth laughed again, hiccupping, her laugh mixed with her tears. She sniffed and wiped the tear tracks from her face, rubbing her nose with her palm. Papa handed her his handkerchief. She wiped her wet nose, and then held onto the cloth, clutching it, a tangible connection to Papa, hoping it could somehow save her.

"Do you want to come back in now and help with trimming the tree?" he asked.

"In a minute. Give me a couple of more minutes out here in the garden."

"Okay. Come join us when you're ready." Papa gave his little one a final squeeze, kissed the top of her head, and started back to the house.

When he was gone Elizabeth turned to her fairies again. "Thank you for helping me, Your Highness, for sending your soldiers," she said to the Queen. "And thank you Olivia, for being here with me when he told me."

"You are special, Elizabeth," said the Queen. "Do not ever forget you are special."

"Thank you, Your Highness."

Olivia chimed in as well, flying to sit on Elizabeth's lap. "We will always be here with you. A boy like that cannot hurt you when we are watching over you. I will not allow it."

Elizabeth reached out a hand and Olivia hopped onto it, her light glowing in Elizabeth's palm. "Thanks, Olivia. You're my best friend ever."

Olivia flew from Elizabeth's hand to her face and kissed her cheek. It felt to Elizabeth like a blown snowflake.

"I think I'll go in with my family now," said Elizabeth.

It was chilly and turning to dusk; the garden grew colder still. Elizabeth stood and strode toward the terrace. She clutched her jacket closed, still grieving for Zach. Crowds of fairies, returned from their pursuit of Zach, trailed behind her, led by Olivia. Some chirped to each other about Zach and how he had mistreated her. She found it comforting.

As she walked, she came across two thick-bodied fairies hard at work in a corner of the garden. They wore stained leather aprons over rough tunics. Intent on their task, they paid no attention as she passed. Their brawny little arms laboring, they sliced along the bellies and around each paw on the bodies of gray mice, using knives with blades made of glass shards. Blood spattered. With the incisions made, they peeled the fur off each of the mice. Beside them lay a pile of pelts ready to be cured and fashioned into winter clothing. Behind them was a line of pale, skinless bodies. Blood stained the ground, dark dirt coated with a glittering frost of ice crystals. Shaken by the gory scene, Elizabeth hurried on to Papa's house.

That night, she hugged Jefferson to her as she fell asleep. Jefferson was old, but he was still there for her when she needed him. Like Papa. And the fairies.

16
Elizabeth – Age Thirty

SUNRISE CREPT INTO THE FRONT bedroom at Papa's house. Elizabeth lazed, dozing in the unaccustomed bed in the room she still thought of as her parents'. Little footsteps scuffed across the hall. Her door opened quietly. She felt a child's heavy breath next to her bed. Elizabeth opened her eyes. Inches away, a little elfish face grinned at her. "Good morning, Mommy!"

Elizabeth scooped Livvy into the bed, dragging her under the covers, tickling. Livvy squealed, screaming and giggling. "Mommy, stop! I can't breathe!"

Elizabeth eased back and held her baby. Livvy was warm, comforting. Elizabeth kissed her. "Did you sleep well?"

"Yes. Did you, Mommy?"

"Yes," Elizabeth lied. She had gotten to bed very late after watching Livvy's secret dash into the midnight garden. Now she felt like she had been awake most of the night, dreaming about her childhood and worrying about how to move on with her life without Lucas and Papa. She had no clear direction, just a list of tasks she needed to do each day.

"Can we make scrambled eggs for breakfast?"

"Well, all right. Scrambled eggs it is. Maybe we can use some of the eggs from the cardinals in the garden. What do you say?"

"No! That's silly. Chickens lay eggs. That's what we eat."

"Okay. Will you help me scramble them?"

"Okay. And then what'll we do? You're not going to work today, right Mommy? Can we do something fun?"

"Of course. Would you like to find a new school to go to here in our new town?"

Livvy lay in the bed, rolled up with her mommy. After a contemplative moment she said, "Well, all my friends are back at my school in Richmond. I'll have to make new friends if we move here."

The little girl paused, mulling, sorting things out with her child's logic. "But it will all be good, Mommy. Do you know why?"

"No. Why, Honey Bunny?"

"Because I'll have Olivia and the other fairies for friends until I meet new friends at my new school."

Elizabeth looked out the window at the sunshine on the front lawn. She pondered again. Should I warn her about the fairies? Should I let it be and allow her to enjoy a few days, maybe a few years, believing in them? She's been through a lot recently. If believing in fairies helps her cope, maybe I should let it go for now.

"Can we make floater pancakes this morning, Mommy? Instead of scrambled eggs?"

"Sure. Now run along and get dressed. I'll be down in the kitchen in a moment."

Livvy jumped from the bed, trailing the covers behind her. The cold morning air hit Elizabeth hard. The child ran back to her room, her narrow bare feet pounding on the hall floor.

When Elizabeth reached the kitchen, there was no sign of Livvy. She knew from her own childhood exactly where to find her daughter. She went out to the terrace and called into the garden. "Livvy? Where are you, sweetheart?"

"Out here with the fairies. Come see the fairies, Mommy."

"No. Come on back now. It's time for breakfast."

Livvy ran through the garden and bounded up the steps to the terrace, her white-blonde hair flying. "Mommy, guess what?"

"What sweetheart?"

"The fairies eat nectar and pollen for breakfast. What's nectar?"

"It's the juice in the flowers. The fairies are sort of like bees."

"Yeah. That's what Olivia said too. I told her we were going to have floater pancakes. She wanted to know what that was. I told her they were really fluffy pancakes. But they don't really float, do they?"

Elizabeth nodded. "No, they don't really float."

Livvy giggled. "Sometimes when I was little, you made me watch them and hold them down with a fork so they wouldn't float away. That was silly."

"The fairies float, don't they? That's not silly?"

"Yeah, sometimes the fairies float. And they can fly too. See, I told you you believed in fairies, Mommy."

"Yes, I used to when I was your age. So, I know all about them."

"But they're real, Mommy. You know they're real. Nobody knows about them but you and me."

"You really shouldn't talk about them. The fairies don't want you telling people about them."

"I'll only tell you. That's because you already know about them. They'll be our secret."

Elizabeth turned away, worrying that some time when Livvy was out among her friends, people might overhear her talking about the fairies and think she was crazy. Elizabeth had dealt with that her whole life and didn't want Livvy to endure the same reactions from her friends.

They prepared breakfast together. Livvy stood on a chair next to the counter so she could reach the bowl and stir the batter with a wooden spoon. Elizabeth took over when the batter was ready to pour on the griddle.

It had rained late at night, and the table on the terrace was still wet. It gave Elizabeth an excuse to stay out of the garden. They ate inside at the dining room table, watching the garden through the window.

As they washed the bowl with the pancake batter and sponged down the griddle, Elizabeth asked Livvy, "We've talked about moving and getting you into a school here in Williamsburg. Would you like to live here at Papa's house next year? We could move down in the next few days."

Livvy looked out the kitchen window at the garden and grinned. "Could we do that? We could live here?"

"Sure. We'd have to move all of your clothes and toys and books here. You could sleep in the room you stayed in last night. But yes, we can move here."

"Hamilton's already here. And he says the other animals want to come too."

"Okay. We'll see about getting you signed up for kindergarten today. And there's a pool. Would you like to take swimming lessons this summer?"

"Yeah. When I grow up, I want to be a mermaid."

After the dishes were in the washer and the kitchen was clean, Livvy curled up in front of the television watching a cartoon about pastel unicorns. Elizabeth poured a second cup of coffee and went out to the terrace. It was a cool morning, and a breeze blew through the trees, the shadows of the leaves shifting across the flowers in the garden beds. She toweled off one of the iron chairs, sat cross-legged at the table, and relaxed. She sipped her steaming cup and sorted through the list of tasks she had been considering for the day. Sunlight warmed her, highlighting her auburn hair with traces of red and gold.

One step at a time, she decided. I can work on making changes in Richmond when I get home tomorrow. Today, I'll deal with things here in Williamsburg. I'll get Livvy enrolled in kindergarten here. And I need to find childcare for the rest of the summer. I go back to work next Monday, and I need to have everything set before then.

Her thoughts strayed to Lucas and how it ended between them. *How did things get to this point with Lucas? How did I lose him? He was away so much, working long hours in Richmond, lobbying at the state house, writing position papers, researching the law on the issues that matter the most to his boss.*

I tried not to worry that he was out so much. He never stayed out overnight, though he said once that if they worked really late, he might have to do it. Now I know he had something going on with that girl who worked in his office. They were together for more than a year. Elizabeth recalled the night it happened, how suddenly it fell apart.

~~~~~

One night, Lucas came home late, as usual. He sat Elizabeth down at the kitchen table and delivered his devastating news. "I think we should get divorced. You're always at your job down in Williamsburg. And I'm busy here in Richmond. We're not doing right by Livvy. Sure, she's in childcare, but it's not right."
~~~~~

Elizabeth was stunned, confused by Lucas' suggestion. "How will a divorce help us with Livvy?" she asked, baffled, crying. Livvy was asleep in her bedroom and heard none of their talk. Yet here, in seconds Elizabeth had gone from believing they had a wonderful life as a family to discovering everything was over.

Desperately, she suggested, "Maybe we should go to a marriage counselor. I don't know what's wrong, but that might help."

"No. I never see you. It's time we both move on."

"What?" Elizabeth couldn't think. She felt chilled. Adrenaline pounded blood through her ears, making them ring. She was numb and confused, at a loss for words.

Lucas paused and then confessed everything, every sad detail. "Okay. I want the divorce because I'm in love with one of the lawyers I work with. Samantha. We've been together for a long time now, working on the same issues, the same cases. And one thing led to another. It's not right for me to be coming home to you late every night. I should be with her."

"So this has nothing to do with me or Livvy? It has to do with you having an affair?"

"I'm in love with Samantha."

"Why do you say this is about how we take care of Livvy? You're having an affair and you want a divorce? And you say it's so we can take better care of Livvy? That makes no sense."

"I'll take good care of both of you with alimony and child support. I'll leave you with the townhouse here in Richmond and plenty of money. You won't have to work. You can stay home and take care of Livvy till next year when she's in kindergarten."

"We can support her without getting divorced. Besides, I love my work at the nursing home. They love me there too. I don't think quitting my job will help anything."

"It would help Livvy."

"How? This is crazy. Lucas, what's the matter? What's happening to us?"

Lucas couldn't meet her eyes. They sat in silence for a long moment at the kitchen table. Finally, he finished the conversation, restating his irrelevant assumption about Livvy. "Yes, this is so you can take better care of Olivia. And I think it would be best if I didn't stay here tonight. I'll grab some of my things and be off. I'll call you later this week."

Lucas rummaged in the bedroom closet while Elizabeth sat speechless at the kitchen table. Then he was gone.

The next month was awful. Elizabeth's thoughts were chaotic, her emotions surging between despair and anger. She withdrew from her parents and her brother, giving them only a terse summary of her situation, afraid to admit to them her marriage was a failure. Even with Papa, she couldn't bear to share more than small hints of her ongoing struggle.   She also cut off contact with Julia.

Every few days, Lucas dropped in unexpectedly to talk with Elizabeth, always staying in the kitchen, sitting at the table, going over legal papers she had to sign. Elizabeth took copies to review with a lawyer she had hired, but she really had no option other than to sign the papers. Lucas offered her everything in the settlement, ample alimony and child support and sole ownership of their townhouse. What he wanted was a quick, trouble-free divorce.

"You took vows in a church," Elizabeth pleaded during one of his visits. "You're a lawyer. Doesn't abiding by the law matter with our marital status?"

Lucas said nothing, just shook his head and left.

When he visited, Lucas was falsely jovial with Livvy, awkwardly joking and teasing. But he wasn't interested at all in fighting for custody or visitation with her.

"I want to get past this time and move on," he said one evening. "I don't need any hassles, here or at work. Let's both move forward." Then he was gone, and Elizabeth was left trying to explain to Livvy what was happening and why Daddy wasn't staying with them.

"Why isn't Daddy here, Mommy?"

"He has things to do somewhere else."

"I want him to stay here."

"I know, sweetheart. I'm sad he's going away too."

"Doesn't he love us anymore?"

"Of course he does. He loves you very much."

The half-truth, half-lie of the answer didn't get by Livvy. "Doesn't he love you too, Mommy?"

"I don't know. Maybe he loves someone else now."

~~~~~

That's all I've ever wanted, all I've ever needed, Elizabeth reflected. Someone to love me.

Now, after Papa's death, she felt abandoned. Elizabeth pushed the terrible memories away, stood, stretched, and started back inside the house. There was motion in the crepe myrtle near her table. Elizabeth stopped and peered into the foliage, praying she wouldn't see the fairies again. Instead she saw two cardinals hopping fluttering, chasing each other through the branches.

Good. It's just two birds, being birds, acting the way birds do in the summertime. Maybe it would have been nice to talk with the fairies about everything that's happened. Back when I was little it helped. No! I'm an adult. Enough of all the foolishness. If I need to talk about it, I can confide in a human. But who? Papa's gone. Where is my old friend Julia when I need her? She was always here for me. She always knew what to say. I've lost touch with her. I need to track her down.
~~~~~

17

ELIZABETH – AGE EIGHTEEN

ELIZABETH SPREAD AN OVERSIZED BEACH towel on the lawn deep in Papa's garden next to the statue of the little dancing girl. She was out of sight of the house, and of anyone outside the high walls of the garden as well. She stretched on the towel, her long bare back gleaming in the hot sunshine filtering through the lacy canopy of new pastel leaves above her. Still prone, she untied the straps of her bikini top and spread them on each side of her. Her auburn hair, lightened by the sun and glowing with threads of bronze, was pulled up and clasped loosely on the back of her head. Her eyes were closed and shielded by opaque black sunglasses. She napped briefly, then roused herself and looked for her fairy friend.

Olivia sat cross-legged, the way she always did, next to Liz in the shade of the low pachysandra plants. The little fairy was plaiting threads from yellow blossoms into a long thin rope. The yellow braid snaked around her in a coil on the garden soil. A pile of dandelion and black-eyed Susan blossoms lay gathered next to her, waiting for her to put to use.

Elizabeth propped herself on her elbows, peeking over the top of her glasses and asked, "What are you doing, Olivia?"

"Braiding blossoms. It is the work I do. This rope will be cut in sections and become sashes for me and other fairies."

"It's your job? Braiding flower blossoms into rope?"

"I do not know if it is what a human would call a job. All fairies have tasks we do to serve the Queen. We all contribute to the prosperity and success of her kingdom. It is good for all of us to be industrious. I like braiding. I am good at braiding. It is what I do. What are you doing?"

"Right now? I'm working on my tan."

"You are working on your tan? I do not understand. It looks like you are sleeping, not working."

Elizabeth laughed. "No, I might have dozed for a moment but I'm trying to get a good tan. I want to look good when I go to the beach."

"But you are tan. Or a pale color like thin honey. And you do look good. Do not the boys appreciate your appearance? Do you not realize that you are pretty when you look in the mirror?"

"Yeah, I guess boys like the way I look. But I think I look better when I get darker in the summer. The sun darkens my skin. So that's why I'm lying out here in the sun. To get a darker tan and look prettier."

Olivia frowned, puzzled, trying to make sense of it. "You have told me you have a boyfriend."

"Yes, Derek. He's in Richmond. He told me he'll be coming here a few times this summer to see me."

"Does Derek like the way you look when he sees you?"

Elizabeth gave a coy smile. "Yes, he tells me I'm beautiful."

"Then why would you want to lie in the sun and get darker and change the way you look? He likes the way you look now. If you change the way you look, Derek might change the way he thinks about you."

Elizabeth was used to questions like this from Olivia. Much about the way humans lived and thought perplexed the little fairy. Elizabeth spent a lot of her time in the garden trying to explain her world to the little fairy. Olivia, in turn, dedicated hours helping Elizabeth come to understand the ways of life in the fairy world.

"I guess I like the way I look with a tan. Anyway, I put on sunscreen so I won't burn."

"I understand that you would not want to burn. That would be a terrible way to die. What is sunscreen?"

"This lotion." She held up the plastic bottle, letting the implicit concern about being burned to death by the sun go unanswered. "I rub it on because too much sun isn't good. It protects me from the sun."

"Oh." The tiny fairy put down the dandelion braid, uncrossed her legs and sat back, leaning on her elbows, sorting through all these new concepts of human behavior. "You lie in the sun because you want the sun to make you darker, because to be darker is to be more beautiful. And you coat yourself with this oil because you do not want to become too beautiful when the sun makes you too dark. It makes no sense."

Elizabeth shook her head. "You're right. But I like lying in the sun. It's warm. It soothes me."

Olivia stood and began to pace slowly beneath the green groundcover, distracted and thinking. "The sun is harmful to fairies. That is why we do so much of our business at night, and at dawn or in the evening. The sun hurts our eyes. Too much sun can make us sick. Summer heat is bad for fairies."

"Well, I have to get ready to go to work now. I'll come see you tonight when I get home."

Still recumbent, Elizabeth reached for the straps to her top and tied them at the nape of her neck and in the middle of her back. She rolled and sat up.

Olivia raised a hand and stopped her. "Work? What is this work? I know you finished your schooling a few weeks ago and came to spend your summer with your grandfather. You come here every summer. But what is your work?"

"I wait on tables in a restaurant."

"This is your job? Someone pays you money to do this? You stand on a table and wait? What do you wait for? I do not understand."

"No. Waiting on tables means I go up to people who are sitting at a table in a restaurant and I take their orders, what they want to eat for dinner. I go back to the kitchen and tell the chef what they want and then I bring them their food when he's finished cooking it. I'm a waitress."

"They give you orders? Is that like what the Queen does when she issues a decree?"

Elizabeth laughed. "Yes, sometimes it feels like that. But it's not so bad. I get their food when it's ready and serve them. If I treat them well, they give me a good tip."

"What is this tip? The tip of what?"

"No. It's extra money the people give me if they like my service. I get paid to do the job. But when I serve people their food, they give me extra money, my tip, if they like how I take care of them."

"Do they tip you more if they think you are pretty?"

Elizabeth laughed again, amused by Olivia's sudden comprehension, how she saw right through to the ugly heart of the ways waitresses worked for tips. "Sometimes. It doesn't hurt to be pretty. And I need the money. I told you I'll be going to college at the end of the summer. I'll need money when I get to college."

"Then you need to work more on your tan. If you get really dark, maybe the people who you wait for will think you are prettier and give you more money, a lot of money for your college."

Elizabeth stood, laughed and said, "I've got to go. I need to be at the restaurant before people start to come in for dinner."

She gathered the towel from the lawn and began to walk back to the house. Olivia trotted along next to her, staying in the shade.

"Have a nice evening waiting," she called as Elizabeth entered the house. "Make a lot of money so you can go to college in the autumn."

<div align="center">~~~~~</div>

"My name is Elizabeth and I'll be taking care of you this evening. Would you care for drinks before dinner?" Elizabeth, dressed all in black, stood next to a table where a man and a woman and four school-age children studied their menus. They had the look of a family of tourists on vacation in Williamsburg.

"Thanks, yes. I'll have a Heineken, a glass of the house rosé for my wife, and four Cokes for the children."

"Very good. I'll get that for you and come back in a couple of minutes for your dinner order." Elizabeth turned and went to the bar.

After she delivered the drinks, she went to the kitchen to check on orders. Julia, another waitress, hurried into the kitchen. She began tying her apron, harried, rushing to be ready to work.

"How're you doing today, Julia?" Elizabeth asked. The clatter of the cooks working around them made it hard to talk. Waitstaff dashed past them carrying plates. Elizabeth stood close to Julia in a corner of the kitchen.

"Living the dream, of course," Julia replied sarcastically, pinning her dark hair on top of her head. "My kids. Couldn't get their stuff packed fast enough and get both of them loaded in the car. And then my mom wasn't ready when I dropped them off. They spend the night with my mom when I'm working. So I'm late for my shift. Caught hell from the boss."

"I'm sorry. The kids are all set now?"

"Yeah. My two girls. I'll see them tomorrow morning."

"You won't pick them up or stay with your mom tonight?"

"No. It's too late when I get out of work to go over there. I hate to wake them. I usually go home, if I go home at all. Most nights my boyfriend picks me up when I'm done here. He's coming by tonight. We'll stay at his place or mine."

"Oh, that's good. So life really is pretty good."

"Yeah, right. It's never easy being a single mom. You be careful when you get off to college. Don't get pregnant. And don't ever get married. Learn a lesson from me."

Elizabeth didn't know how to respond. She smiled weakly and said, "I don't have any plans to do that right now. Maybe when the right guy comes along. But not now."

Julia paused. "I thought you said you have a boyfriend."

"I do. But he's just a guy I know from high school. We went to prom together and all that. But we're not serious."

Julia pointed a finger at Elizabeth, stressing her lesson. "Sure, that's what you say now. But next thing you know, you'll be all hearts and roses and thinking 'he's the one'. You need to keep your head out of the clouds and your feet on the ground. Life isn't a fantasy."

"Oh, I know that. That's why I'm going to college in the fall. I want to be a doctor, maybe."

"That's right. You're off to college. I'll still be here working in this restaurant. Scraping by with my girls. You'll do better someday as long as you don't get in trouble. I wanted to be a teacher. I was in college too, back then. But I got pregnant and here I am. And my kids' father split, right after my youngest was born. This is all I've got. What do you want to do after college? A doctor?"

"Something with medicine. Maybe a doctor. I'm enrolling as a freshman in chemistry, pre-med."

"Keep your eyes on that goal. Don't let some boy turn you away from that. They're all bastards."

"Thanks. I'll try." Elizabeth headed back out to the table with the tourist family and to her other diners.

"Have we decided what we're having for dinner this evening?" she asked the father.

Elizabeth took their order, delivered it to the kitchen and returned to the dining area to check on her other tables. When the meals were ready for the family, she carried the plates out on a large tray and served them. She chatted with the family, easy banter about their vacation and her college plans. The father appreciated that Elizabeth was a college student and left a big tip. She brought more drinks and dinners to her other tables. She made them all feel they were her most important customers. Elizabeth was always moving, always cheerful, and sometimes flirtatious. Her tips were very good.

18
Elizabeth – Age Thirty

THE KINDERGARTEN WAS LESS THAN a mile from Elizabeth's job at the nursing home. The director gave Elizabeth and Livvy a brief tour. Then she sat with them, talking about her school, extolling its standing among other nearby schools, answering Elizabeth's questions. All the while, Elizabeth sensed from the director's attentive looks and note-taking that she and Livvy were being evaluated, that the director was assessing her soon-to-be-divorced parental status and her quiet daughter's adjustment to her new life. Then the director nodded and smiled. Elizabeth felt that the director had judged them to be good people, and she was sensitive to the grief they were sharing because of the recent passing of Livvy's great-grandfather. The director assured them Livvy could attend the summer programs if they needed childcare before the beginning of the school year.

Elizabeth asked for a day to think it over. She wanted to discuss such an important decision in private with Livvy before she committed. A few months ago, Lucas would have been included in the discussion. Years ago, with any important decision, she would have consulted with the fairies, or Papa, but rarely her parents. It came to her suddenly that she had never made significant decisions on her own. She always turned to others for affirmation with any of the big moves in her life. Now she was going to ask her daughter, a child, for advice. Where was Julia? Until recently, when Elizabeth became overwhelmed by Lucas' leaving, Julia had been Elizabeth's confidant. Julia had always been a good person to turn to whenever Elizabeth needed help. But Elizabeth had been reluctant to talk about the failure of her marriage, and now she and Julia had lost touch with each other.

They drove in silence for a few minutes before Elizabeth asked, "What did you think of the school, Honey Bunny?"

"I like it. There were lots of kids there. They seemed nice. I think I'll like some of them."

Elizabeth noted the assumption in Livvy's answer that she would be attending the school. "If you go here, it'll be close to Papa's house," Elizabeth said. "And it's right around the corner from where I work."

"Maybe sometime, if I go there, you can come see me when it's lunchtime where you work."

"I could do that," said Elizabeth. She was pleased with how Livvy's mind worked, sorting things out, making decisions the way an adult would. She imagined they would both be happy once Livvy was settled at the school.

"Mommy, I'm hungry. Can we go somewhere for lunch? Can we go to McDonalds?"

"Sure we can go out for lunch. I know a place that's even better than McDonalds."

"Okay. And then can we go to the beach this afternoon? It's hot. I want to go swimming."

"Maybe we can do something this afternoon, but probably not the beach."

"Aw. Why not?"

"Two reasons. First, I didn't pack our swimsuits when we came down from Richmond for Papa's funeral. Maybe we can go back tomorrow and pack up the rest of our things. But you and I don't have our swimsuits here."

"Oh, okay. But can we go to the beach anyway?"

"We'll see. There's also this. You don't really know how to swim."

"I can dog paddle. You know that. Can you teach me to swim for real this summer? Daddy told me you're a really good swimmer."

"Yes, I can teach you. Or maybe I'll sign you up for swim lessons with a real swimming teacher. Do you remember there's a pool right in Papa's neighborhood? I went there all the time when I was a little girl."

"Yeah. You told me about the pool and you took me there once. It's cool."

They went to a restaurant for lunch. As soon as they came through the door, they were surrounded by the clatter of silverware on plates and the loud voices of the diners. From the midst of the raucous, convivial din came a shout from the back of the room. "Elizabeth! Oh Elizabeth, I'm so glad you're here!"

Julia rushed up to greet them. She embraced Elizabeth and leaned down to greet Livvy. "How are you, young lady?"

Livvy leaned into her mother's leg, watching this ebullient stranger cautiously. "Fine."

Julia smiled at the little girl. Then she stood, placing a hand on Elizabeth's shoulder. "I'm so sorry about your Papa. I read about it in the paper and I went to the funeral."

"You were there? I didn't see you," Elizabeth said.

"Yes, I was in the back of the church. I had to leave right after the service to get to work. But I was there. I wanted to see you. And Olivia too," she added, smiling again down at Livvy.

"I didn't know you worked here. I thought you would still be at our old restaurant."

"Yeah. I'm still there a couple of nights a week. But I'm here for lunches most days. I finish in time to pick up my kids from school, and I'm home most nights with them and Greg. You remember Greg, my boyfriend?"

"Ah, yes. Greg. It sounds like things turned out well for you."

"Yeah, things are good. Listen, I'll get you seated, but I've got to get back to my other customers. Are you in town for a while?"

"Yes, we're staying at Papa's old house for a couple of more days, trying to sort things out. Papa left it to me. Livvy and I might be moving here to stay now."

"That's wonderful! But what about Lucas?" Julia asked, suddenly serious.

Elizabeth gave a short, quiet laugh and smiled.

Julia nodded. "Oh, I see. Well, okay. The bastard!" She caught herself and looked again at Livvy. "I'm sorry, sweetheart. I shouldn't have said that."

Livvy grinned, feeling a part of the grownups' conversation. "That's all right," she said. "Daddy is a bastard."

"Olivia!" Elizabeth tried to scold, but she felt herself smiling, almost laughing. "Daddy's not really a bastard. He's just moved out. He's still your daddy, so don't talk like that."

Livvy pouted, and then she giggled.

Julia led them to a table and seated them with menus. "I've got to get back," she said. "Work, work, work, you know. Can I stop by tonight?"

"Sure. We'll be there."

When Julia left, Livvy leaned across the table and whispered, "Who was that Mommy?"

"That's Julia. She's an old friend, a very good old friend. You'll like her."

19

Elizabeth – Age Eighteen

ELIZABETH AND JULIA SET UP the restaurant tables for the next day's shift. Finally, near midnight, they were ready to leave. Elizabeth hung up her black apron and tucked her tips in her purse. As Elizabeth went to her car, she saw Julia get in a car with a bearded, heavy-set man. Elizabeth arrived home well after midnight. Papa had gone to bed.

She turned off the hall light Papa left on for her, dropped her purse on the sofa, tiptoed through the living room, slipped out to the terrace, and down the steps, into the garden. Elizabeth had visited the garden every summer and every vacation over the past years but usually during the daytime at dawn, sometimes in the evening. Her visits in the middle of the night had been mostly for formal meetings, summoned by the Queen to discuss important matters, flown from her bedroom by Olivia. The Queen always asked about her boyfriends, her studies in school, her emerging interest in healthcare and medicine. Rarely had she been in the garden this late at night without being escorted by Olivia.

Elizabeth was surprised to see how, on this, an ordinary night with no ceremonies, the town and the marketplace were lit and bustling. During the day, the shops and the carts were open for business and a few fairies moved about slowly, but it was usually quiet. Now, on what might be a typical night, the garden was a hive of activity.

A small fairy orchestra had set up in a circle in the middle of the town square and performed high-pitched, celestial music on reed pipes and trumpets, stringed instruments, drums, and chimes. Elizabeth had heard the fairy music before at their parades and celebrations, but this was her first time hearing them play less formal music. Fairies danced to the music in the town square. Crowds of fairies moved about the streets, carrying bundles and baskets, running errands, sitting on benches, and standing in groups talking and laughing. For the first time, Elizabeth noticed the small shops and vending carts floating above the garden, nestled in the shrubbery and trees. Fairies flew to these elevated enterprises to shop, just as they walked to the ones on the ground. The town was busy, filled with a sparkling, festive mood. Elizabeth had seen their midsummer-eve celebration in past years as an invited guest of the Queen and of Olivia. Even now, on an ordinary night, the garden conveyed a sense of gaiety.

Near the armillary, Thomas stood on the top step of the town hall, his arms folded. He saw Elizabeth and nodded, unsmiling, all business in his officious way. His posture made him an imposing presence among the little fairies around him, but to Elizabeth he was still only ankle high. He turned back to surveying the fairies as they worked and played in the town square.

All the fairies had bright yellow sashes wrapping their short summer tunics. She thought of Olivia hard at work braiding the blossoms. Then she saw Olivia giggling with a cluster of fairies near one of the vending carts. Olivia spied Elizabeth and came running to her from the middle of the market.

"You came! What a wonderful surprise."

"When I was going to work, I said I'd stop by tonight."

"Yes, you did say that. A promise is just a promise. Sometimes humans are not very good at abiding by their promises. Zach did not abide by his promises to you when you were young and he was your boyfriend. It is known by the fairies that humans do not always live by the vows they make. I did not know if you really would be here tonight. Did you have a nice evening waiting? Did the people reward you with lots of tips?"

"Yes. I did well tonight, but it was a long night. I went to work at four in the afternoon and we didn't close till eleven. So that's a seven-hour shift, and I had to close the restaurant. It was midnight by the time I left there. I'm exhausted."

"There is an interesting aroma. Is that from your working?"

Elizabeth sniffed her hands. "Yes, it's garlic. And maybe seafood. I can't help it. I get it on my hands when I serve the meals and pick up the dirty plates."

She held her hands out and Olivia flew over to check them. "I like the smell. I might like the human food. It smells similar to the way we prepare mice on the festival days. But it does not smell as fragrant as pollen or nectar. So you received good tips. That will be useful when you go to the college."

"I hope so."

"There is a college near to us. William and Mary. That is where you will attend college?"

"William and Mary? No. I got accepted there, but I'm going to the University of Virginia. It has a good medical school. I'll be majoring in Chemistry and studying in the pre-med program. UVA isn't near here. There are lots of colleges."

"Oh. The only college I know is William and Mary. We have a small fairy outpost there, a few fairies who live at that place. But you will study medical things at a different college, this University of Virginia. What is medical school, and what will you do when you finish learning?"

"I'll be studying medicine, how to help people stay healthy. I might become a doctor when I graduate, maybe do medical research."

"Your grandfather was a doctor."

"Yes, Papa was a dentist, a special kind of doctor. He helped people with their teeth."

"You will become a tooth doctor like him? We have a tooth fairy who lives here. Her work is to help us with our teeth."

"No, I'm not sure what kind of doctor I might be. I hope I'll figure it out in the next year or so."

"You are learning this medical thing, but you do not know what you want to do with it?"

"Yes. That's the problem. I did very well in high school. I got almost perfect grades and was near the top of my class. It worries me sometimes, when I think about all the things I still need to learn. Getting ready for med school will be different. Chemistry is a hard major."

"So what do you do when you finish with this college?"

"That's when I might start medical school. That's how I get ready to become a doctor. Doctors help sick people get better. I think I might prefer research so I could discover things we can do so nobody ever gets sick in the first place. We'll see."

"Fairies never get sick. We use magic to be healthy. You should learn fairy magic to stay healthy. Fairies live forever."

"Humans don't. That's not a problem for me now. I'm still young and healthy. But there's so much I have to learn to become a good doctor. That's why I'm going to the University of Virginia."

"I will ask the Queen if she knows of this college. The Queen knows many things."

Elizabeth looked over the bright nighttime fairy town then turned back to Papa's house. "I'm tired. I've got to get to bed. My brother Michael is coming to visit tomorrow with his girlfriend."

"Goodnight, Elizabeth." Olivia darted back into the market as Elizabeth walked up the steps to the dark house.

~~~~~

Michael had loved technology since he was little. Now he was studying computer programming at James Madison University in Harrisonburg, a town set along the mountains on the western edge of Virginia. To help pay his tuition, he worked as an on-call software technician, sent out throughout the Shenandoah Valley by a computer store to help people with technology problems. He stunned Elizabeth when he confided to her he had a girlfriend. He had had few girlfriends in the past, and none of the relationships lasted for long. He had teased Elizabeth about the many boys she dated. Now, suddenly, he had this new woman, and he seemed to mention her whenever he called Elizabeth.

Several days ago, he called Elizabeth. "I'd like you to meet my girlfriend. Her name is Evelyn. Eve for short. Are you going to be around this weekend? We can come to Williamsburg and meet you at Papa's house."

"Sure," Elizabeth replied. "But what about Mom and Dad? They won't be coming down till the Fourth of July."

"I'm not ready for that yet. All they know is I stayed at school to work this
~~~~~

summer. They don't know I'm living with Eve in Staunton. They think I'm still living up in Harrisonburg in the apartment with my roommates. They don't even know I've got a girlfriend."

That they were living together astonished Elizabeth. Her brow creased. She shook her head and almost laughed. *Finally! Michael has a significant girlfriend. And living with her too! Michael must be in love!*

Now Michael and Eve were on their way, driving across the state to spend the weekend. Papa had prepared two bedrooms, one for each of them since he was not yet aware of their living arrangement. He had stocked up on beer for when he and Michael watched baseball on TV. Elizabeth was ready as well; curious to see what sort of woman had turned Michael's head.

They arrived late in the morning after the drive from Staunton. Like many college students, Michael owned a rusted and dented used car, but they arrived in a pristine new, dark-blue hybrid, the sunroof open. Michael got out and trotted to the driver's side to open the door for his girlfriend, the driver. Elizabeth noticed he wore baggy shorts and a plain black t-shirt; not his typical summer wardrobe of a button-up short-sleeved shirt and jeans. The woman for whom he held the car door was pleasantly attractive but looked older than Michael. Her straight dark hair was combed back and pinned with a silver filigree clasp. She wore a loose, long-sleeved white cotton blouse over a long batik-print blue skirt. They both had leather sandals.

Michael grabbed two bags from the car; his own canvas backpack and a large flowered, cloth duffle bag. He slung the bags awkwardly over his shoulders, one on each side. They strode together deliberately toward the front door where Papa and Elizabeth waited, the woman's long skirt swinging around her legs as they walked. Her arm was tucked through Michael's at the elbow. Michael grinned. "Hey, Grandpa. Hi, Elizabeth. This is my girlfriend, Evelyn."

Evelyn smiled warmly and extended her hand to Papa, the thin back of the hand facing up as though she expected Papa to kiss it. She took his hand just by the fingertips and squeezed. "Call me Eve. Please," she said. She turned to Elizabeth and gave a graceful, but remote hug, one hand on each of Elizabeth's shoulder blades. Their bodies didn't touch. "It's so nice to meet you both."

Up close, Elizabeth noticed Eve's black hair was laced with white. The faint beginnings of wrinkles creased her face.

After introductions, Papa led them out to the terrace. They sat in the shade at the table. "Drinks?" Papa asked. "What would you like Eve?"

"Do you have any iced tea? Something without caffeine would be delightful."

"I have bottled iced tea or I can brew some fresh for you and put it over ice. But I'm afraid it's standard tea, not something herbal or floral like chamomile. Would Earl Grey do?"

Eve answered pleasantly. "No, thank you. Ice water will be fine."

Papa tried again. "How about you, Michael? It's almost noon. The sun's almost past the yardarm so it's okay for something stronger. A beer before lunch?"

"No thanks. I'll have ice water as well."

"Sure. And Elizabeth?"

"I'll have the iced tea."

"Okay good. I'll be right back with the drinks." Papa returned to the kitchen.

Olivia's bell-chiming voice came from somewhere deep in the garden. "Be sure to tip your grandfather well, Elizabeth. He will have to work hard to please your brother and his girlfriend."

Elizabeth laughed, a quick chuckle.

Michael asked defensively, his face reddening. "What? What's the joke?"

"Oh, it's nothing. I was remembering something funny that happened yesterday. Something someone said. It has to do with my job at the restaurant. About what we have to do for good tips."

Papa returned with a tray of drinks: two ice waters and two iced teas. As he handed them around, he asked, "So Michael, Eve. How did you meet?"

Michael turned and let Eve answer, watching her and beaming. "I have an antique business I run out of my house in Staunton," she said. "It's a beautiful old Victorian and the whole first floor is my store. But my computer is upstairs where I live, and I couldn't get it to work when I upgraded. Michael was sent out to get me set up. It took him a couple of hours working upstairs while I was downstairs minding the store. By the time he was done, I was closing for the day and it was time for dinner."

Michael picked up the story, eager to inform Papa of his new living situation. "So I asked if I could take her to dinner, and she said yes."

Eve folded her hands serenely in her lap. "We had to drive all the way over to Charlottesville for dinner. There are good organic restaurants in Staunton, but there's a vegetarian place in Charlottesville I like better. So I drove him over and we had dinner. Then, of course, it was late when we finished dinner, and I had to drive Michael back to Staunton to pick up his car. So…"

Michael interrupted, looking slyly at Elizabeth, avoiding eye contact with Papa. "So I ended up staying the night. I've been living there ever since. When college starts again in the fall, I expect we'll still be there together. It's a bit of a drive, getting up to Harrisonburg, to James Madison from Staunton every day, but that won't come between us."

Eve nodded. "We plan to stay together for at least the near future."

There was silence. Elizabeth remembered Julia and her warning the night before to keep her feet on the ground and not to let love distract her from her goals in college.

Papa spoke, his face impassive. "I see. Do your mom and dad know of your plans yet, Michael?"

Michael looked hard at the wrought-iron table top. "No, I haven't told them about Eve yet. I will. Sometime this summer. They'll be fine with it once they meet her."

Papa nodded, unsmiling. He shifted the conversation. "How about lunch? I have sliced turkey. Would turkey sandwiches on whole wheat do?"

Eve smiled politely. "We don't eat meat. Do you have salad?"

"Of course. Lettuce and tomato for the sandwiches, but you can turn it into a salad if you'd prefer."

"Thank you. Yes, I can do that. I'll come help in the kitchen. Do you have black olives? Hummus?"

"I've got olives," Papa offered as they started for the French doors to the house.

Michael remained seated. "I'll stay and catch up with my sister."

With Papa and Eve inside, he turned to Elizabeth, grinning. "Well? What do you think? Isn't she great?"

Elizabeth nodded. "She seems nice. But you've changed. This is so unlike you. You used to drink beer with Papa and Dad when you watched the ball games on TV. And you used to eat meat. What happened?"

"Eve happened. She's the one who's changed, though. She used to be vegan. Now she's just a vegetarian. And she's even started eating a little fish. She believes eating what she calls 'the processed flesh of dead animals' is morally wrong and unhealthy. They put too many chemicals in our food these days. It's genetically altered and not healthy. And I have to say that since I've started eating like her, I feel so much better, so much more energetic."

"You're staying in school, right? It's like she's leading you down the garden path. Don't let her steer you away from the things you've always wanted to do." Elizabeth thought again of Julia's words of caution.

"Oh, that won't happen. I help her a bit in her antique business, watch the store, keep inventory, that sort of thing. But I've loved computers my whole life. That's what I'll do when I graduate in a couple of years."

"Okay. Keep your eyes on that goal. A woman I work with told me not to let my boyfriend distract me from my goals."

"How is your boyfriend? What's his name? Derek?"

"Yes, Derek. He'll be at Virginia Tech next year. He's got a football scholarship."

Michael laughed. "Yeah, you always hung around the athletes. I never understood it. You, the perfect student, hanging out with guys who play sports but maybe can't even read."

"Michael! Derek's a good student. We met in math class. Don't assume because he's an athlete he's stupid."

"Yeah? What's he majoring in at Virginia Tech? Football?"

"No. Sociology. He wants to do something to help inner-city kids when he graduates."

"Sure." Michael remained unconvinced. He gave a short, sarcastic laugh.

Papa and Eve returned with four plates. Two had salads; the other two had turkey sandwiches and potato chips. When everyone was served and settled at the table, Papa asked, "You're both here for two days? What are your plans?"

Michael spoke first, Eve allowing him to lead this conversation. "I figure we'll go over to Colonial Williamsburg this afternoon and walk around. We'll check out some of the old furniture and things. Tomorrow I think we'll take the ferry across the river and have a look in the antique shops in Smithfield."

There was a squeal from within the greenery of the garden. Olivia called to Elizabeth. "He wants to take a fairy across the river? He can't! The Queen doesn't allow us to leave the garden."

Quickly Elizabeth answered Michael, mostly to clarify for Olivia. "So, you'll take the boat across the river. The ferry boat. And go to Smithfield."

"Yes, Eve says there are some nice stores there. Do you want to join us?"

"I'd love to, but I'm scheduled to work."

In the garden Elizabeth heard Olivia. "Oh. It is just a boat. That is good. I was ready to go tell the Queen what your brother was planning to do."

Papa continued. "After lunch, I can show you to your rooms. Michael, you'll be in your usual room. And Eve, I'm putting you in the big guest room, the one Michael's mom and dad usually have when they visit."

Michael protested. "Papa, you need to understand. Eve and I are living together. We can share a room."

Eve reached over and patted Michael's arm, a gesture of a parent soothing a child. "Oh, Michael. If it makes your grandfather more comfortable for us to be in separate bedrooms for a few nights, that's all right. I'll take the big guest room."

Michael nodded. "Sure, that'll be fine Papa."

<p style="text-align:center">~~~~~</p>

Elizabeth stood quietly near the bar with Julia. It was a slow night; only three tables had people seated for dinner. They had time for talk. "I've thought about some of the things you said the other night," said Elizabeth. "About keeping focused on my studies in college. I plan to do that. But I can see how easily a person could get distracted from that."

"Oh? How is that? What made you see it my way?" Julia turned to Elizabeth like an older sister ready to offer more guidance.

"My brother Michael. He's always been a computer nerd and not very involved with girls. Now he's visiting for the weekend, and he's brought his girlfriend with him. Turns out they're living together. He's got two more years to go in college and now he's off living with this girlfriend, miles away from his college."

"There you go. And if a girl can do that to someone like your brother, imagine what a guy could do to a girl like you."

"Yeah. I've thought about it." Elizabeth turned the conversation away from Michael and Eve. "A couple of nights ago when we were going home, I saw you get in a car with a man. Your boyfriend, I assume?"

"Yes, Greg."

"Are you and he serious?"

"I don't know. We've been together almost two years, several nights a week, whenever I can drop my girls at my mom's house. Yeah. I guess you'd call that serious."

"You think you'll marry him?"

"Are you kidding? Like I said the other night, I'll never do that again. Too many hassles being married. Too hard to break it off. Nothing lasts forever."

"You think you'll break up with him then?"

Julia looked away, checking on the customers at her table. She shook her head. "No. I want us to stay together. He treats me right. He's a good guy. He's asked me a couple of times to marry him, and I said no. I don't need that headache. And he's fresh out of his divorce anyway."

"Have your kids met him?"

"Yeah. They like him. He's really good with them. But I don't want them to see me living with him. They can't wake up in the morning and find him hanging around. I don't want them growing up thinking that's okay. They're little girls, you know. Very impressionable."

"So what are you going to do?"

"Aw, hell, I don't know. It's no picnic living with a guy for a night here and there. And it's no good wanting to make it full-time and not doing it. God, you've got a lot of questions."

Julia hustled over to her table and chatted, smiling with her customers. It was an excuse to end the conversation with Elizabeth. But later, when they had another quiet moment, Elizabeth started up again.

"I apologize if I asked so many questions earlier," she said. "This is all new to me. I've had boyfriends, and I have Derek now. But what do I do as things get more serious? This is something I don't have answers for."

"I don't think I've got the answer either. Just be careful. You see what my life is like. And now you see what's happening with your brother. Be careful with Derek."

<div align="center">~~~~~</div>

Michael and Eve were about to leave at the end of the weekend. Elizabeth and Papa walked with them to Eve's car.

"When are you two planning to meet your parents, Michael?" asked Papa.

"I don't know. Maybe we can come back on the Fourth of July?"

Eve interrupted. "Michael, that's one of my busiest weekends of the summer. I don't think we can get enough free time to come over for a whole weekend."

"Maybe we can just stop by for a day," Michael said. "With Mom and Dad staying here, there wouldn't be a spare room for you anyway."

Eve nodded. "Sure. I can get someone to cover the shop for a day."

Papa hugged Eve. "It's been good to meet you Eve."

"My pleasure," she replied. Then she hugged Elizabeth as well, a hug less stiff than when she arrived.

Papa turned to Michael and put an arm around his shoulder. "You need to tell your mom and dad about Eve. They need to meet her."

"We'll come on the Fourth."

"Good. Call them first and tell them all about her before they meet her." It was a pointed comment, a demand. The intent was not lost on Michael. He nodded to Papa.

Michael turned to Elizabeth and hugged her. He whispered, "How come, with all the boys you've dated, you never got the hassle I get now with Eve?"

Elizabeth held onto him. "I've never lived with a boy. Be careful. And if she's this special to you, you've got nothing to hide. It'll be okay to tell Mom and Dad about her."

"Okay. It's just that you've always been the one to do stuff like this before me. You're younger, but you're the one who breaks the rules, sets new boundaries. Eve's my first real girlfriend."

"Enjoy it, big brother. Love her." Elizabeth kissed him and let him go to Eve and her car.

They slammed the car doors then rolled the windows down to wave as they pulled away. Papa and Elizabeth heard Eve speak over the quiet sound of the hybrid engine. "What was all that whispering with your sister?"

"Nothing. Just some brother-sister talk."

"What was it about? I need to know."

20
Elizabeth – Age Thirty

AS ELIZABETH DROVE, LIVVY SLEPT in her car seat in the back of the car. Elizabeth reflected on her past loves. When she was young, Zach had been everything to her for almost a year. She remembered the Queen's words of caution when she was still young and in love for the first time. "All they want to do is breed," the Queen had warned.

Was that the best explanation for all her troubles with men? With Zach, maybe not; he was too young to really be a problem. It certainly could have been the root of the issue with Derek. And now learning Lucas had left her to run around with that woman from work? What was wrong with men? And what, Elizabeth wondered, was wrong with her?

Maybe the Queen had been right. Of course, by admitting she was now remembering the Queen's advice was to acknowledge the fairies were real. At least, they had seemed to be real. Elizabeth now considered the Queen's wisdom from a more mature perspective and with a new appreciation.

Couldn't a man and a woman have a relationship, be friends, without sex complicating things? She could think of many men with whom she had been friends, fellow students in college, other men she worked with. It was possible to have common interests, to enjoy each other's company without a physical component becoming a part of the friendship. She could think of times when a friendship evolved into a deeper, emotional connection. She remembered a male nurse, Steve. She had spent a lot of time with him, their shifts matching for weeks while she was in grad school. They felt a common bond. They truly understood each other. There were moments, talking with Steve when they were on break together, when they each shared their deepest dreams and fears. But she had been living with Lucas and wouldn't have cheated on him.

Not that Elizabeth didn't enjoy the physical side of a relationship. She did. But it had messed up so much of her life. Was it always about sex with men? Could she ever have a close friendship with a man without sex getting in the way? Elizabeth didn't believe it had to be that way. Why were men so foolish?

21

ELIZABETH – AGE EIGHTEEN

DEREK PLANNED TO COME FOR the long Fourth of July weekend. Since Michael and Eve would only be stopping by for the day and not spending the night, Michael's room was open for him. It would be the first time since Elizabeth left Richmond for the summer that she and Derek could see each other.

Elizabeth met him at the train station. He got off the train, tall, black, and noticeably athletic with his erect posture and taut body. As he approached her, he dropped his duffle bag and produced a bouquet from behind his back with a flourish. "For my beautiful lady," he said with an exaggerated bow, one arm presenting the flowers to Elizabeth, the other gallantly flung wide.

"Derek, you're amazing," she said, accepting the flowers. They shared a long kiss. Then she took him, walking arm-in-arm, to her car for the short ride back to Papa's house.

"My parents will be coming tomorrow. And Michael and his girlfriend Eve will stop by on the Fourth just for the day."

Derek smiled. "So it's just us and your granddaddy right now?" With a slight arch to his eyebrows, he asked, "Where will I be sleeping?" He grinned and reached over, a hand on her knee while she drove.

"In Michael's room, the room he usually sleeps in when he's here."

"And where will you be?"

"Down the hall. And don't get any ideas. Nothing's going to happen with my Papa there, and then, when my parents come tomorrow, they'll be in the house with us too."

"Sure." Derek looked out the window, watching the town roll by. "I was hoping, you know. It's been a long time since we've seen each other."

"Yeah, me too, but not with my Papa in the house. We can't. It'll be great though, the two of us being together."

"Yeah. Sure. It's going to be great."

When they arrived at the house, they walked hand-in-hand to the front door. Inside, Derek dropped his bag at the foot of the stairs, and Elizabeth led him out to the terrace. Papa was cleaning the iron table, wiping it down with paper towels, getting ready to set up for lunch.

"Papa, this is Derek," Elizabeth said.

Papa looked up from the table, wiped his hands and reached out to shake Derek's hand. "Very nice to meet you," he said. "Elizabeth told me a bit about you. You'll be playing football in college this fall?"

"Yes sir. Wide receiver at Virginia Tech."

"Very good. When do you go to school? I expect you have to go early to prepare for the season."

"Yeah. A couple of weeks from now. I've been working out every day all summer. Lifting, running, doing drills. I'm working at a camp for kids in Richmond too, but most of my time is spent getting ready for football."

After lunch, Papa stood. "I've got to go buy groceries to have everything ready for the Fourth of July. Elizabeth, you can show Derek around the garden or drive him over to Colonial Williamsburg if you'd like. I'll be back in an hour or so."

Papa left. Elizabeth took Derek's hand and led him down the terrace steps into the garden. She saw Olivia perched on a branch in a crepe myrtle tree. Cardinals fluttered nearby. A hummingbird paused at a blossom, and then darted to another, and then another. Olivia saw Derek and gasped. "Oh, Elizabeth! Is he not handsome? He is the darkest man I have seen with you. You have told me that to have a dark tan is considered beautiful. He has a very dark tan."

Without thinking about how Derek might respond, Elizabeth explained to Olivia, "He's black."

Puzzled, Derek asked, "What?"

Elizabeth covered. She couldn't let Derek know about the fairies, and she didn't want him to hear her talking to nobody. "I said, 'he's back'. I thought for a moment I heard my Papa coming back out to the garden. But I guess I was mistaken."

"Yeah," said Derek. "I heard his car leaving. We're alone."

"Yes." Elizabeth shifted to Derek, leaning against his tall frame.

He looked down and kissed her. His arms pulled her closer. "So, what do you say girl? We have an hour till your granddaddy gets back. You want to show me your room? Did you bring that teddy bear down here to Williamsburg with you?"

"His name is Jefferson. And, of course, he's here on my bed. He's an old faithful friend."

"So let's go see about Jefferson."

He stroked her back, then let his hands drift lower, cupping, feeling, squeezing. Elizabeth sucked in her breath and couldn't help smiling. Now Derek's hands slid forward under her arms, up to her breasts. She sighed and settled in, feeling the pleasure.

Elizabeth was distracted by movement. Olivia darted closer, wary. Other fairies began to gather, pausing in the slow mid-day heat in the marketplace and town center. They all watched. Fairy soldiers began to appear, hovering nearby, alone and by twos and threes. Faintly, Elizabeth heard the tin sound of a fairy bugle inside the palace at the back of the garden. The clarion was answered by the rhythmic stamping of small boots behind the palace wall. Through the tree branches, Elizabeth saw the palace door burst open. Lines of fairy soldiers began marching out. In the courtyard they lifted, floating to fly, clearing the outer fortification wall, not bothering with the gate. They spread into wide regiments in the air, gathered and settled in ranks on the ground close to Elizabeth and Derek. A shrill command pierced the air, and the soldiers shifted into parade rest, each with their feet spread, one hand behind their armored backs, the other hand holding a slender spear.

It had been weeks since Elizabeth had seen Derek. She leaned up and kissed him, lingering, enjoying the way his body moved against hers. Then she considered her fairy friends. She looked down, saw their stern faces watching her, and she stopped.

"We can't," she said. "Not out here in the garden."

"Okay. Let's go back inside. We still have time till your granddaddy gets back."

"No. Someone might be watching. Inside or outside."

"Out here? In a walled-in garden? We're alone. Let's do it right here on the lawn."

"No!" She pushed him back, though she was flushed, excited and wanting Derek as much as he wanted her.

"Why not?"

She turned away, exasperated. She knew she shouldn't tell him about the fairies, but right now she was angry with them for being here and interfering. And she was angry at Derek for pushing her, and also at herself for wanting him.

"No. This garden has fairies in it. They're always watching. We can't do it in front of the fairies." She recalled Olivia telling her how the fairies had watched and laughed when they caught Papa and Nana in the garden.

Derek laughed. "What? You believe in fairies? I mean, I kind of like your teddy bear. What's his name again?"

"Jefferson."

"Yeah, Jefferson. It's cool getting it on with you when you still have a teddy bear on the bed with us. But now you tell me you still believe in fairies? And that's why we can't get things going? Come on, girl. You didn't complain at the after-prom party. Or that other time we did it. I've been thinking about this ever since you left to come down here, and now I'm here. Let's go. Out here or up with the bear in your room. I don't care. Let's get it started."

"No!"

"Why not?"

"The fairies. You don't want to mess with them."

"Huh." Derek laughed and started to slip his hand inside Elizabeth's shirt. Suddenly he tumbled, his feet pulled out from under him. In an instinctive movement, he tucked a shoulder and hit the ground rolling. Elizabeth watched the buildings in the fairy town fade for a second as they slipped beneath his body. She saw them reappear, bright as ever, the moment he crashed past. Fairies in the marketplace ran screaming. The soldiers massed closer and started to advance.

Derek finished his roll, flowing into a quick pop back to his feet. He looked at Elizabeth, angrily.

"What the fuck? Why'd you do that? Pushing me, tripping me? I mean if you don't want to do it right now that's fine. But come on, girl. No need to throw me down like that."

"I didn't touch you. The fairies did it. I warned you not to mess with them."

"You're crazy!"

"You think so? You're the one they just knocked over."

Derek took a deep breath and stepped toward her.

"Okay, Elizabeth." He leaned closer, one finger raised, pointing to emphasize his words. "I respect you. You're a very special girlfriend. If you don't want it here in the garden, that's okay. Maybe we can go someplace where you'll feel more comfortable than here with your make-believe fairy friends. Okay?"

"Okay. You still love me?" she asked.

"Of course. You still love me?"

"Yes." Elizabeth stepped up to Derek, wrapped her arms around him and kissed him quickly on the cheek.

"Let's go for a ride," she suggested.

They drove along the parkway next to the river and parked in a lot intended for river-bank picnickers and fishermen. Next to the parking lot, a few people sat in folding chairs viewing the river from the shade. More were on a beach on the shore of the river, some of them fishing. Small children splashed in the shallow water and played on the sand, their voices shrill, like sparrows. Quietly taking him by the hand, Elizabeth led Derek from the car, down to the river, then along the bank until they were far from any other people. When they were out of sight and alone, she sat in the shadow of a low-hanging oak on a narrow clay and sand beach. Derek sat next to her. They kissed. Again, he began to search her body with his hands. She allowed him. His hand slid up her thigh to the hem of her shorts and began to move under. Her legs spread.

Elizabeth heard a splash in the river, a sound like a jumping fish, and she looked aside for a moment. There in the shallow water, she saw three small, fairy-like figures dressed in long, white and aqua gowns that flowed to their ankles and clung, wet, to their slender torsos. They rose from the water, dripping, and walked on tiptoes across the river surface, finally striding on the beach itself, leaving tiny footprints on the mud. When the water-nymphs were at Elizabeth's feet, they stopped and watched her and Derek without saying a word. She looked up and saw more fairies, not her usual garden fairies, but rustic fairies here in the woods, dressed in rough, earth-tone tunics, gathering above her on the oak branches. Elizabeth noted they all stared at Derek, not her. A dragonfly darted by and soared off high above them, heading away from the river toward the town.

"This is no good," she said glumly, pushing his hand down. "I love you and I want you, but this is no good."

"Damn it! You're the ultimate tease. What's your problem?"

"Do you have a condom?" She knew he never used a condom. At least he didn't the other two times, but she was safe at those times. This question could buy her time till later, when they might find a way to be truly alone.

"No. I don't like condoms. I don't want anything between me and you. Aren't you on the pill?"

"No. And this isn't a good time for us to do it without protection."

"Son of a bitch!" Derek stood up, hands on his hips, towering over her. He paced on the bank. "Why do you think I came all the way down here to see you? Why do you think I bought you those flowers? Damn, girl!"

"Come on, Derek. You know I love you. We have that whether or not we make love."

"Sure. I don't think so. There's a train to Richmond later this afternoon. Why don't you stop by your granddaddy's house so I can grab my bag? And then take me back to the station."

He stormed back along the beach to where they left the car. Elizabeth had no choice but to follow. She dragged herself to her feet and chased after him. The river nymphs and wood fairies trailed them. She found him leaning against her locked car in the parking lot, head down, hands on the roof. An hour later she dropped him at the train station with his bag.

She pulled back into the driveway at Papa's and came in the house, slamming the door. Papa looked up from where he sat on the couch with a book. For a moment, Elizabeth headed toward the stairs and began to stamp up to her room. But she saw Papa and stopped. He would ask her about all the trouble later if she ran to her room. She might as well face it with him now. She gave a hard sigh and turned into the living room.

"Where's Derek?" Papa asked, his face creased with concern.

"Gone. We had a fight." She fell into an armchair across from the couch, leaning her forehead on one hand, pushing her bronze hair back from her face with the other.

"Oh, I'm sorry. Can I ask what happened?"

"The fairies." Elizabeth looked up and sat back, confronting her grandfather. "I'm not supposed to talk about them. You know that. But they messed with Derek, just like they did with that boy Zach back when I was a kid."

"Oh. I'd almost forgotten about the fairies. And about Zach. They got involved with him that day? Ah. It makes sense." Papa nodded, absorbing this new understanding of the events that had happened years before in his backyard.

Then Papa continued. "Sometimes I still dream the fairies are out there, but somehow I'd guessed you'd outgrown them, moved on, when you became an adult."

"No, they're always here," she said, her voice filled with exasperation. "Whenever I come to visit, they're out there in the garden, sometimes inside the house too. I can never seem to get away from them."

"I see."

"Papa, can I ask you something?"

"Of course. Anything."

"Am I crazy? I want to believe I'm not crazy. I mean, the only way I might still be seeing the fairies at my age is if I was insane. Right?"

"I don't know. Maybe they're real. I don't think you're insane. And like I said, I dream about them too. We can't both be crazy, can we?"

"No." Elizabeth almost laughed. "Okay, maybe I'm not crazy. Maybe they're real. I saw them beat up on Derek. I couldn't do to him what I saw happen."

"Maybe, whenever you have things that bother you, things you worry about, maybe you use the fairies to help you sort everything out in your head."

Elizabeth leaned back in her chair, thinking. "No," she said. "No! I can handle problems like Derek without their interference. But why would I think the fairies are real? That's kids' stuff. I'm supposed to be an adult, right?"

She looked out the window across the terrace into the garden. It appeared so commonplace, a sunny spot with the flowers, the shrubbery, the insects and birds. But even from within the living room she could see fairies flitting by the window, intent on fairy business.

Grudgingly, she shook her head. Papa's last suggestion might make sense after all. Maybe the fairies were nothing more than a means of coping with problems in her life.

"Yeah, that could be it. Right now, things with Derek aren't so good. He's a great guy and he'll always be special to me. But I don't know if it would have lasted with him. Maybe I used the fairies to deal with that. It could have been the same with some of the other times when things worried me. Like with Zach, years ago."

"It could be." Papa chuckled and winked at her. "Or maybe they are real. But either way, you're not crazy."

"Thanks. I know I'm not. It's nice to have you confirm it, though."

"Are you okay with losing Derek? He seemed like a decent guy, maybe just not the right guy for you."

"Yeah. I don't know if I lost him, if it's over. Right now I'm mostly angry with him. I don't want to go into it with you, but he did and said some really dumb things today."

"Okay. Give it some time. Your parents have finished working and called to say they're on their way. They should be here in a few minutes."

"That's good. Don't tell them about Derek and all this. I don't think they knew he was coming today. They like him. We don't need to tell them Derek and I had a fight."

<div align="center">~~~~~</div>

Mom and Dad arrived at Papa's in time for dinner. After dinner, the family remained at the table on the terrace, enjoying the peaceful garden. Dad started to talk about Michael. Mom sat stoic and silent, focused on the garden, listening intently to her husband.

"Michael called yesterday," Dad began. "He told us he has a girlfriend."

Papa nodded and replied. "Yes, her name is Eve. He brought her here to meet Elizabeth and me a couple of weeks ago."

"What did you think of her?" Dad asked, seeking affirmation the family was united against Michael's living arrangement with Eve. He reached his hand toward Mom to give her the support he knew she needed.

"She seems like a nice girl," Papa continued. "Pleasant, polite. She and Michael seem to be very much in love."

"Did he tell you they're living together?"

Mom shifted in her seat and clasped her hands in her lap. Still silent, she looked away, her jaw set, her brow wrinkled.

"Yes," Papa replied, calmly. "They told us that."

Dad shifted forward in his seat, ready to attack this trouble. "And what do you think about it?" he challenged his father. "I mean, that's not how we raised him. Or you, Elizabeth. This is not what we'd expect from either of you. Certainly not from Michael. For him to have a girlfriend is fine. But he knows better than to move in with her. And what about college? She doesn't live anywhere near his college. How's he going to manage that?"

Papa was about to give his opinion when Elizabeth interrupted. "I agree with Papa. I think they're in love," she said. "Michael would never live with a woman unless he was in love with her. It's not like him. You'll understand when you see them together tomorrow."

Mom looked up. Her face was creased with worry. Her eyes shone with tears that wouldn't flow. Finally, she spoke. "Oh, Elizabeth. I know you would never do this. You'll be the one to wait till you're married. Like with your boyfriend Derek, you've always been respectable and done the right thing. I just never thought Michael was the kind of boy to…" Mom broke off, unable to say what she thought about her son's behavior, to give words to his new lifestyle.

"He's in love. Wait till you meet her," Elizabeth repeated.

Mom's attitude was disturbing but not unexpected. Mom had judged every boy Elizabeth had ever dated, advising her to maintain her virtue regardless of the boy's character. Now, she and Mom rarely talked about her boyfriends.

Papa concluded the discussion. "He'll be okay. He's a grown adult. Let him make his own decisions about his life, even if some might be mistakes. He'll work it out."

Elizabeth kept quiet. But she was thinking. *He's not making decisions for himself. Eve's making his decisions for him. If anyone works it out, it will be Eve, and that might not be the best thing for Michael.*

"They'll be here in a bit and you'll have a chance to meet Eve," Papa said. "For now, let's all relax and enjoy our time together."

Dad and Mom were happy to change the subject and talk about other things; the family's Fourth of July traditions, or baseball, or anything other than Michael and Eve. Still, Michael's plans loomed over the table. They all knew it would come up again when Michael arrived with Eve.

~~~~~

Late at night, Elizabeth was woken by a light and a buzz next to her bed. She expected it to be Olivia, angry about Elizabeth's conversations about the fairies, first with Derek and then with Papa. Instead it was her phone, buzzing on the bedside table. Derek's name popped up on her phone screen. She answered the call quietly in the dark.

"Hey, Babe, I've been up all night thinking about you. I was a fool this afternoon. I want to apologize."

"Okay."

"I mean I was really looking forward to seeing you and spending a couple of days with you. But then, I don't know. I got carried away. I wanted you so much and I acted like a fool. I thought about it all the way back on the train. So, can we still be together? Can you forgive me?"

"I don't know. Maybe. Let's give it a couple of days and see how we're feeling then."

"That's right. Can you come up to Richmond and see me in a few days? I promise to treat you right this time."

"Maybe. You need to remember there's more to me than just sex. You're the only boy I've gone all the way with, and you're special. But there's more to me than that."

"I know. You're an amazing girl. And not just because you believe in fairies."

"Leave the fairies out of this. You don't want to tangle with them again."

"Yeah. I still don't know how you did that to me in the garden this afternoon. I mean, linebackers have a tough time getting me down."

"You better start believing in fairies too then, because I didn't touch you."

"Yeah, that's right. I do believe in fairies. I do, I do, I do believe in fairies." Derek chuckled.

Elizabeth shook her head, frustrated. "I've got to get back to sleep. Thanks
~~~~~

for calling, Derek. I'll let you know if I can come to Richmond. Good night."

"Good night. I love you."

Elizabeth hung up, exasperated by Derek again, still sorting out her feelings for him. She reflected on the after-dinner discussion with her parents about Michael and Eve. She felt relief her parents weren't aware of the truth about her relationship with Derek. But she knew the fairies did. Now she thought about their response that afternoon, the soldiers attacking Derek, and how the nymphs and the fairies had intervened on the riverbank. It was after three in the morning. The house was silent. She was the only one awake.

She got out of bed and looked out at the garden, half expecting the fairy kingdom might have vanished because she had talked about it that afternoon. But she remembered that, when she was talking with Papa, after dropping Derek at the train, she had still seen fairies flying outside the window. She was relieved to see the lights and the tops of fairy buildings shining through the trees.

Then her anger at what the fairies had done that afternoon returned. She slipped out of her bedroom, down the stairs and out the door into the garden, ready to confront Olivia and the Queen. As she approached the marketplace, she heard the music stumble for a moment, then stop and the usual bustle of excited fairies subsided. Fairies paused and watched her in silence.

Olivia flew up and spoke, her head down, her tinkling voice subdued. "Good evening, Elizabeth. I am glad you have come into the garden. I was not sent to summon you. The Queen is not pleased with you and she wants to speak with you. But she wanted to leave it to you to come to the garden on your own."

"Well, I'm here. Will the Queen come?"

"She knows you have come. She will be here in a small moment."

The Queen walked slowly through the town. She was accompanied only by Thomas, no soldiers, no dignitaries, no parade tonight. Fairies in the market knelt as she passed. It was still and quiet in the garden. No nighttime birds called, no insects hummed, no more fairy music played. She stopped in front of Elizabeth and floated till she was level with Elizabeth's face. Thomas joined her, floating until he was just below her right hand. Olivia remained on the lawn below them.

"Good evening, Your Highness," said Elizabeth sarcastically. She deliberately didn't curtsy or kneel but remained standing, hands on her hips, gazing straight into the minute regal fairy's eyes.

The stern queen returned Elizabeth's look. It was a frozen stare that compelled Elizabeth to turn away, but Elizabeth steadied herself and forced herself to look again into the Queen's face. "Good evening, Elizabeth," said the Queen. "We need to discuss some of the things you have done today."

"I understand." Elizabeth held her pose and continued her defiant approach to the little queen. It flashed through her mind the Queen might deprive her again of the ability to see her kingdom. *That would be all right*, thought Elizabeth. *I'll miss you and your fairies, I suppose, but I'm done with all of you.*

"I'm angry with the fairies for the way they interfered today."

"You talked with the dark-skinned boy about my kingdom. And then you talked about us again this afternoon with your grandfather."

"Yes I did. Derek, my boyfriend, needed to know. All of your fairies were there watching him."

"This is true."

"And your fairies tripped him up, set him falling right into the marketplace. He needed to understand what was happening to him."

"I agree. This is why I will not censure you for your actions with the boy."

"You need to stop," Elizabeth demanded. Her anger at the fairies' interference returned. "Whether I'm with Derek, or any other boy I might bring into the garden, you need to leave us alone."

"I disagree. We need to protect you from the things a boy could do to you. That boy, or any other boy who might not have your welfare in mind."

Elizabeth's voice rose in anger. "No, you don't." She quieted her tone, afraid of waking her parents or Papa. She glanced back at Papa's window and at the side of the house where her parents slept, but no lights flashed on. "It's my life. It's my body. I make my own decisions. Not you. If I choose to make love with a boy, I can do so. And I will. You have to leave him alone and let me do what I want."

"No. You are special, Elizabeth. But you sometimes make foolish decisions. We need to take care of you."

"You keep saying 'you are special'. What do you mean?"

The Queen paused, taking a deep breath, considering her words. "There are a very few humans who have a trace of fairy magic in them. You were conceived here in this house above my garden and so you are one of those few. So is your grandfather, though there is not as much magic in him as there is in you. You are capable of achieving magnificent things in your life because of your fairy powers. And I must take care of you to enable you to do these things, just as I take care of all my subjects."

"Okay. That's fine. But let me pick my boyfriends and decide what I do with them. You can't interfere with that. Even down by the river after we left here, fairies were watching us."

"This also is true. The water-nymphs and the woodland fairies are friends of ours. I sent them a message by dragonfly to watch over and protect you."

"You shouldn't have. You don't need to do that. I want you to leave me alone."

"You need to know this, Elizabeth. If you had done the human breeding activity with this dark-skinned boy Derek today, if you had 'made love' with him as you call it, you would have become pregnant. He wanted to do it with you. And I feel what you feel, so I know that you wanted to do that thing with him as well. It wouldn't have mattered if you had made love with him here in the garden, or up in your room with Jefferson the bear watching you, or on the mud bank of the river. You would have become pregnant with Derek's child. And you would have quit the college you plan to attend. You would have lived a life like your friend from your work, Julia, waiting at the side of tables and going home to take care of a baby girl. You are better than that. You are worth more. You are capable of much more. You are special, born with special fairy powers. I will only permit you to bear a child when I know you are ready and when I see it is time. Not before that time."

Elizabeth flared. "Permit me to have a baby? Permit me? I don't need your permission."

"Then you need to be more sensible about what you do with boys and when you do those things. You need to become more careful. You need to become responsible for yourself and your actions."

"I guess I need to do something so I won't get pregnant. I expect I will make love again; maybe with Derek, maybe with someone else. And you're right. I don't want to get pregnant at this point in my life."

Beginning to use birth control was a decision Elizabeth had already made.

She was conceding nothing to the Queen by telling her.

"That would be a prudent decision."

"If I get birth control, a pill to prevent pregnancy, will you leave me alone the next time I am with a boyfriend?"

"Yes. I will know when you have done this. We will let you do what you want to do with a boyfriend when you have taken this pill. You must also consider other consequences of this behavior and take additional precautions. There are more dangers than only pregnancy to be considered."

"Thanks." Elizabeth felt for the first time that she had faced the Queen and won a small victory.

"There is one more thing I must discuss with you Elizabeth."

"What?"

"You spoke of us with your grandfather today."

"Yes."

"It has been many years since you did this thing, speaking with him about us. I understand you were angry today and so you said some things without thinking before you spoke. And I do not believe any damage was done by your actions or your conversation with your grandfather. He does know of us. So, I am forgiving you."

"Thank you, Your Highness," said Elizabeth contritely. She bowed her head for a moment, abandoning her defiant posture, and relieved that she would still be able to enjoy contact with the fairy kingdom.

The Queen nodded solemnly. "When you were talking about fairies with your grandfather this afternoon, you expressed a concern that you must be insane because you still know of my kingdom."

"Yes. Most adult people don't see fairies flying around in gardens."

"That is true. You are not insane, Elizabeth. We are real. Let me demonstrate. Watch the sky above you."

Elizabeth looked up to see a shooting star. Then another, then a silent shower of falling stars, almost like the fireworks she would watch the next day on the Fourth of July. As suddenly as the star shower began, it ended. One last star continued to fall, coming closer, a tight dot of light floating to a stop, glowing in front of the small fairy Queen. Calmly, the Queen reached out, touching it with a fingertip. The star flared and then popped like a soap bubble. Out of the flash, a white bird flew away into the night.

"The falling stars really happened, Elizabeth. And yes, I turned the last little star into a dove. I can change the forms of things. Animals are not always what they appear to be. That is only a small display of my power. We are real. Your other idea? That we are here to help you understand the complicated things that happen in your life? That is also true."

"Okay. I believe you." Elizabeth nodded and curtsied to the Queen, recognizing her immense power once again.

"You are tired, dear Elizabeth. It is almost dawn. See how the sky is growing light through the trees? I must go now. Come along, Thomas. Olivia, see Elizabeth back to her bed."

Led by Olivia, Elizabeth flew back to her bed and fell immediately asleep. She woke in the morning dreaming of Derek. They were in the garden making love. But there would be no babies.

~~~~~

Elizabeth, Papa, Mom, and Dad were finishing their morning coffee on the terrace when Michael and Eve arrived at Papa's, purring up the driveway in Eve's hybrid. When Papa heard the car on the gravel, he went through the house to greet them at the front door. He hugged Michael. Then he encouraged them, his tone jovial. "Come on out back. Everyone's outside. I bought decaffeinated herbal teas for you, Eve. Would you two each like a cup?"

"That would be lovely," Eve said. "First, let's go meet your parents, Michael."

Papa led them to the door to the garden, pointed to two empty chairs waiting for them at the table, and returned to the kitchen to prepare the tea. Dad stood as they came through the French doors to the terrace. Mom stayed seated, studying her hands in her lap. Elizabeth hurried to her brother, hugged him, and whispered, "I'm glad you came. It's great you're introducing Eve to Mom and Dad. They need to get to know her."

"Hi, son." Dad shook Michael's hand first and then clasped Eve's fingertips as he sat back down. "And you must be Eve? It's nice to meet you."

Eve withdrew her hand, leaned down and gave Michael's father one of her graceful, but remote hugs. She turned to his mother. Mother stayed seated and looked away when Eve extended her hand to her. Eve smoothly retracted her outstretched hand.

Michael was anxious, sweat beading on his upper lip. "Yeah, Mom, Dad,
~~~~~

this is Eve." Needlessly, he explained. "She's my girlfriend. I told you about her on the phone the other day."

The conversation stalled as Michael and Eve took the empty seats at the table. Elizabeth fiddled with the napkin in front of her, the tense silence around them deepening. In the garden, Olivia nestled nearby on a boxwood bush, perched on a low branch in the shade. She observed the family, but seemed detached from the drama, consumed by playing with a tiny blue butterfly.

Papa returned, carrying a tray with two cups of herbal tea and set them down, one in front of Eve, the other for Michael. Empty coffee cups, stained with the last dregs, sat in front of the rest of the family.

Michael's father opened the conversation, steering the direction to a safe topic. "Tell us how your classes went this spring, son."

"Good. I got my grades. I did well. Two years to go till graduation."

"And you're all set for the fall semester?"

"Yup. I'm all enrolled, ready to go." Then Michael dove in, indirectly confronting the topic on everyone's mind. "And Dad, I think I can save you a few dollars this fall and for the next two years. You have money set aside for my housing? I'll be staying with Eve, so you don't need to spend that money. I've told my old roommates, and they've already found a new guy to move in and share the apartment rent. So you can stop worrying about paying my share of the rent for my old place in Harrisonburg."

Mom was flushed, staring at the table, unable to speak to her boy or make eye contact with his girlfriend.

Dad continued, speaking as though Eve weren't there. "You told us she lives in Staunton. That's a long drive up to Harrisonburg every day. We'd rather you stay in your apartment near the campus."

"It's not that bad. A little over a half an hour on the interstate. More if there's traffic, but there never is."

"What if the weather's bad? What if it snows?"

"My buddies have already told me I can crash there for the night if that happens. And the college cancels classes if it's really bad."

Mom finally broke down. "Oh Michael. We just don't know if you're making a big mistake." She looked finally at Eve and said, "I'm sure you're a wonderful young lady but we're just now meeting you. This is such a big step for Michael to be taking."

Eve tried to soothe her. She reached over, putting a slim hand on his mother's forearm. Mom recoiled. "Your son will be fine," Eve said, taking her hand back. "If it helps, I'm a good cook. He'll eat better staying with me than if he were on his own. He's in good hands."

Mom held in her tears. "This is all so sudden. What if it doesn't work out with Eve?" she asked Michael, also speaking as though Eve weren't even at the table with them. "You've already told your roommates you're moving out? Where would you stay if you and Eve break up?"

"We won't. Eve and I have already talked about getting married. Our meeting each other was the most amazing thing that's ever happened to either of us. We're thinking maybe a winter wedding, right before Christmas. The Winter Solstice is an important date for us. That's when we're thinking."

Silence.

Eve picked up the conversation. "We would like your blessing."

Mom protested. "We don't even know you." Her voice was high-pitched, her tone was pleading. There was more silence as everyone processed what was being asked.

Elizabeth interceded. "I think this is wonderful. I believe you're very much in love with each other. You have my blessing." She looked to her parents, evaluating their response to her comment. She was secretly pleased to note they were distressed again by her support of her brother. If this situation directed their attention to Michael, any future time when she might find herself in a similar situation, this fight would already have been fought. It would be easier now for her to bring her boyfriends and her relationships with them to her parents.

"Could you wait maybe till spring?" Dad suggested. "There's no need to rush into this. Take some time. See how it goes this winter."

Papa intervened. "I agree with you, son," he said to Michael's father, taking him by the hand.

Papa turned to Michael and Eve, appeasing, extending his other hand to them. "Marriage is a big step. Take some time, Michael. Eve, there's no reason to rush. Stay together this winter. You've known each other a few months. See how it goes. We can start making all the wedding plans during the winter and have the preparations in place for a wedding next spring."

"That's good," Eve agreed. "You're right. We can wait till spring. Maybe we could do it on the summer solstice. I still need to tell my family, anyway. I know they'll be surprised. They've probably given up on the idea of me ever finding a man and getting married."

Michael gave in to Eve. If she said spring was a good time for their wedding, then he agreed. "Perfect!" he said.

"There. It's settled," Papa said. "Let's move on. Let's put together our plan for the day. We'll do a cookout here for lunch. I have vegetables we can grill, Eve. There's even a separate grill; one for meat, another one for the vegetables. Then maybe we could take it easy this afternoon, watch a ball game on television. And I thought we could take a picnic with us down to the green in front of the Governor's Palace and set up there to be ready for the fireworks tonight."

Michael protested. "The fireworks are late. By the time we get out it'll be too late to drive back to Staunton."

"Oh Michael," said Eve. "Relax. We don't open the shop till ten. We can sleep here tonight. I'll sleep on the couch downstairs and you can be up in your room. Then we can get out early, first thing in the morning and be back to Staunton by ten." It was too logical for Michael to protest. Eve had decided. They would stay the night.

Later, Elizabeth realized that the concession on the date of the wedding made everyone forget that the point of the conversation was simply to get agreement on the whole idea of Michael and Eve getting married.

<center>~~~~~</center>

Only a few days were left to the summer. Soon Elizabeth would leave, moving to Charlottesville to begin her first year at the University of Virginia. She sat on the terrace sharing a glass of wine with Papa after dinner. Olivia reclined on the wall of the terrace, always present, watching and listening.

"How are you feeling about starting college?" asked Papa. "Are you excited?"

"I guess." There was no excitement in Elizabeth's voice.

Papa shook his head, smiling slightly. "Come on now. I know you. I can tell when things are worrying you. What's the problem?"

"I'm a little nervous," she confessed.

"Why?"

Elizabeth stared into the garden for a moment. Olivia sat up, attentive, ready to help if she was needed. "I don't know. In high school I always got good grades. I was almost perfect. It wasn't hard for me, and it all made sense. I studied and learned what I needed to in order to ace the tests. But college is going to be different. I don't know how hard college will be. Everybody there'll be smart. What if I can't do it?"

"You'll be fine. It's a new place and a big step but you'll be fine."

"I hope so. I'll be in pre-med. Dad and Mom are all excited I'll become a doctor. But I don't even know what type of medicine I want to study or what direction I should take."

"You'll discover your passion while you're there. Follow your passion."

"I don't even know what I don't know. There are so many things I'll need to learn to be a doctor, and I'm not even sure what I'm lacking. As much as I do know, I still have a lot to learn. It's so much to think about."

"Relax. You'll do well. Call me if you need any advice. I'm always here."

"Tomorrow's my last day waiting tables at the restaurant. I'm ready to get on with school. One thing I do know is being a waitress is not my life's calling. It's a good summer job, but it's not my destiny."

"That's right. So, go to UVA. You'll have a fine year there."

They stood and started for the door to the house, bringing their empty wine glasses.

Olivia called after Elizabeth. "The Queen has sent a message to the University of Virginia. The Queen wishes for me to tell you there is a large community of fairies on that college campus. You will never see them, but they will be protecting you, watching you. You will do well there. You will be safe."

~~~~~

The next evening was Elizabeth's last at the restaurant for the summer. It was late, almost closing time. Only one table still had diners, two couples lingering over drinks and talking noisily. Elizabeth and Julia sat across from each other at a table in the back, rolling silverware into white cloth napkins, getting ready to set up for the next day.

"When do you leave for college?" asked Julia.

"In the morning. I'll meet my parents in Richmond, and they'll follow me in my car to Charlottesville. I move into my dorm tomorrow afternoon."

"Are you ready?"
~~~~~

"As ready as I'll ever be." Elizabeth paused before confiding, "I'm a little nervous."

"You'll do fine. You're smart enough. And you've been away from home every summer for years, staying with your grandfather. A lot of freshmen struggle being away from home for the first time. That won't be a problem for you."

"Yeah, you're right. I've never had a roommate before, but the college put me in touch with the girl I'll be rooming with, and we talked on the phone. She seems nice."

"There you go. You'll have fun. You'll get good grades. And remember what I said about the boyfriends?"

"Yeah. I'm okay with that. I know what to do and what not to."

"What about your boyfriend Derek?"

"I haven't talked to him in weeks. Not since he left here back at the start of the summer. He's been at Virginia Tech getting ready for football."

"Are you going to see him once school starts?"

"I don't know. I don't think so. He wanted me to go see him in Richmond this summer, but I decided not to. And since then, if he hasn't bothered to call all summer, why should I get back with him?"

As if summoned, Derek appeared in the entrance to the restaurant. He looked around, saw Elizabeth, and strode past the empty tables with his rolling, bouncing, long-limbed gait, grinning.

Julia saw him first. She had never met him, but she could guess who he was by the way he approached Elizabeth. She looked Derek over, evaluating his perfectly symmetrical mahogany face, his wide shoulders and his hard, lean body. He was impressive, though she was put off by the arrogant way he looked at Elizabeth.

Elizabeth turned and saw him. "Speak of the devil," she said. "We were just talking about you."

Derek's smile grew bigger. "I bet you were. You telling her what a great guy I am?"

He stretched his long arm out to Julia, offering to shake her hand. "Hi, I'm Derek, Elizabeth's boyfriend. It's great to meet you. And you are?"

"Julia." She shook his wide hand, watching him, but showing no emotion.

Derek turned back to Elizabeth. "I got a couple of days off from practice before school starts. I thought I'd come down and see you. I swung by your granddaddy's house. He said you were here, so…" He spread his arms, filling the room, "…so I'm here." His presence was overwhelming. The late diners watched him as did Elizabeth and Julia.

"Why?" Elizabeth asked. "I haven't heard from you since early July. I called you a couple of times, but you never returned my calls. So why come now?"

"Because I've missed you. I've been busy. Practice and everything."

"And after practice and in the evening?"

"Like I said, I've been busy. Most nights I go out with a bunch of guys from the team. But I'm always thinking about you."

"Sure. So, what do you want?"

"I wanted to see you. And I've got these." He held up three tickets, fanning them out. They were glossy and colorful, showing a photograph of a football player in the Virginia Tech Hokie maroon. "These are prime seats for three of our games. I want you to come down to Blacksburg and watch me play."

Elizabeth looked at the tickets, but she didn't reach for them. Derek waited for her reaction, still holding the fanned tickets out to her. Julia also watched and waited. Elizabeth's face was blank. After a moment, she pushed Derek's hand back. "No. I expect I'll be busy with my studies. I'm not sure I would be able to come to Blacksburg."

"You don't even know what days they're for. One's a Thursday night game, but the other two are on Saturdays. You wouldn't miss a class for the Saturday games. Come on. You always loved watching me play in high school. Why not now?"

"I'd need to drive there and get a hotel and everything. It's too much money. I don't think so."

Derek gave a wink. "You can stay with me. Right there in my dorm room."

"No. Keep the tickets."

"Come on, baby," he said, embarrassed to be rejected by her in front of Julia and the four late diners. "What's the problem?"

"I don't want to come down to Virginia Tech to watch a game. And I don't want to come down and shack up with you for a weekend. We're done Derek. You need to go now."

"Come on. It's not like that. All I want is for you to come watch me play football. Okay? Why this attitude?"

"We're done. Please go."

He looked down. He was beaten but he tried one last time. "Okay. I'll sell these. But tickets like these aren't easy to get. Let me know if you change your mind, and I'll see what I can do."

"Sure. Okay. Now go."

"Okay. Could I ask one small favor?"

"What?"

"It's late. I'm really tired. And Richmond is an hour away. I'm wondering if I could—"

"No!" Elizabeth interrupted him. "Get out of here!"

He turned and rushed from the restaurant. Elizabeth let out her breath and slumped at the table for a moment, her head in her hands.

"Atta girl," Julia cheered. "You'll be fine in college. Let's keep in touch."

22
Elizabeth – Age Twenty-two

ELIZABETH LOOKED OUT AT THE sodden garden. Late-spring rain fell, a gentle shower puddling on the crushed-shell paths, leaving shallow pools bound by the brick borders of the walkways. Moss on the aged brick walls seemed luminous in the ambient light. The thin rain stopped from time to time, but the sound of falling water continued, dripping from the sweeping live-oak branches and the broad magnolia leaves. Beads of water clung to the myrtle and dogwood blossoms. Everywhere, aside from the white and pink flowers, the garden was painted with hues of green.

Elizabeth felt smothered within the walls of Papa's house. Papa was there for her, as he always had been. She liked that. But she needed time to be alone to sort things out. Tomorrow, when her parents came, she would have to tell them.

She had already told them she planned to become a nurse rather than a doctor. They were disappointed, having hoped she would become a doctor, possibly a surgeon. Her grades were good enough—she could have gone to med school rather than choosing to study nursing. But she wanted nursing.

Her parents' response when she told them of her plans with Lucas was her most essential worry. They had met Lucas several times, even inviting him along to a celebratory dinner in Charlottesville after he and Elizabeth graduated from UVA. They liked him, but she knew they would be upset when she and Lucas shared their dreams. She remembered how it was when Michael laid out his plans with Eve, how her parents had resisted, voicing their displeasure with his decision to abandon their high-tech goals for him and choosing to live with Eve and help run her antique store.

Elizabeth pulled on calf-high rubber boots, odd attire for a grown-up, but utilitarian footwear that served two purposes. Of course, the boots were necessary in the puddles that dotted the garden today. But the boots also made Elizabeth laugh, harkening back to playtime in her childhood. Her friends, even Lucas, teased her whenever she wore them. The boots were dark gray with sassy, fun little yellow rubber duckies printed all over them. Some of the duckies held umbrellas. Others wore rain hats and slickers. Consumed with her worries, it made her happy to be wearing the ducky boots today.

Above the boots she wore a navy, orange, and white University of Virginia sweatshirt and khaki shorts. She took an oversize green and white golf umbrella from Papa's closet and found a thick green towel in the bathroom. Then she was out the French doors, across the brick terrace, down the steps and into the garden. She slopped along the puddled paths in her boots until she came to a circle on the far side of the garden facing one of the statues, the dancing boy. She toweled the wetness off a bench, folded the towel as a seat cushion, and sat, leaning the unfurled umbrella against her shoulder, sheltered beneath it from the incessant dripping off the trees.

Within moments, Olivia appeared. A red hat covered her head; possibly crafted from a flower petal. Rainwater dripped from the petal onto a wide, white cloak, edged with red and blue embroidery. The cloak, made of the hairless skin of an indefinable animal, wrapped around her shoulders and hung to her thighs. Olivia's legs were bare beneath the folds of the cloak. Her feet were in her customary summer footwear, red, pointed-toed slippers.

"Elizabeth!" Olivia called. "You so seldom come to the garden when the rain is falling. Why do you come today?"

"I need some time alone to think. To plan what I'll say tomorrow when Mom and Dad get here."

"You want to be alone? Should I leave?"

"No. Stay. It always helps me work things out when I talk with you. But why are you here? Most of the fairies don't seem to be outside today."

"Fairies do not like the rain. It is hard to fly with the water always bringing us down. Fairies like to stay inside on days like this and play games."

Elizabeth smiled, welcoming the diversion of learning something new about her fairies. "What kind of games do fairies play on rainy days?"

"Guessing games, riddles, and games of chance are fairy favorites. I am not very good at these games. I am not a lucky fairy. And I am always watching for you when I know you are visiting your grandfather. I was happy when I saw you coming out of your grandfather's house because it gave me a reason to leave the palace and come see you. I will play no more games today."

"I'm glad I gave you a reason to get outside, even in the rain."

"That is why I am here. Now what is distressing you so much that you come outside in the wetness?"

"There's a lot going on right now. You know I graduated college last week?"

"Yes. All of the fairy world is proud of you. We discussed holding a festival one night while you are here. Fairies love a celebration, and we must celebrate this achievement with you. To graduate is a good experience, is it not?"

"Yes. And I'll start college again at a new school at the end of the summer."

"Why will you do this? I thought you would become a doctor when you finished college."

"No. I'd need several more years of college to become a doctor. I've decided I'd rather be a nurse. But that means I'll have to go to college for a couple of more years. I'll be twenty-four years old when I finish nursing school."

"A nurse." Olivia sat down with her legs drawn up in front of her, elbows on knees, arms crossed, her chin resting on her slim forearms. She was contemplative, perplexed. "Nursing is how human mothers feed their newborn young. This is what you will do? You are pregnant? How could you have become pregnant?"

Elizabeth laughed. "No. I'm not pregnant. I've got that all taken care of. A nurse is someone who tends to sick people. The doctor makes the big decisions about how a sick person is to be treated, but nurses do most of the direct care, the actual treatment. I want to be a geriatric nurse, someone who cares for old people."

"That sounds like a marvelous idea. So, you will go to school to learn how to become a nurse?"

"Yes, at Old Dominion University. It's in the city of Norfolk, not far from here."

"I am not familiar with this college. I know so little about all the different colleges. Is there a New Dominion University that I also do not know of?"

"I don't think so. Anyway, Mom and Dad still think I should be a doctor. And they don't think Old Dominion is as good a school as UVA or William and Mary. But it's a great school for geriatric nursing."

"Geriatric nursing. Caring for old people. I would imagine that would be difficult. If they are old, they must be so near to their death. How can you help when you know that about them?"

"That's exactly why I like it. I took a class in it back at UVA, and I spent a semester working in a senior care center. I find it very rewarding to help people enjoy their last years as much as they can. I'll be working at a center for the elderly here in Williamsburg while I'm in school at ODU."

"ODU? UVA?" asked a puzzled Olivia.

"ODU is what people call Old Dominion. It's the school's initials. And UVA is the University of Virginia. But what matters is I want to study how to be a geriatric nurse."

"Oh, then this is a good thing you will be telling your parents. They will come to understand how you feel about this geriatric nursing."

"I hope so. But Lucas will be here, and he and I will be sharing other news with them. It's another thing I expect they won't like."

"I recall that this Lucas is your boyfriend. You have told me of him, and we have seen him here with you several times. What is this news? And why would it upset them?"

"Well, Lucas and I have been together for the last two years at UVA. My parents believe he's just my boyfriend, but we've been living together for most of the last year. Do you remember how upset they were when my brother Michael moved in with Eve? Now it'll all happen again but this time with me and Lucas."

"I cannot imagine your parents will be upset with you for this information. Everything worked out so well for Michael and Eve. They lived together for a year. Then they married. Now they have a little boy. What is his name?"

"Solomon."

"Yes, Solomon. He is a good little boy, almost three years old now. It is sad that he does not know there are fairies. He is too serious about his young life. He is too logical. Logical humans, even young ones, cannot accept a world that includes fairies. That is all right with the fairies. We do not mind. He leaves us alone when he plays in the garden. But he can be a noisy child. He gets into things when he runs in the garden. He can be a nuisance."

"Yes, it worked out for Michael. But my parents aren't happy he's working with Eve in her antique store, not with computers. Mom and Dad had plans for Michael and me. He was going to be a software developer, and I was going to be a doctor. And they still think people shouldn't live together before they get married. They seem to believe that so many people my age are doing things they shouldn't do, like living together but not getting married first. It's true that living together doesn't always work out. Neither docs marriage. But Lucas and I are committed to each other. We're getting an apartment together here in Williamsburg in the fall. Mom and Dad will be angry with me about that, too."

"Will Lucas become a nurse too?"

"No, he'll be in law school at William and Mary. He wants to go into politics."

"What is politics?"

"It's how we run our country. It's about laws, our rules."

"Oh. So, Lucas could become a king someday."

"No. Remember we have presidents, and senators and representatives, not kings. It's kind of like your Queen and her council. Lucas might become someone like the fairies on the Queen's council when he finishes law school. He wants to be a lawyer or go into government."

"That sounds like a noble idea. The world always needs more lawyers to make laws, to make sure that people do what they should do. Humans are not like fairies. Humans don't always do what is best or what is right. They need to have their laws. But why would your parents be upset that you and Lucas will live together? They do not know that you and he have done this for a year?"

"No. We each had separate apartments back in Charlottesville. But we spent most nights together in one apartment or the other."

"I have seen this Lucas when he comes to visit here, but I have not truly met him. I do not know what kind of a boy he really is. You have not had another boyfriend that I know of since that dark-skinned boy Derek."

"No, actually I've had several boyfriends since Derek and before Lucas. I just never brought any of them here to Papa's garden."

"Why not?"

"Remember what you and the rest of the fairies did to Derek? And to Zach, way back years ago?"

"Yes. We protected you from these boys."

"I worried you would do something like that again. I didn't want that to happen, so I didn't bring any of my boyfriends here. That's why I kept Lucas away from the garden most of the time when he came with me to see Papa."

"Oh, I see. We will leave the boys alone if you wish us to do so. We have told you this. I would like to meet this Lucas. When we meet Lucas, we will do as you wish with him. We have no reason to be concerned about the boys who you befriend if they are good to you. And now you are prepared not to become pregnant?"

"That's right. I want you to tell the Queen to leave Lucas alone when he comes to visit. I love him, and I want him to be safe here with the fairies."

"I will inform the Queen. It will go well for you and your Lucas. We will watch him, but we will not bother him if you love him. Perhaps we will leave both of you alone when he is here with you. You have nothing to fear."

They heard a door open and close. Through the dripping shrubbery, Julia stepped carefully around the puddles, following the pathway into the garden. She tugged a shiny blue rain jacket close to her chest and fumbled with a small, collapsed umbrella.

"Elizabeth," she called. "Why are you out here in all this rain? Where are you?"

"Over here, to your right. Follow the path and you'll see me."

Olivia ducked into the pachysandra. "Someone is coming. I do not want them to see me. I will leave you to your visitor." She hurried off into the shimmering, wet shrubbery.

Julia walked up, hunched under the small umbrella. "I came as soon as I could after you called me. Your grandfather said you were out here. What are you doing sitting out here alone in the rain?"

"It's almost stopped. And I like it here in the garden. It's a good place for me to think."

Julia surveyed the garden. "It's beautiful, almost a magical place even in the rain. I can see why you like it here. So, what's on your mind? Is this about Lucas?"

"Yes. My parents will be here tomorrow, and Lucas will be coming by. They like Lucas. But they don't know we're getting an apartment together. They're going to go crazy."

"Come on. They don't know about you and him back in Charlottesville?"

"No. The only people who know about that are a few of our friends from Charlottesville and you. All my parents know is he's my boyfriend. And when we tell them we're planning to get married when I finish nursing school…"

Elizabeth heard Olivia squeal off in the trees. "Married? Oh, what a wonderful thing! I cannot wait to tell the Queen about this. The whole kingdom will celebrate on the day of your wedding."

Julia continued. "That should make it easier for them, when they find out you two are engaged. They'll be fine with it then, won't they?"

"No. They'll still think we should wait to live together till after we're married."

"Yeah. I get it. Remember how I was trying to hide from my daughters that Greg and I were sleeping together? People think things like that matter. So everyone goes around pretending everything's all proper, even though they all know what's really going on."

"That's right. But now you're living with Greg all the time, just like a regular family. And your girls love him."

"True, and we're not married; just happily ever-aftering with no vows. It works for us."

"So, there's that. But the whole situation, me going to ODU for nursing, living with Lucas. They're going to be opposed to all of it. It's not going to be fun telling them."

"They're coming tomorrow?

"Yes. And Lucas will be with me. And my brother and his family will be here. And Papa, of course. It'll be crazy with everyone involved."

"You're working tomorrow night? So you'll have been through it all with your mom and dad before you come to work? You can tell me how it went when you get to work."

"Sure. I'm working full time at the restaurant this summer to put some money aside before I start nursing school. And I'll work one or two nights a week while I'm in school next fall. Can I lean on you for advice when it gets messy?"

"Of course. Let me know any time if I can help."

"Thanks. You're the best." Elizabeth leaned over and hugged Julia, needing to be close to her friend. "You're one of the only real people I can count on for support with these things. You, and my Papa too, but some things I can't share with him."

Julia missed the off-hand mention of her as a "real person". It was enough she and Elizabeth shared secrets about their boyfriends, their lives, their dreams. Elizabeth had been there for her as she worked things out with Greg.

They walked back to the house together, noting the rain had almost stopped. The sun broke through the scudding clouds, brightening the garden. The forecast was for sunny weather the next day when Elizabeth's family arrived. Elizabeth took it as a good omen.

<div align="center">~~~~~</div>

The garden baked in hot sunshine. No fairies could be seen. They would only come out at night in this heat. It was mid-afternoon, the first time Elizabeth had been able to call everyone together. Her family gathered on the brick-paved terrace in the shade next to the house at the black iron table. Elizabeth had taken a seat at the head of the table to deliver her big news. Papa sat in his usual place at the other end of the table. Mom and Dad sat side-by-side with Lucas next to them. He was tall, a handsome man with short, sandy hair and soft, dark eyes. He wore a pastel green polo shirt, pressed white shorts, and leather loafers with no socks. Michael and Eve were along the other side of the table with Solomon squirming on their laps, crawling back and forth between the two of them. Solomon had the face of a cherub, dark curls hanging to his shoulders. Michael and Eve were dressed identically; leather sandals, baggy white cotton shorts, and gray t-shirts.

Everyone had cold drinks sweating in chilled glasses. Michael and Eve drank herbal iced tea, ice cubes rattling when they raised their glasses. Papa, Lucas, Elizabeth, and Dad sipped dark beer, each glass capped with a thin layer of beige foam. Mom nursed an icy Sauvignon Blanc. Solomon had a plastic Sippy cup with apple juice.

Elizabeth began to speak, trying to contain her smile, but her face was flushed, and her eyes sparkled, betraying her excitement.

"Mom, Dad, everyone, Lucas and I have some news." They all turned to her expectantly. She and Lucas had been together for more than two years. The announcement they expected Elizabeth to deliver would not be a surprise. Lucas beamed beside Elizabeth, holding her hand beneath the table.

"We're planning to get married! We want to wait two years till we both finish grad school. Then I'll become a nurse and he'll find a position in a law firm, maybe up in Washington. That's when we'll get married."

Elizabeth saw Olivia grinning, darting through the tree branches, rushing to her to offer support. Olivia lit on the end of the terrace wall and slipped into the shade of a potted begonia on the ledge. She sat, red-faced with the heat, eagerly waiting for more news and more excitement.

Dad reacted first. "This is great news. Lucas, I would have liked it if you could have come to me first to ask for her hand. It's traditional, of course. But you're a good man, from a good family, heading toward a successful legal career I'm sure, maybe even in politics. And we can see you and Elizabeth are in love. This is wonderful."

Mom leaned across Lucas to her daughter and tried to hug her, putting a thin hand on her shoulder. "Honey, yes, this is a wonderful thing you're doing. We're so happy for both of you. Lucas, welcome to our family. We're so glad you're waiting two years for the wedding. It's the way it should be done." She shot a significant glance at Michael and Eve.

"Congratulations," Michael said, happy for his little sister and ignoring Mom's comment.

"You have our best wishes," Eve added with a demure smile.

"Mommy, can I have more juice?" Solomon held up his empty cup. Eve took the cup inside, leaving Solomon fidgeting on Michael's lap.

Elizabeth, knowing it was going well, decided to forge ahead with the rest of her news. "So, this year, Lucas will be in law school here at William and Mary. And I'll be down at ODU in the geriatric nursing program."

Dad interrupted. "You won't consider going back to UVA for Med School?"

"No, Dad. I want to go into geriatric nursing. I'll be at ODU. Anyway, while Lucas and I are in grad school, and both of us are studying right here, we're planning to get an apartment together a block or so from the William and Mary campus."

Silence.

Finally, Mom spoke. "Oh, Elizabeth. We're thrilled you and Lucas are getting married in a few years. But you don't have to live together before you're married, do you? Why can't you wait?"

Lucas stared stone-faced down at the black tabletop, letting Elizabeth deal with her parents' reaction. She had warned him to expect this.

Eve returned with Solomon's cup. She realized she had missed something in the short interlude while she was in the kitchen. Now she watched the family drama playing out around her, fascinated.

Michael grinned, waiting to see how his sister would respond.

Dad reached to his wife and rested a comforting hand on her arm.

Elizabeth replied. "Why should we wait? We love each other. We want to be together. But we don't want to get married till we finish grad school."

Again, silence.

Elizabeth glanced at Olivia sitting on the ledge, stirring but staying where she was, watching her. "We're being careful, so I won't get pregnant till after we're married if that's what you're worried about," Elizabeth concluded petulantly. "We won't do anything scandalous," she added with a dismissive wave of her hands.

"Oh, Elizabeth," Mom repeated. "You make it sound like you and Lucas are already living together."

Elizabeth looked away from her parents, quietly considering whether to come out and tell them she and Lucas had been living together for months while they finished school at UVA.

Finally, Lucas stepped in, hoping to cover for Elizabeth. "Not right now, not today," he confessed, telling a lawyer-like, carefully worded half-lie. "But we've already scouted out a few apartments. Elizabeth and I like one, and we have a lease that starts the first of July."

Elizabeth picked up from there. "So Papa, I'll be living here in town, nearby. We'll stop over to see you all the time. And in a couple of weeks we'll be moving in together."

Papa nodded. "Whatever I can do to help."

Mom's eyes filled with tears. "Oh, Elizabeth. Darling. Why can't you wait?"

Dad said nothing. He attended to his wife, stroking her hand, watching her, ready to comfort her anyway he could. He recognized this battle was lost. Probably the whole war was lost. His daughter was head strong. She would become a nurse, not a doctor. She'd go to ODU, not UVA. She would live the next two years with Lucas before they got married. There was no way he could change any of it in his daughter's mind.

"Why, Elizabeth?" Mom repeated. "Why?"

"Because we're in love. This is how we'll live while we're in grad school."

~~~~~

Solomon wandered alone into the garden on the white, crushed-shell path, cradling an inflated red rubber ball in his arms.

"Be careful in the garden, Solomon," Eve called after him from her seat at the table on the terrace with the other adults. "You can play, but stay on the paths and out of the gardens."

"Yes, Mommy," the boy shouted back. He always tried to be obedient. It wasn't easy, but he wanted so badly to be a good little boy. He wanted to be loved by his Mommy and Daddy. He knew they adored him, but he craved their love anyway, every day. He would do anything to please them.

Once he was deep in the garden, out of sight of the grownups, Solomon ran to the back wall where there was a wide space without plantings, nothing but packed white gravel and bare dirt. He began playing alone, bouncing the ball on the dirt, catching it before it rolled into the gardens, chasing it when he missed. Once, when it bounced into the thick groundcover, Solomon looked around anxiously, saw no one, and then tiptoed in to retrieve it. He checked again when he was out of the pachysandra. No grownups had seen him and the plants all looked the same. Back on the dirt, he bounced the ball again, this time against the ivy-covered brick wall. The ball rang like a bell when it hit the wall. He smiled, almost laughed at the sound, and threw the ball again.

Solomon couldn't see the fairies or any of the buildings of the fairy kingdom. For him, just as it was for his daddy, they didn't exist. But a legion of fairy warriors swarmed from the part of the garden wall that was the palace, marshalling in the courtyard of the castle. They rose into the air, a flying battalion ready to guard the palace, wary, watching Solomon, tracking his ball each time he threw it against the garden wall. The ball bounced back
~~~~~

to him and Solomon tossed it again. He was unaware of the fairy palace, but his ball shot directly at the tallest tower. The fairy guards flew in an echelon, swifter than the thrown ball, diverting it, tipping it high, over the wall and into the wilderness of the woods beyond. For the fairy soldiers, it was an easy, practiced defensive maneuver, something they did to ward off hawks.

Solomon stood, stunned, watching his ball change direction and vanish. He ran to the wall and reached for the top, his chubby fingers barely reaching the rim. He pulled himself up, trying to climb, but his sneakers slipped against the bottom bricks and his knee scraped against the rough wall. He sat back on the bare dirt and assessed his skinned knee. It was scuffed and it hurt, but there was no blood. He scrambled to his feet and ran back to where the grownups were.

"What happened to your ball, Solomon?" Michael asked.

"It bounced over the wall," Solomon said. Then he waited, desperately hoping he wouldn't be scolded. His knee hurt, but he knew this was not a time to seek sympathy.

Eve shook her head. "Oh, Solomon. It's always something with you, isn't it?"

Papa spoke calmly, wrapping a reassuring arm around the little boy. "That's okay. You were down at the back of the garden? There's nothing but woods on the other side of the wall there. We can get the ball later today."

Then Papa saw the scuffed knee. "What happened to your knee?" he asked.

"Nothing."

"Is it okay?" Papa looked into Solomon's eyes, seeking the truth.

"Yes." Solomon walked away to seek new diversions.

Michael looked at Eve and shook his head. "What are we going to do with that boy?" he asked.

"All we can do is try to raise him to be responsible," Eve replied.

~~~~~

Later in the afternoon, Michael and Eve strolled with Lucas and Elizabeth along the paths into the suffocating heat of the garden, talking quietly. Solomon was down for his nap. On the terrace, Papa took Mom and Dad aside, asking them to stay with him in the shade at the table.

"They're all still children." Mom watched the four young ones walking away among the flowers. Her eyes began to glass over with tears as she
~~~~~

thought of their long-abandoned childhoods and her lost dreams for them.

Dad nodded. He spoke to his wife, consoling her, while still trying to put things right in his own mind. "They're almost grown. We can't keep calling them children. I suppose we ought to begin thinking of them as adults. They're making their own decisions. Michael and Eve have their business and a child of their own. It's time we let them go."

"That's right," Papa said. "Children need to be able to do what they want to do when they grow up. They won't always end up doing what we as their parents hope they'll do. I always thought you'd be a doctor too." He looked at Dad, smiling. "I wanted to have you as a partner in my dental practice. Then you went into sales. And you've done very well. Keep that in mind. Michael and Eve aren't going in the direction you wanted for him, but they're doing fine. Elizabeth is following her dreams too, just like Michael. She'll become a nurse, and she'll be okay. You're right. You have to let them go."

"But think about Michael," Mom continued. "He could have done so much with his software skills. He always loved that before he met Eve."

Dad interjected. "And now Elizabeth, chasing her nursing dreams when she could have been a doctor. She's settling for less than what she could have been, just like Michael."

Papa repeated, "They're both happy with what they're doing. And I expect they'll both be successful."

"It's not just their career choices," said Mom. "It's that Elizabeth and Lucas seem so intent on living together before they get married. It's not how we raised them. We tried to teach them to have better values. They know better. Why can't they wait?"

"Did you two?" asked Papa. It was a hard, direct question that was met with uncomfortable silence.

Mom and Dad looked embarrassed and said nothing. Finally, Dad answered. "You knew?"

"Yes. Of course. You didn't get an apartment together or live together, the way Michael did with Eve. And now, Elizabeth and Lucas. But your mother and I knew you were spending nights together. Nobody talked about it back in those days. That's the only difference. I won't comment about what your mother and I did in our day, before we were married. I will say I find it refreshing that it's out in the open now. Whether it's right or wrong, there's less tiptoeing around, less hypocrisy these days."

Mom and Dad sat at a loss for words, trying not to make eye contact with Papa.

The heat drove the children back up to the shade of the terrace. In spite of his attempt to accept everything, Dad went after Michael again. He was in the moment after the discussion with his father, and he couldn't let things drop. "Michael, do you ever do anything with your software background, your high-tech skills? You got a degree in software. Have you put it to any useful purpose?"

"The degree's in Computer Science. And yes, I do a bit with it. Not much. I manage the internet for our business. I put the inventory and all our financials for the antique store on spread sheets. There's that. And I have a contract job with a store in Staunton to do tech support work. They send me out once or twice a week to fix issues with some of the programs and systems people buy in their store. That's about it."

"You could do better than the antique business. Are you two making an adequate living selling old furniture?"

Eve looked frustrated, maybe even angry. Michael rested a quieting hand on her forearm and remained calm as he answered. "Yes, we're doing very well. It's a good business for us. And it really works nicely with Solomon upstairs in our apartment or playing with us in the store. But it is a departure for me. I always loved the cutting-edge aspect of technology, the novelty, how everything is new and innovative. Then, when I met Eve and started to learn about antiques, it really opened my eyes."

Dad nodded, but the set of his face showed he was still not pleased, still not understanding.

Michael continued, excitement animating his words. "I mean, you look at an old piece of furniture, a dresser for example. We sold one a couple of days ago. You could see the craftsmanship. I look at the cabinetmaking, the grain of the wood, how carefully that dresser had been put together. I imagine the time someone took so many years ago to make this thing, carving the curve of the top by hand, making sure the drawers move in and out smoothly. I think about the care the carpenter took to make sure it was just right, dovetailing the joints in every drawer."

Michael had never been one to talk a lot, but he continued, his voice rapturous as he explained his newfound passion for antiques. "And I think of the people who bought this dresser for their house so long ago when it was new. I like to imagine the lives they led with this as a part of their home. I love the stories that come to me when I see these fine old things! I see a small nick on the top where someone dropped something maybe, or bumped the dresser with a vase. The piece might not be perfect because of the little dent, but it has character, it has a history.

"You don't get that with new furniture or with a computer," he explained. "A lot of the furniture's not even made with real, solid wood anymore. The junk they make today, it's plywood or particle board covered with a laminate layer, a veneer to make it look like real wood. Everything's the same, slapped out and mass produced. And computers are so predictable. They all use the same codes, follow the same rules, work the same way. Nothing's unique or original these days. And it's made with built-in obsolescence. They don't even expect it to last. They want you to upgrade every year or so. But that dresser we sold this week? It was over a hundred years old."

"There's more money in technology," Dad fussed. "You could be doing so much better."

"You love your business, don't you Michael?" Papa asked.

"Yes."

"And you love Eve and Solomon, your new family."

"Of course."

Papa turned to Elizabeth. "And you and Lucas love each other too. You'll be in the same place as Michael and Eve in a few years. You and Lucas will have your careers, and you'll get married, maybe start a family together. You both have to work at it. But it's all there waiting for you to make it happen."

Elizabeth smiled. Lucas took her hand.

Before Elizabeth could respond, Michael changed the subject. "Hey, here's something we can do with my high-tech skills. How about all of you join my fantasy football league?"

It was an odd, irrelevant question, but it took the conversation away from the tension of Michael's and Elizabeth's life choices. Except for his passion for watching baseball on television, Michael had never cared for sports, never played them after two sad years in little league, rarely gone to games as a spectator.

Lucas leaned forward with interest. If this deflected the conversation away from his impending living arrangements with Elizabeth, he was all for it.

Dad remained icy, still intent on trying to save the lives and career aspirations of his two children. Mom had tuned out of the conversation an hour ago, feeling nothing but dismay about her daughter's improper life choices. She gave up, sighed, and turned away.

"Tell me about it. How does it work?" Papa asked, following the diversion. "Explain fantasy football. I keep hearing about it, but I don't quite get it."

"It's like this. Before the pro football season starts, we all pick teams. Quarterbacks, running backs, wide receivers. Defensive players, too. It's based on the real players on all the teams. Everyone drafts their teams made up of the best guys in pro football. Then we all place money on each of our teams to make it interesting. Each week, once the season starts, we see how each of our players does in the real games, and we score points based on their performance, their statistics. It's fun! I never really followed sports at all till I discovered fantasy football. A few of my old friends from college and some of the guys from my tech store ran a fantasy football league last year. I played along and I finished third. I won a bit of money and a small trophy."

"Not for me," Papa said. "I don't think I'll do it. I have enough trouble understanding reality without trying to figure out and place bets on fantasy."

"Dad, how about you?"

"No thanks." Dad's answer was terse. The day had not gone the way Mom or he had planned. He couldn't bring himself to go along with any of his son's ideas. Today nothing was acceptable.

"Lucas? Are you in? Elizabeth, you'll like this," Michael continued. "Remember your old boyfriend from high school, Derek? He's only a rookie, but he got drafted so high by the NFL that he's on the fantasy list of wide receivers we get to pick from. You could have Derek on your team."

Elizabeth shook her head. "Nope. Not for me. I don't want to have Derek."

Lucas grinned. "I'm in. Do I give you my money now or later? And when do we draft our teams?"

~~~~~

The summertime grad student life was idyllic for Lucas and Elizabeth. They took the small apartment on a side street near the William and Mary campus, a living room, an eat-in kitchen, a single bedroom and a
~~~~~

bathroom on the second floor of an old house. They outfitted it with old furniture from yard sales and consignment stores. They adopted a dog from a shelter, a happy-go-lucky black mutt they named Loki after the Norse God of mischief. They eased through the summer, settling into a full-time life together, visiting Papa several times a week, whenever Elizabeth wasn't working at the restaurant. The three of them enjoyed dinner and relaxing evenings together on the garden terrace. The fairies left them alone but were never far away, watching from a respectful distance.

As summer ended and classes began, Lucas and Elizabeth found themselves too busy for regular visits to Papa's house. Elizabeth continued working two nights a week at the restaurant and spent one afternoon each week working at a nursing home in Williamsburg. Her classes consumed the rest of her weekdays. Lucas spent all day at law school and in the library. In the evenings, they shared the apartment and their lives side-by-side, eating dinner together whenever they could. They always seemed to be studying, finding too little time to be with each other. It was a life together but with no time for conversation except on weekends.

On most Saturday mornings, they took Loki on a leash and walked to the farmers' market in Merchants Square to stock up on fresh vegetables for the week ahead. Sharing coffee with Lucas on a bench behind a farmer's booth one morning, Elizabeth remembered when she was a child, and she and Papa had met with Santa on the same bench. She recalled the Queen's decree and the years without the fairies that followed that day. She looked around now and saw a fairy here and there in the trimmed shrubbery in the square. Now she knew fairies were everywhere there were gardens.

While they walked back to their apartment with their bags of vegetables, Loki stopped to inspect a flat-topped boxwood bush planted next to the sidewalk. He sniffed and prepared to mark the bush as his own. Elizabeth couldn't contain herself and laughed as she saw fairies run from the bush screaming and flying into the trees.

"It is a dog!" screamed one of the fairies. "It is disgusting, disgraceful. Why cannot dogs be more refined like cats?"

"Cats are worse," cried a second fairy. "They are strange creatures, silent, capricious and unpredictable. Even fairies never know what cats are thinking."

"What's the joke?" asked Lucas. "Why are you laughing?"

"It's nothing. Just Loki." Elizabeth was tempted to explain about the fairies to Lucas. If they were going to get married, shouldn't he know? But even as an adult, she remembered the Queen's decree. She knew she ought to abide by what the Queen told her. Still, if they were a couple, married and raising a family, Lucas ought to know.

Elizabeth, Lucas, and Loki climbed the stairs to their apartment. While Elizabeth and Lucas busied themselves putting the vegetables away, Loki lapped noisily at his water bowl.

Elizabeth paused, put down a bag of tomatoes and turned. "Lucas, I have to tell you something about myself."

Lucas stopped and looked at her. The way she opened the conversation suggested what she had to say was significant.

Elizabeth took his hands and continued. "I believe fairies are real. I see them. They're everywhere, mostly in gardens. They're all over in my Papa's garden. Most people can't see them but they *are* there. I'm not crazy. I've seen them since I was little. I still see them even now that I'm an adult. They're real."

Lucas smiled slowly, watching her eyes, and spoke deliberately. "Okay, then. You see fairies. Okay. If you believe in them, I can accept that. I love you, so I can believe in your fairies. I've got a confession too. One time, back when I was still in high school, I think I saw a flying saucer. There was a bright light in the sky. It moved back and forth slowly for several minutes and then just like that it darted off and was gone. Airplanes don't move like that. It had to be a flying saucer. What else could it have been?"

"Maybe it was a fairy."

"No. It was too high up in the sky. Fairies couldn't possibly fly that high with their little wings. You don't think I'm crazy because I believe in flying saucers, do you?"

"No. And you don't think I'm crazy about the fairies?"

"No."

"Oh, and fairies can fly, but they don't have wings. They don't need them to fly."

Lucas laughed and nodded. "Of course they don't."

23
Elizabeth – Age Thirty

ELIZABETH AND LIVVY WERE SETTING out food from the refrigerator, starting to prepare their dinner when the doorbell rang. Elizabeth went to the door, followed by Livvy. Julia stood on the doorstep, holding a big brown paper bag.

"I brought fried chicken, a salad, and some snacks," she said. "I hope you haven't eaten yet. Dinner is served. I've got wine, too."

Livvy hid behind her mom, wrapping her arms around Elizabeth's thigh, peeking out at their visitor. "Mommy, this is the lady from the restaurant where we had lunch. Why is she here?"

Elizabeth looked down at her daughter and placed a reassuring hand on her head. "Yes, this is Julia. She's brought us something for dinner because she's a friend. That's what friends do for each other."

Julia bent down, eye level to Livvy. "That's right. Your mom and I worked together a few years ago at a restaurant. We always looked out for each other. I've got your dinner here in the bag. Where do you think we should eat?"

"Outside in the garden! Come on!" Livvy shouted. Off she went, running for the terrace doors.

Julia followed, calling back to Elizabeth, "Bring place settings and a corkscrew. It looks like I've got a guide to help me find my way out back!"

Elizabeth would have preferred eating inside. She was still tired of the garden and its fairies, but Livvy was already outside and Julia followed, right on her heels. The decision had been made. Elizabeth went to the kitchen, put the food she and Livvy had taken out for dinner back in the refrigerator, and gathered a stack of three plates, placemats, and silverware. She got a glass and a bottle of juice for Livvy along with the corkscrew and two wine glasses for Julia and herself. She set everything on a tray and followed Julia and Livvy to the terrace, pushing the door open with her hip.

They settled in at the table, enjoying the summer warmth of the garden, the late afternoon sunshine sifting through the crepe myrtle blossoms. The garden surrounded them with the hum of bees, the constant motion of the birds, butterflies, and dragonflies. Julia took a box of fried chicken out of the bag and began to serve it. She added macaroni salad and bread to the meal. Livvy opened her bottle and carefully poured the juice into her glass. Elizabeth worked the cork out of the wine bottle and poured white wine into the two wine glasses.

"Greg is watching my girls tonight," said Julia. "You and I didn't have time to really talk in the restaurant today, and I wanted to see you. How are you two doing?" She carefully included Livvy in the conversation.

"Good!" Elizabeth tried to sound optimistic. "I mean, losing Papa was hard. I was so very close to him. But I think Livvy and I are both doing well."

Livvy chimed in. "We're going to come and live in Williamsburg, and I'm going to go to school here."

"Really?" Julia smiled and looked to Elizabeth for confirmation.

"Yes, I think so. Papa left me the house in his will. My job is here, and there's no reason for us to stay in Richmond. We checked out an after-school program for Livvy this morning. She'll be in kindergarten most of the day while I'm at work."

"Really!" Julia started to grin, her voice affirming. "When do you think you'll move?"

"Soon. We're going back to our house in Richmond tomorrow to pick up some of our things, our clothes and a few personal items."

Livvy joined in again. "I need my swimming suit. And my clothes and my toys and my animals. They want to move here too."

"Your animals?" Julia asked.

"Yes. I have lots of animals. Hamilton, my bear, is already here. He always goes wherever I go because he gets scared at night if I'm not with him. And all my other animals are coming too. I have a pig named Oscar Mayer. He's annoying because he always makes a mess. But I'm bringing him anyway."

Julia smiled. "Oh, that's good. I don't think Oscar would want to be the only animal left behind."

"His name is Oscar Mayer. And he's bossy, but the other animals don't listen to him. I'll bring Sarah too."

"Tell me about Sarah," Julia said. "Who is Sarah?"

"Sarah's my cow. She's sad right now because Daddy left. And she doesn't know that Papa died yet. She'll be more sad when I tell her Papa died."

"Well, you need to take care of Sarah and cheer her up."

"That's why Mommy and me are going back to our house in Richmond tomorrow. To get my clothes and my swim suit and my animals. When my animals come here, that's when I can cheer up Sarah."

Elizabeth had been sitting watching and listening as Julia and Livvy discussed the situation. She suddenly realized neither she nor Julia had started eating. Livvy, sometimes talking with her mouth full, was done.

"I'm all finished, Mommy. Can I go play in the garden?"

Normally Elizabeth would have insisted Livvy stay at the table till everyone was finished, but she wanted some time alone to talk with Julia. "Sure. You go play, Honey Bunny."

Livvy scrambled off her chair and ran down the steps into the garden, trotting along the path.

Once Livvy was gone, Julia began. "What an adorable little girl! You called her Olivia when she was first born. I remember all about her birth. Livvy seems to be doing pretty well with all the changes you've both been through. How about you?"

Elizabeth dodged the question and turned the conversation to her daughter. "Livvy's still sad at times. You heard what she said about Sarah the cow? I think she uses the cow to tell me how she's really feeling. But she does seem to be coping."

"That's good. And you?"

Elizabeth sighed, gave in, and began to talk about her emotions. It was the first time she had allowed herself to think in detail about everything that happened with Lucas and Papa. Her words, once they started, rushed out.

"I'm getting by a day at a time. It would all have been so much easier if Lucas had still been with me at Papa's funeral. I'm trying to do something to move forward each day. There isn't a lot to do, but I feel overwhelmed at times. I can't always decide where to start each morning. It's all so chaotic. I don't know what direction to go sometimes. Tomorrow I have to confirm with the school we visited this morning that Livvy will be there next year for the after-school program. That might just be a phone call, but I expect I'll have to pay for a few days or maybe a week up front, and I'll have to fill out some papers too. I'll have her enrolled in the kindergarten here in town. And I have to get our townhouse in Richmond listed with a real estate agent and start moving our things down here. I go back to work at the nursing home next Monday. There's really not a lot to do, but I have to move fast and sometimes when I wake up in the morning, all I want to do is go back to sleep for a few hours."

"I understand." Julia nodded. "I was like that when I went through my divorce. I try not to think about it anymore, but it's always there."

Elizabeth sipped her wine, holding it in her mouth, lingering with the flavor while she decided what to say next. Julia waited. After a moment, Elizabeth continued. "Little things stop me dead in my tracks. You heard Livvy going on about her swimsuit? She wanted to go to the beach or the pool. But neither of us had our suits. It seemed like a huge problem at first. I almost lost it and yelled at her. But she's a little girl. She wasn't the problem, and I caught myself. We went to a park by the river and sat for a while. It was nice. But when it was happening, and she wanted to go swimming and we didn't have our swim suits, it seemed like the end of the world."

"How did Livvy deal with it?"

"She simply said, 'let's not forget our swim suits when we go back to Richmond tomorrow.' You heard her just now. For her, we're going to Richmond to get our suits and her animals. Maybe she's coping better than I am." Elizabeth gave a quick shake of her head.

"So you go back tomorrow and you pack some clothes and your swimming suits. And don't forget Oscar Mayer or Sarah the cow."

"Yes. We can't forget Oscar Mayer or Sarah!"

Julia spoke quietly. "What happened with Lucas? Can you talk about it?"

"Of course. With you." Elizabeth hadn't talked much about what happened. Not with her parents, certainly not with the fairies, not even with Papa. She realized she was finally ready to let it all go.

"You met a couple of my boyfriends. Derek and one or two others. You remember what they were like. Lucas seemed different. He was so good with me, so smart, and funny, and caring. He was going places in life, becoming a lawyer and getting involved with politics. I thought I loved him. I thought we had it all. You know him. You were in our wedding. You understand."

Julia nodded and waited for Elizabeth to continue.

"Once we got settled in Richmond, he always worked late. Lawyers do that. Work at the State House can take hold of your life, I guess. And I worked down here at the nursing home. I've been there since grad school, and I do enjoy working there. It got even crazier after Olivia was born. We got her into a childcare center in Richmond and kept up with our jobs."

Julia nodded again. "So, what happened?"

"I don't know. He came home one night just a few months ago and asked for a divorce. He'd had an affair, and he wanted out of our marriage."

"Just like that?"

"Yes. Just like that. I was caught off guard. Maybe I'm still dazed by how fast it ended. But the good thing is, in politics they don't want any scandals so it's been easy as far as custody and all that. He simply ended it and gave me the townhouse and alimony and child support and anything I wanted. He doesn't want any problems or publicity that could haunt his career or hurt the aspirations of his boss."

"I guess that's a good thing. You don't have to fight him for anything? I had to go to court to get my ex to pay child support."

"No. Lucas took care of everything. The odd thing is with my job, and with Papa leaving me the house, and with Lucas doing his part, I've landed on my feet financially. Money won't be a problem. But the money isn't what matters to me. I've lost Lucas and now Papa. That's the hard part. I feel very alone right now."

Livvy trotted up the garden path and hopped up the steps.

"Mommy, does Julia know about the fairies?"

Elizabeth paused, deciding how to respond. She knew the fairies enforced their rules and guarded their need for privacy. It gave her an easy response.

"Livvy, haven't the fairies told you not to talk about them? I don't think they want you talking about them with people who don't know."

"Yes. The Queen told me. But you already know about them and Julia's our friend, so I guessed she knew too."

"No, Julia doesn't know about the fairies. And you better check with Olivia and the Queen to be sure they're okay with you talking about them, even with me. They like to be kept a secret."

"I know." Livvy began to pout, crossing her arms. "But it's fun to talk about them with you. I still want you to come and play with them. You told me you played with them when you were little."

"That was when I was little. I know they're fun. Why don't you run along now and make sure they're not upset because you told Julia about them. You should apologize to them so they're not angry."

"Okay." Livvy skipped down the steps and trotted back into the garden.

Julia looked at Elizabeth, smiling. She took another sip of her wine. "What was that all about?" she asked.

"Oh, when I was Livvy's age, I believed there was a whole town of fairies living in the garden. I believed the Queen and other special fairies lived there with a palace and everything." Even now as she was telling Julia, Elizabeth felt the worry she always felt whenever she told anyone about the fairies.

Julia nodded, still smiling. "Children do that. Just like Livvy with her stuffed animals."

Elizabeth stared hard at the black wrought iron of the table top, frowning and not looking at Julia. She traced the edge of the table with her finger, debating whether to continue. Then she started again.

"I still believed in the fairies when I was older. I still saw them and talked with them here in this garden until a few months ago. I stopped when Lucas left. And now after Papa. But I believed in them most of my life."

"Really." Julia put down her wine glass and leaned back in her chair, assessing her friend. She knew this was not a time to joke about it or tease. Elizabeth was dealing with enough with her divorce and her grandfather's death. But Julia wanted to ask a lot of questions.

"Yes." Elizabeth looked up at her friend. "Am I crazy? Nobody sees things like fairies after they grow up. But here I am telling you that, as an adult, I still saw them and talked with them, doing things with them. I must be insane, right?"

"No." Julia reached out, resting a comforting hand on top of Elizabeth's. "If they seemed real to you, if you believed in them, they must have been real. At least for you."

"And now they're real for Livvy. I named her after my best friend fairy, Olivia, my special fairy. But I've made myself move on. The fairies used to help me when things got hard. So, where were they when things went wrong with Lucas? They didn't help me with Lucas, so I gave them up. It feels good to be handling problems like Lucas without the fairies. And now Papa. They were useless when he had his heart attack."

"Okay. So now you don't believe in fairies. That's good, right?"

Elizabeth looked at Julia. It was a relief to see Julia took her assertion about the fairies seriously. "Yeah. Finally. I've grown up."

"But you remember them. So you know what it's like for your daughter out there imagining a garden full of fairies."

"Yeah, I remember them. Livvy tells me I still believe in them and maybe she's right. They were real for me then, but not anymore. They're real for children. And you're right too—I'm not crazy. I don't see them anymore. But I worry Livvy won't outgrow them, the way I never did. I don't want her depending on them when she grows up."

Julia nodded. "Let her enjoy believing in them while she's still young."

"I guess. It's just… the fairies always helped me; for most of my life, but not with Lucas and not now with Papa. They failed me. They let me down when it mattered most." Elizabeth shook her head.

"With Lucas, they ignored what he was doing," Elizabeth continued. "They must have known, and they could have warned me. They could have done something to him to make him stop seeing that woman and make him come back to me. Maybe we were too far away from this garden where they live. But they have a network to talk with fairies in gardens everywhere. So why didn't they tell me he was having an affair? Why didn't they stop him? They let it all happen."

"I guess they left it up to you to figure that out."

"It feels like the whole mess is my fault." For a moment Elizabeth almost cried, filled with the mix of dismay and anger that had fought for her mind ever since the night Lucas left her. Elizabeth's shoulders shook, a quick shudder, but she regained control and looked into the garden for a moment to steady herself.

Julia nodded but said nothing, waiting and letting her friend unburden herself.

Elizabeth continued. "My parents weren't helpful. They live across town in Richmond and could have done something, but they blamed me for the failed marriage. Lucas is wealthy and powerful and successful, so they said I shouldn't have let our marriage fail. I should have made it work. Looking back, I realize they've been unhappy with so much I've done with my life. They were never there to support me when I was growing up. They disapproved of my decision to become a nurse. Now, at this difficult time, when I've needed their help, I'm disappointed they offered so little."

Julia replied, "The divorce, your Papa's death, none of it is your fault. Your Papa had a heart attack. It's unfortunate and it's sad, but it's not anybody's fault. And certainly, you're not to blame for what Lucas did."

"I should have done something sooner. That's what Mom and Dad said. I should have been home for Lucas, maybe taken a job in Richmond instead of working here in Williamsburg. I could have been home every night and always picked up Livvy from child care and been there waiting for him with his dinner ready. Maybe I wasn't supportive enough of Lucas' career working in the Statehouse. That's what my parents said."

"Lucas had an affair. That's not on you. That's his fault."

"I know. I love my job. But I worry that somehow I'm to blame. Maybe if I had done enough for him at home, he wouldn't have gone looking elsewhere for love. I thought we were fine. I must have done something wrong."

"You can't do that. He messed up, not you. Don't blame yourself for his mistake. Let it go. You'll land on your feet."

"What was it like when you got divorced?" Elizabeth asked. It was a topic they had never discussed.

"It was awful. I felt like my life had ended. I blamed myself too, just the way you're doing. I held it together for my little girls. I was fine when it was all over. You will be too."

"I guess so. I've got to keep my life together, keep moving forward for Livvy. And I know we'll be okay. I want this time to be finished so I can move on. I can't wait for us to move here and get back to the regular day-to-day routine of going to work each morning and picking up Livvy from school at the end of the day."

Julia reached across and took her hand. "That's right. It's rough water right now, but it'll all smooth out in a week or two when she starts school."

They gathered the dirty dishes and took them inside to the kitchen. They poured the last of the wine in their glasses and returned to the terrace. The sun was setting and Livvy, deep in the garden, could be heard singing. Her voice had the gentle sound of faraway bells. Julia and Elizabeth sat enjoying the evening together. Elizabeth leaned to her friend and gave her a hug. They were quiet now. They had said everything that needed to be said.

<div align="center">~~~~~</div>

They finished cleaning up after dinner, and Julia left. Her daughters were teenagers now, self-reliant, but Julia still wanted to be home with them when she could. Greg would make sure they did their chores and finished their homework during the school year. He sent the girls to bed if Julia was late, but Julia wanted the time with her girls. She wanted to spend the evening with Greg as well.

With Julia gone, Elizabeth put Livvy to bed. Her little girl was exhausted after all the activity of the past days. She fell asleep halfway through the story Elizabeth was reading to her.

Elizabeth, too, was worn out by the funeral and all the emotions of the past week. The day itself had also been hard. They had committed to the decision to move from Richmond and made the preliminary arrangements for Livvy at the childcare center and the kindergarten in Williamsburg. It was still earlier than her usual bedtime when she decided to forego her nighttime cup of tea and go to bed in her new bedroom at the front of the house. She fell immediately into a dreamless sleep.

In the middle of the night, Elizabeth woke with her mind racing. She couldn't fall back asleep, chasing all her thoughts, sure she was forgetting important details. *What do I have to do tomorrow? Now it's past midnight, so it's not tomorrow anymore. It's today already. There's so much to do. I'll have to start right after breakfast. We'll finalize our plans for Livvy with the childcare center and enroll her in kindergarten. Then we'll go to Richmond and find a real estate agent and list the townhouse. And we'll pack for the move to Williamsburg. What else do I need to do? There must be something I'm missing.*

Finally, she gave in to her restlessness and got up. She slipped across the hall to check on Livvy. Her child sprawled sideways across the bed on her back, the covers everywhere. Gently, trying not to wake her, Elizabeth rearranged Livvy, and pulled the covers back over her. Livvy squirmed for a moment, mumbled something, pushed the covers away, and slept.

Elizabeth went back to her bedroom. She paused for a moment by the window, looking out at the front lawn. The yard was still and bright with white light, painted silver by a full moon. Shadows were distinct, crisp areas of darkness beneath the trees that rimmed the yard. Suddenly, out of the black shadows, a dark mass dropped from a tree to the shining lawn below. She heard screeching howls and saw a shadowy, tumbling fight between the dark beast from the tree and another animal on the moonlit grass. She remembered the evil thing she had seen in the garden treetops only one night ago. Was this the owl again? Was it killing a rabbit? The screeching continued. Then, abruptly, the noises stopped. There was only silence.

Elizabeth, a hand at her mouth, continued to watch the horrifying death scene playing out in front of her. Finally, the black beast flapped twice and lifted above the yard, carrying a limp object in its talons. Then it was gone, blending into the darkness and the trees across the street. In the bright moonlight, the lawn was empty. Nothing was left. Nothing moved.

Elizabeth sat back on her bed, lifted her legs beneath the blanket and lay down. *I came to believe the garden in the backyard was the most dangerous part of the house. I believed the fairies were evil, with all of their powers, all the things I saw them do out there. But the real danger is outside the garden. The fairies never hurt me. They didn't always do what I wanted, and they didn't always help me, but they always meant well. There was never anything malevolent about them. Now I see the front yard is different. I just watched a life end in a moment on the lawn. Maybe the real evil is outside my garden.*

She fell anxiously back to sleep and, restless, dreamed of the violent death of a bunny.

24

ELIZABETH – AGE TWENTY-FOUR

THEIR GRAD SCHOOL YEARS FLEW by. As Elizabeth approached graduation, Lucas accepted a position working as an aide on the staff of a young representative in the State House in Richmond and decided to leave law school. Elizabeth was offered a full-time job as a nurse at the nursing home in Williamsburg where she had worked part time the past two years.

They planned an early fall wedding. The marriage ceremony would be at their church in Williamsburg. Since the guest list for the wedding was small, Papa's garden would be large enough for the reception.

During the spring before the wedding, Elizabeth and Lucas invited Julia and Greg out to dinner at a seafood restaurant near Colonial Williamsburg. Over drinks before dinner, Elizabeth asked the question that was the reason for them getting together. "Julia, you've seen me through a lot these past few years. You're my best friend. We've told you we're getting married next October. Would you be my maid of honor?"

Julia laughed. Then she cried. She stood and leaned around the table to hug Elizabeth. "Oh, Elizabeth. Of course I will! You're like my little sister. I'm thrilled."

Greg and Lucas sat back watching their women, both of them pleased. They were a contrast, Lucas handsome, smooth, very much a lawyer, Greg heavy set, bearded, his hands thick and calloused from his work.

Lucas rested his hand on Greg's meaty shoulder. "It's great we've all become good friends."

Greg replied, "True. You and I don't have much in common. You in law school, me working as a plumber. But we do hit it off, don't we?"

"Sure. Our girlfriends are best of friends so we are too."

The four of them relaxed, enjoying the comfort they found together. They shared a toast to the future wedding.

A tall man and a woman on the far side of the restaurant paid their bill and prepared to leave, walking by Elizabeth on their way out. The man stopped suddenly and turned. "Liz? Is that you? Are you Liz?" he asked.

Elizabeth looked up at the man. He seemed familiar, but at first she couldn't place him. Tall, receding blond hair trimmed short, his face tanned, but creased by too much sun. Then she caught his eyes. They were intense green. "He has green fairy eyes," she recalled Olivia saying back when Elizabeth and the man were both younger.

"Zach?" she inquired, uncertainly.

"Yes! Liz! How are you?" He leaned down and kissed her on the cheek, an easy casual gesture between old friends.

"Good! Good! How are you?" Elizabeth stood and was immediately aware how tall Zach had become as an adult.

"I'm doing okay," he answered. "This is my girlfriend, Stacy. What are you up to?"

"I'm in grad school down at ODU. I'll be graduating in a few weeks. This is my fiancé, Lucas. And these are our friends, Julia and Greg."

"Nice to meet all of you. Liz and I swam together on a team, years ago in middle school."

"So what are you doing these days, Zach?"

"I'm in insurance. And I'm divorced. Well, almost. It'll be final in a month."

"Oh. Well, it's good to see you, Zach."

"Sure. Maybe we should all get together some time."

"Sure," she said, though they all knew it probably would never happen. "But Lucas and I are both pretty busy with school and with the wedding coming up and all."

"Well, maybe we'll see each other again. Give me a call. Take care, Liz."

Zach and Stacy left. He had asked her to call but hadn't left his number. Her friends turned to Elizabeth.

"Liz?" Lucas asked, laughing.

"Yeah. Liz. That's what people called me when I was in junior high. I had a huge crush on Zach back then. We hung out a bit."

"He's a good-looking guy," Julia said. "Those eyes!"

"Yeah. You should have seen him then. Long hair, and the eyes. And he could really swim. I thought I was in love." Elizabeth laughed.

Lucas took her hand. "Everybody's got a past. For me, it was Tricia. She broke my heart one summer. I thought I'd never find another girl."

"Mine was a girl named Sue," Greg added.

"There was my husband," Julia contributed. "But I'm not going to drag him into this. The bastard!"

"Everybody's got a past," Lucas repeated.

"And we've all got futures!" Elizabeth spoke confidently, optimistically, like most lovers before their wedding.

<p style="text-align:center">~~~~~</p>

Two days before the wedding, Elizabeth and Lucas met with the caterer in Papa's garden to review final details for the reception; how the tables would be set, where the bar would be, when the food would be served. Papa was spending the day shopping in town, running some last-minute errands to prepare for the wedding.

The planning completed, Lucas led the caterer to the driveway. When she was gone, Lucas returned to the garden. Elizabeth sat on the bench next to the armillary, leaning back, her legs stretched out and crossed at the ankles, basking in the cool autumn sunshine. He sat beside her.

"It's so beautiful out here." He put an arm around her shoulder. "The leaves on the trees are just starting to turn colors, but there are still a few flowers blooming in the beds. It's perfect. The best of both summer and autumn."

Elizabeth shifted closer, their bodies merging perfectly, settling into what had become a familiar position. "Yes, that's why I wanted the reception out here," she said. "The caterer will set up a tent over the garden tomorrow just in case. But the day of the wedding is supposed to be sunny and warm."

"Will your fairy friends be here?" Lucas asked. Elizabeth turned to look at him, checking to see if he was serious. His demeanor showed he was. He smiled, but his eyes searched Elizabeth's face for a clue to her thoughts.

"Of course. They're always here." She looked around. "It's odd. I don't see any right now. But they're usually here whenever we come out to the garden together. They follow us around. I don't know why they're giving us space."

"So, they're leaving us alone today? That's good. And with your Papa away for a while, we're totally alone here in this paradise of a garden? What should we do?" He left his questions as an implied suggestion.

Elizabeth smiled. She looked up at Lucas and kissed him. "That's right! Alone at last! Papa won't be back for several hours."

Hurrying to be sure they finished before Papa returned, they began to make love on the thick lawn next to the armillary. Once, quickly, in the moment, Elizabeth looked up into the turning colors of the leaves. She saw no fairies, only a swirling kaleidoscope of autumn colors. Suddenly, it seemed as though she was floating in the air, dizzy and out of touch with the world. Her body tingled, her ears rang. Every molecule of her body exploded, shattering into countless bright fragments and rainbow-colored prisms. It left her shuddering.

Afterward, still breathless as they got dressed, Elizabeth heard Olivia far off in the garden calling to her. "Oh, Elizabeth! I am so happy for you and your boyfriend Lucas. We know that you have given up taking those pills, the ones you take so you won't get pregnant. They do not protect you now. Oh, Elizabeth, when you are married you will bear a baby girl. You have done the human breeding thing with your Lucas here in our garden, and now you are pregnant. This is so wonderful."

Looking around her again, Elizabeth now saw the sparkle of millions of fairy lights twinkling everywhere; in the trees, the shrubs, the flowers, even on the lawn where she and Lucas had lain together. She heard choruses of fairies singing wordless songs, pure, magical fairy music. Olivia called out again. "Oh, Elizabeth, this is how it happened when your mother and father conceived you in your father's house, above the garden. Fairies were a part of their time too, though your parents did not know it. Your baby girl will be special. Just the way you are."

That night, asleep next to Lucas in their apartment, Elizabeth dreamed she was nursing a baby girl.

~~~~~
~~~~~

They decided to keep the wedding party small. They wanted Lucas' oldest brother Matthew to be the best man. Julia, of course, was the maid of honor. Michael and Eve would be groomsman and bridesmaid, and Solomon was to serve as the ring bearer.

The wedding guests filled only a few rows of the vast church. Neither of their families was large. A few friends from the University of Virginia and some from their two years in Williamsburg made up the rest of the guests.

Lucas had never been a man for romance or creativity with what he said. His vow was short, simple, to the point, drawing on his legal view of the world. He spoke quietly so that few except the wedding party and Elizabeth could hear him. "Ever since the moment I first met you, I wanted to marry you. I will honor the vows we take today for the rest of our lives. From this moment forward, I will always honor and cherish you. I love you, Elizabeth."

Elizabeth had turned to her special source of inspiration for her vow; she consulted with Olivia and the Queen. "Today is a fairy-tale day for both of us," she announced in a clear voice, ringing to the back of the church. "This is the kind of moment only be imagined in a dream. It is magical. It is a fantasy. I will love you forever and ever and live with you happily ever after."

For the reception in Papa's garden, a table for the wedding party was set on the terrace. Under a wide white tent, round tables for the wedding guests ringed a small dance floor placed next to the armillary. The musicians set up on the lawn below the terrace to play.

Only Elizabeth could see more clusters of tiny tables for all the fairies, spread out in the garden beyond, floating among the tree branches and high next to the roof of the tent. Her fairy guests far outnumbered the human ones. It appeared the whole fairy town had turned out for her wedding day. Crowds of excited fairies flew about the garden and sat at their tables. They toasted Elizabeth by raising tiny cups filled with what she assumed must be nectar. The Queen, Thomas, Olivia, and several important ministers of the fairy realm sat at the largest table, floating near the top of the tent.

When the music started, a fairy orchestra combining pipes, reeds, chimes and flutes, played along with the small human band. Somehow, the fairy music, which only Elizabeth among the humans could hear, harmonized smoothly with the melodies played by the human band, a perfect counterpoint of merged notes. Following tradition, Elizabeth and Lucas danced the first dance alone. They were as beautiful a wedding couple as the plastic figures that danced on top of their wedding cake. There was a second dance, Elizabeth with her father. He smiled proudly, sweeping his beautiful daughter around the small dance floor, aware of the watching guests and the photographer. Then it was Lucas' turn with his mother, a slower, slightly awkward dance. Finally, the rest of their guests joined the dancing.

Fairies too began dancing throughout the garden, among the late-blooming flowers, along the paths and up among the autumn leaves. The fairies continued dancing late into the evening, long after the humans had stopped. Elizabeth recalled Olivia telling her fairies loved dancing more than any other pastime, even more than their rainy-day games of chance.

The guests began to prepare for Elizabeth and Lucas' departure. The band packed and the caterers quietly began to clean up. Elizabeth heard Olivia whispering to her fairy friends in the garden. "It is time we stop our dancing. We usually dance until dawn. But the humans are leaving the party. Soon Elizabeth will leave with Lucas."

As the guests waved, Elizabeth and Lucas drove away from Papa's house. Elizabeth turned and saw Olivia perched alone on top of the porch light. Her hands were clasped joyously in front of her, and she beamed.

<div align="center">~~~~~</div>

For their wedding night, they stayed in a bed-and-breakfast in Williamsburg, not far from Papa's house. Very late, with dawn beginning to tint the eastern horizon the color of pearl, Elizabeth woke with Olivia's light glowing in the bedroom. Olivia silently floated Elizabeth out of the wide four-post bed, the sheet trailing behind. Elizabeth looked back as they flew out the window and saw Lucas lying on the bed, his bare back partly covered by the rumpled sheet. He slept soundly, snoring quietly.

"There was no time to see you after the wedding," explained Olivia in her melodic chiming voice. "The Queen has come with me to talk to you. I am so rarely able to leave the garden. This is an exciting night for me, first with your wedding and now to be here with you outside our garden."

The bed-and-breakfast had a garden too, smaller than Papa's, but well-tended, the bushes neatly trimmed. Olivia dropped to the center of the garden, settling Elizabeth on the lawn next to her. The Queen stood at the far end of the garden under a dogwood next to a stone birdbath. She was still dressed in her finest gown, the one she wore for the wedding reception, golden, embroidered with patterns in an array of colors, shimmering like a rainbow, sprinkled with jewels. Thomas was there too, still in his wedding finery; a long, dark blue coat and a ruffled white shirt. He wore a wide-brimmed hat with a curling white feather. With the hat, he reminded Elizabeth of the University of Virginia mascot, the Cavalier. Thomas held a staff as he always did, this one tipped with a golden crest. Fairies Elizabeth had never seen before knelt deferentially around Thomas and the Queen. Elizabeth assumed these unfamiliar fairies must be residents of the bed-and-breakfast garden, distant subjects of the Queen's realm.

Olivia flew again, lifting Elizabeth and transporting her to a spot in the garden in front of the Queen. "Good evening, your majesty." Elizabeth gave a formal curtsy, holding out the hem of her short, lacy wedding nightgown between her thumbs and index fingers.

"Good evening, Elizabeth. I wish you all happiness with your marriage to your young man, Lucas."

"Thank you."

Thomas smiled, something he rarely did, and bowed deeply, holding his staff to the side with one hand, sweeping his hat off his head with his other hand, throwing his arm wide. "And might I also congratulate you on your matrimony. May you enjoy many years of bliss together with your Lucas."

"Thank you as well, Thomas."

Olivia grinned. "Oh, Elizabeth! I am so happy for you and Lucas." She flew to her and kissed Elizabeth lightly on the cheek.

The Queen spoke. "We have watched over you for more than twenty-four years now. Ever since you were born, we have been with you. Even when you lived with your family in Richmond and when you went to the University of Virginia, we had fairies there. Now you will be going far away with your Lucas on a special trip."

"Yes. It's our honeymoon. We'll leave in two days and be gone for a week."

Olivia laughed. "A honey moon. What an unusual idea! Both of these are special to fairies. Fairies love honey and the moon is important to us. Our lives follow the cycles of the moon. What a romantic trip a honey moon will be!"

"Enough! No more of your nonsense, Olivia," commanded the Queen, turning impatiently on the tiny fairy. "A honeymoon is a special trip a newly married couple takes. It really has nothing to do with honey. Or the moon."

Olivia looked embarrassed to have been corrected by the Queen in front of Elizabeth. She hung her head, blushed, and seemed to be on the edge of tears. "Of course, Your Majesty." She stepped back deferentially.

"That's okay, Olivia," soothed Elizabeth. "I would have explained it to you. I know some of the things we humans say are a little confusing to fairies."

Olivia smiled again. "They are so often confusing to me. I am embarrassed." She settled cross-legged on the ground next to the Queen.

"Where will you go for the honeymoon?" The Queen ignored poor Olivia.

"Lucas and I are going to Kauai. It's one of the islands of Hawaii. They call it the garden island. It's supposed to be very wild and unspoiled. Most of the island is still not settled by people and has jungles and mountains and waterfalls and beautiful scenery. We plan to go hiking and snorkeling."

"I have heard of this place. I am told there are fairies there. But I have no contact with this place. It is too far away, across a wide ocean. My fairies and I would need to travel many days on a boat to reach this place."

"That's true," confirmed Elizabeth.

"I cannot take care of you there. I cannot protect you or Lucas or your unborn daughter while you are there."

"My unborn daughter? I'm pregnant?"

"Yes, do you not remember Olivia telling you this after you and Lucas did your breeding activity in the garden two days ago?"

"Oh. Yes. But I didn't know for sure."

"Yes. You are pregnant. And I cannot protect you in this island nation of Kauai. Be careful and stay safe."

"I will."

"You must also know this, Elizabeth. When you have returned, if you do not visit my garden often, I cannot watch over you even if you are as close as Richmond. My power diminishes, the connection with you weakens when you are far away for a long time. You remember when you were young and I decreed you would not see us for five years?"

"Yes."

"It will be like that. You and Lucas will move away soon to live near his work in Richmond. My power with you will last for only five years if you do not return to my garden frequently. After that time has passed, I will not be able to help you."

"But when I come back to visit Papa?"

"Yes. Whenever you come back to my garden, we will be here for you. Our power within you will be restored each time you visit your Papa. Be sure to visit often, so we remain connected. You will always have us with you when you come to my garden. But when you have been away for five years, if you do not return to visit, my power will dwindle within you. Now go, Elizabeth. You are strong. You should live happily with your Lucas. Be well."

Elizabeth floated up from the garden supported by Olivia, flying through the wall of the bed-and-breakfast. When she was back in bed, she noted that Lucas was still sleeping, still snoring. She rolled to him, wrapped a cool arm around his warm torso and fell asleep again. She dreamed of an enchanted love.

~~~~~

Elizabeth was home from the honeymoon and back at work. She left work early and stopped to visit Papa on the way to her new townhouse in Richmond. Papa went to the kitchen to prepare iced tea for the two of them. Lucas was still at work in his new job at the statehouse in Richmond, and planning to get home late, so Elizabeth had time to share with Papa.

They sat at the table on the terrace, chatting about the wedding and the honeymoon, gazing into the garden. When the tea was gone, Papa took the empty glasses back inside the house. Elizabeth stood and went into the garden, seeking the peace she always found there. Olivia fluttered up to her.

"How was your honey moon in the nation of Kauai?" Olivia sat on a yellow leaf next to the edge of the white shell walking path. Elizabeth sat across from her on a bench near the statue of the dancing girl. Late autumn chilled the setting afternoon sun.

Elizabeth grinned. "Amazing! And guess what we did?"

"Oh, you know I do not like these guessing games. Most fairies enjoy playing these games. I do not. Let me see. You have asked me a question, but I will answer with a question of my own to help me guess. You did the human breeding activity with Lucas while you traveled?"

"Yes. Of course. Guess what else?"

"You swam with dolphins? Dolphins are sea creatures that are much alike
~~~~~

fairies in many ways. The Queen told me there are many dolphins near this nation of Kauai."

"No, I didn't swim with them, but I saw dolphins near a beach we went to. Guess what else I saw?"

"Oh, I do not like these questions. I always get them wrong. Farm animals. Cows? Pigs? Chickens perhaps?"

"Oh yes. There were lots of chickens walking all over the island. Wild chickens. People said there were also big wild pigs, boars, but we didn't see them. They must have been off in the forests."

"It is my turn to ask a question because I answered correctly. Did you see other wild farm animals? Were there also wild cows and ducks and sheep?"

"No. I don't think so. But there was this big pond near the town. It was called the Menehune Fish Pond. The legend is the Menehune were magical little people who lived in the forest and built the fish pond and walls and other things all over the island. They were sort of like fairies."

"I have heard of these creatures. The Queen told me of them after you said you were going to the nation of Kauai. They have lived in that place for many, many years. They are mostly good, very hard-working little fairies."

"It was a wonderful place to visit. But I have more news. Lucas and I moved to Richmond for his job. It's like what the Queen said would happen when we met on my wedding night. I'll still work at the nursing home here in Williamsburg. I'll drive back and forth every day, living there and working near here."

"Tell me again about this nursing home. What is it?"

"It's a place where older people go to live where they can remain independent, living as much as possible the way they always have. But people like me help them when they need medical care or assistance. It will be a great job for me, full time, now I've graduated. I worked there part time while I was in graduate school. So I'll be nearby every day, but I won't be able to visit here as often as I have been. I might be too busy to visit even as much as I did when I was little."

"Yes. I know of this. The Queen has also told me this will happen."

"Yes. She told me too, on my wedding night in the garden at the bed-and-breakfast. I don't know how she knew everything that was going to happen. It was all just a plan back then. I didn't even have the new job confirmed on the day I got married. And Lucas and I hadn't yet bought the townhouse where we'll live in Richmond."

"The Queen is very wise. She knows of many things before they happen."

"I'll miss you, Olivia. I'll still come see you as often as I can."

Olivia flew up to Elizabeth and snuggled in under her chin, embracing Elizabeth's neck with her tiny arms. "I'll miss you too. Never forget me."

25

ELIZABETH - AGE TWENTY-FIVE

JULIA AND ELIZABETH SAT AT a small, round table on the sidewalk outside a coffee shop near the College of William and Mary. The shop had been a favorite haunt of Elizabeth's while she was in grad school at Old Dominion and Lucas was at William and Mary. She still enjoyed meeting friends there when she could. It was late May, after graduation, and the college students had, for the most part, left Williamsburg. The coffee shop was not busy. A few local business people and a scattering of tourists sat at nearby tables. A warm breeze, scented with new flowers, merged with the smells of coffee and pastries. Elizabeth sipped a large decaf coffee with cream. Julia had a cappuccino. The barista smiled at her as he prepared it and stirred a heart into the foam.

"Flattering, isn't it?" Julia laughed. "Look what he did with the foam."

"You've still got it." Elizabeth giggled as though they were two girls sharing their life's dramas at a cafeteria table in junior high school. "I think that boy likes you."

"Yep. Nice. But he's just a boy, a child, and I'm all set with Greg. How are you and Lucas doing?"

"We're doing well," Elizabeth declared with a satisfied smile. "I never see him, though. I'm always working here at the nursing home and he's spending all his time at the State House or his office up in Richmond. But we're good. He takes time off and meets me at the doctor's office whenever I have my checkups. We have the weekends together, and he's home for dinner most nights. I try to get back early enough to have dinner waiting for him in the evening."

"When's the baby's due date?"

"August 8. The doctor said it's not unusual if first babies are a week or two late, so we'll see."

Julia nodded. "That's common. But check the calendar. See when the moon will be full. I think that has more to do with when babies arrive than anything else. The moon was full when my girls were born, and the maternity unit was packed both times. I had false labor with my first and went in early. There was a new moon and the place was deserted. They sent me home. A couple of weeks later, when I really was ready for the baby to come, the moon was full, and it was so crowded at the hospital they could hardly find a bed for me."

Elizabeth shifted her ample body on her small metal chair, its legs scraping and rocking on the brick sidewalk. She leaned forward, elbows on the tiny table. "I feel like I'm ready now but I still have two months to go. I'm never comfortable, and I'm tired all the time. The drive to work every day from Richmond is really getting to me. I have to pee as soon as I get here in the morning and first thing when I get back to Richmond at night."

"You're going to have the baby in Richmond?"

"Yes. My doctor's up there. And it will be easier for Lucas to be there with me. Mom and Dad, too."

"That's good. But what do you do if you go into labor while you're at work here?"

"I guess I'll get in my car and drive to Richmond."

Julia watched a sparrow hopping beneath their table gathering, crumbs. She looked up at Elizabeth, reached across the table, and took her hand. "No, you won't," she said. "If you go into labor here, you'll give me a call and I'll drive you to Richmond."

<div align="center">~~~~~</div>

Two months later, on a steamy late July afternoon, Julia drove to Richmond with Elizabeth reclining on the back seat.

"I've called Lucas," Elizabeth said between deep breaths following a contraction. She pursed her cheeks, blew air out slowly, and drew in fresh oxygen. "He's going to meet us when we get to the hospital."

"That's good. Now try to relax. We're almost there."

"I'm so sorry, Julia. Dragging you away from work and probably messing up the back seat of your car."

"Not to worry. I put a couple of towels in the car two months ago in case you needed me."

"I'm a mess, and now, so is your car."

"That's okay. Relax."

They drove the rest of the way in silence, punctuated every few minutes by Elizabeth's panting breaths when a contraction took hold. They arrived at the hospital, and Elizabeth was rushed through the emergency doors while Julia parked the car. Julia hurried back into the hospital and went to Maternity.

Now, wearing light blue hospital scrubs, she sat with Elizabeth, wiping her face with a cool wash cloth, and feeding her ice chips from a plastic cup. Elizabeth squeezed Julia's hand whenever she had a contraction.

"Lucas is going to be here, right?" Julia questioned between contractions.

"He said he's on his way," Elizabeth fretted, on the edge of tears. "He said he had a couple of things to wrap up and he'd be right here. There's some big, important piece of legislation they're working on."

"The baby is on its way, too. That's what you need to focus on—your body and your baby. When Lucas gets here, I'll hand you off. But until he does, I'm here for you."

Elizabeth gave in and wept for a moment. "I'm so glad you came, Julia. But what about work? And your girls? And Greg?"

"Stop it. No need to apologize. I'm fine. I made some calls. Greg's with the girls tonight, and my mom picked them up and she'll take care of them before he gets off work. You have a lot of people looking out for you today. And you're more important than my job. I told my boss what's happening, and he gave me the afternoon off."

An hour later, Elizabeth was in the delivery room with Julia at her side. They still hadn't seen Lucas.

"Push! Push!" Nurses and the doctor, all gowned and masked, crowded around Elizabeth. Julia sat beside her. Between her legs, the doctor spoke, intent on his work but maintaining a calm voice. "The head has crowned. One more push and the head will be out," he urged.

As Elizabeth pushed, her eyes squeezed shut, she heard a growing swell of chiming, humming fairy music, tinkling somewhere nearby. Fairy voices sang, their voices harmonizing.

"There's the head," shouted a masked nurse.

"She is beautiful," sang the celestial fairy voices. "She is another one of us, just like her mother."

"Push again, Elizabeth! Give us one more good push for the shoulders."

Elizabeth pushed again and saw the magical sparkle of fairy lights all around her, spangling the ceiling of the delivery room, festoons of brilliance in the corners. She felt sharp pain, then something slipping and wriggling between her spread thighs. Crying mingled with the fairy singing.

"You have a baby daughter!" announced her doctor, placing a slick bundle on Elizabeth's gowned breast.

"She's beautiful!" Elizabeth wept, stroking her daughter's back and head.

"She's perfect," Julia said.

"Hello, little Olivia. Welcome to your new home." Elizabeth cried as she held her daughter, overcome with new love. The incredibly tiny baby girl cried also, clenching her fists, squinting her eyes, and snuggling close to Elizabeth's breast, craving her mother's comforting touch.

"Her name is Olivia?" Julia asked. "Is it a family name?"

Elizabeth smiled serenely, and for a moment she gave in to her fatigue and emotions, still weeping silently. "Yes. It's an old family name," she said.

~~~~~

Later in the evening, Lucas arrived. "The baby came already?" he asked, stating the obvious. "I expected it to take hours."

Julia still sat at Elizabeth's bedside in Maternity. She got up and stood by the window, leaving her chair for Lucas. He took it. The baby slept next to Elizabeth, bundled in soft, white blankets. Lucas leaned down and kissed first Elizabeth and then the baby.

"She couldn't wait," Elizabeth said. "She was born at 6:34 this evening."

"I was still in a meeting. I wish I could have been here."

"So do I. It's one of those 'once in a lifetime' moments. You missed it."
~~~~~

"I'll make sure I won't miss it when you have my next baby."

Julia chuckled quietly for a brief moment, shaking her head. "…when *you* have *my* next baby?" she whispered to herself.

Elizabeth quietly scolded Lucas. "You should have been here. You could have told them what was going on. They would have let you come."

"I tried. We're working on an important bill. And then I had to rush home and take Loki for a walk. At least I was there for the conception." Lucas laughed at his joke for a moment, but then saw Elizabeth wasn't amused. He turned and caught Julia's dark, icy look. He looked back to his wife.

"I'm here now. We decided on a name, right? I know we talked about it. My grandmother's name was Angela. I think she looks like an Angela."

"Her name is Olivia." Elizabeth looked Lucas dead in the eyes as she said it.

"Olivia? Where did you ever get a name like Olivia? I like Angela."

"It's an old family name," interjected Julia, unsmiling.

Lucas turned again and saw Julia's cold face. He looked back at Elizabeth. He suddenly found himself flanked by two grimly serious women calling his new daughter Olivia. He conceded.

"Olivia it is," he said.

Later in the night, Julia left for Williamsburg and her family. Elizabeth's parents, along with Michael and Eve, had come, spent some time with the baby, and gone home. Lucas also went home to prepare for his next day's work. Elizabeth was finally alone with baby Olivia. Outside the window, a full moon shone through tree branches. Elizabeth saw throngs of fairies gathered among the leaves, their lights twinkling. When she wasn't sleeping, awakened in spite of the painkillers by the tearing pain from the birth, Elizabeth and the fairies watched each other through the hospital window. The fairies stayed with her throughout the long night.

Elizabeth left the hospital and settled at home in the townhouse with baby Olivia and Lucas and Loki. For the next few weeks, she remained in Richmond, on leave from her job in Williamsburg. Her family and friends had visited every day during the short time she was in the hospital. At home, the visits were less frequent. She recovered at the townhouse, depending on Lucas for support whenever he wasn't at the statehouse or his office.

Elizabeth's parents doted when they did visit, fussing over their new granddaughter. Her mother obsessed over every detail of being a grandmother. She prepared bottles and rocked baby Olivia for hours. Elizabeth's father held the baby when she was awake, watching her face shift, dodging her erratic arm swings. There was no lack of love between the grandparents and baby Olivia. Elizabeth wondered if, finally, by giving birth to their granddaughter, she had become closer to her parents.

Michael and Eve came twice, bringing Solomon. Solomon was overwhelmed by the experience of having a baby cousin. He gave her a small pink plush bear and was entranced when Olivia fell asleep with it.

Julia visited twice as well, bringing baby clothes, a stuffed plush pig, and a soft picture book for Olivia. She also brought a bottle of wine for Elizabeth and Lucas to share. She stayed briefly, noting Elizabeth was exhausted and falling asleep. She promised to call and did almost daily for the first few weeks.

Lucas made sure to be home with his new family every evening, tending to Elizabeth's every need, doing small tasks to make her comfortable, and taking care of the daily household chores; the dishes, laundry, making beds. He acted partly out of love, but also out of guilt for having missed the birth. He adored his daughter. In the second week, he hired a nurse to help Elizabeth a few hours each day while he was at work, giving Elizabeth a respite from the constant care of the baby. Money was not a problem and nothing could be enough for his new family.

All the visits stopped in the third week. The novelty of Olivia had worn off, even for Elizabeth's family. After eight weeks, Elizabeth was ready to return to work at the nursing home in Williamsburg. Her mother was working temporarily from her home office, and Elizabeth made arrangements to leave Olivia with her when she returned to work.

The day before she started, Lucas drove Elizabeth and Olivia back to Williamsburg. Elizabeth had been able to leave her car at the nursing home eight weeks earlier when Julia drove her to the hospital. Now, Elizabeth picked up her car, and followed Lucas and baby Olivia back to Papa's house.

It was an unbearably hot August day, the sun searing through the humidity. As soon as they arrived, Elizabeth announced, "I want to go for a walk in the garden with Olivia."

"It's too warm out there," Papa urged. "Why don't you wait till it cools off in the evening?"

"No, I want to go out there now. I haven't been in the garden in weeks. You both know it's my favorite place."

Lucas implored her. "It's better if you stay in the air conditioning. It's healthier for both you and Olivia to stay inside."

"No. I need to show Olivia the garden. If it's too warm out there, I won't stay long."

Papa nodded, understanding. Lucas shook his head. "I'll walk Loki while you're out there," he said. He let her go.

With Olivia tucked in the curve of her left arm, Elizabeth opened the door to the terrace and went out. She walked slowly, cautiously through the heat, following the white shell path to the shade deep in the garden. Fairies began to gather, following her, chattering with excitement as they walked and flew behind her. Swarms of dragonflies flashed to the back of the garden, to the palace, carrying the news of Olivia's arrival. When she came to the armillary, Elizabeth sat in the shade of the crepe myrtle and live oak trees on one of the benches with baby Olivia on her lap.

In moments, joyous crowds of fairies clustered, animated and singing. Olivia came running, staying in the shadows beneath the pachysandra. She flew when she was near and landed on Elizabeth's shoulder. Far away, at the palace in the back of the garden, trumpets played a fanfare. The Queen was coming.

"We heard from the fairies in Richmond," Olivia said excitedly. "We have been waiting for you to bring us your baby. What have you named her?"

"Olivia," Elizabeth said with a smile.

"Yes. I am here. But what have you named your baby girl?"

"She is named Olivia."

Slowly comprehending, the fairy Olivia began to giggle, her laughter bubbling like flowing water. "That is my name! Did you name her after me?"

"Of course." Elizabeth smiled serenely.

Olivia slid down Elizabeth's arm and tiptoed across her wrist to the baby. She reached out and touched baby Olivia, floating up to inspect her face, her arms, and her downy white hair. The baby watched the fairy, intrigued, possibly puzzled. It stunned Elizabeth to see that her daughter already seemed to be aware of the fairies.

Olivia the fairy spoke, tinkling notes of excitement. "She is so lovely. She is soft, but she is a little slippery with sweat right now. She smells like perfumed powder and spit. She is wondrous!"

The Queen arrived, trailed by a solemn Thomas. The Queen, too, floated up to Elizabeth and her baby. Thomas remained on the ground at her feet; this was a matter to be dealt with by females, by the Queen and Olivia and Elizabeth, not him.

"So, this is young Olivia," said the Queen, admiringly. She turned for a moment to her fairy ambassador. "She is named after you, Olivia. This is a great honor. It is not at all common for a human even to know we exist, and it is extremely rare for the few humans who know of us to name their child for a fairy."

Olivia bowed her head. "I understand. I am humbled and honored."

The Queen turned back to Elizabeth. "I have been informed that the birth occurred safely for you. There were no complications. And about your little girl Olivia; you must know this. Fairy essence and power are in her too. She has as much fairy magic in her as do you Elizabeth, perhaps even more since she was born to you, a human already possessed with fairy power. She will know of us in her own time. Right now, she is scarcely aware of our being here, except for perhaps a faint perception of her namesake, your fairy friend Olivia. It would be too much for her to comprehend at this early moment in her life. The world of the humans is enough for her to discover today. She will learn more about us when she is older and able to understand."

"That's very good," said Elizabeth. "I expect she'll enjoy your company as much as I do. Lucas and I are spending the night here with baby Olivia. Maybe you can visit us tonight?"

"Perhaps. Now go," commanded The Queen. "It is much too warm in my garden today for fairies to be outside. It is also not healthful for either you or for your baby Olivia. She is like a fairy at this moment in her life with little tolerance for the heat. Go back to your grandfather's house and remain cool. We will watch over you and baby Olivia all day and night while you remain here."

"I will spend tonight in your room, watching our baby Olivia," Olivia said. The Queen nodded her assent. Then she, Thomas, Olivia and the rest of the fairies dispersed, sifting deep into the cool, moist shade of the garden foliage. The palace door banged shut at the back of the garden. Elizabeth stood, settled Olivia on her shoulder, and took her back to the cool air inside the house.

"Too hot?" asked Lucas. "Why were you so eager to get out there in this heat?"

"I was only in the garden a few minutes," Elizabeth protested.

"What was it? You wanted to introduce Olivia to your little fairy friends?" Lucas smiled.

"Yes."

Papa looked from Lucas to Elizabeth. "You told him about the fairies?"

"Yes. He was marrying me. He needed to know. Now let's not talk about it."

Papa nodded and chuckled. "That's right, Lucas. We don't talk about the fairies. But we know about them. They're really there. Don't you doubt it for a minute."

"Oh, I don't!" Lucas laughed. "If Elizabeth believes in her fairies, I do too."

Elizabeth spread a soft blanket on the rug and laid Olivia on it with some toys. They all sat with glasses of cold white wine and watched the baby. She was the center of everyone's attention.

That night, Elizabeth fell asleep in her old room, lying next to Lucas. Olivia the baby girl slept in a portable crib at the foot of the bed. Olivia the fairy curled up and slept on the pillow beside Elizabeth. Elizabeth dreamed of a blissful future with her young family. In her dreams, they would live happily ever after, like in a fairy tale, just like in her wedding vows.

26

ELIZABETH - AGE THIRTY

THE NEXT TWO DAYS WERE frenetic, filled with non-stop activity. Elizabeth and her daughter visited the child-care center and confirmed Livvy's attendance in the fall. They also enrolled her in kindergarten for the coming year. Finally, they made arrangements for Livvy to attend the child-care center's summer program in the few remaining weeks before school began. It eased Elizabeth's mind to have a plan in place to care for Livvy.

The next day, they drove to Richmond and met with the realtor she had called. The agent viewed their townhouse, agreed with Elizabeth on a listing price, and they signed an agreement. Elizabeth sent a terse email to Lucas.

I've listed our townhouse for sale. Livvy and I will live in Williamsburg at Papa's old house. I'm taking the few things I want from the townhouse. You should stop by to pick up anything you want. Whatever is left in the townhouse when the place sells, the realtor will arrange to sell for me.

With business taken care of, Elizabeth and Livvy sorted through their belongings. Papa's house was fully furnished, so the battered, grad-student furniture in the townhouse was not needed. Even Livvy's bedroom furniture could be left behind since she would be staying in Elizabeth's old bedroom at Papa's. They began loading the car with big, black plastic bags and cardboard boxes filled with things to take back to Papa's house. They started by packing their clothes in boxes, some of them folded, some still on the hangers. They made sure to include their swimsuits.

"For mermaid practice," Livvy announced.

Elizabeth carried boxes of a few serving dishes and kitchen items out to the car, filling the trunk. Papa's house was filled with his dishes, so they didn't need much. Livvy gathered her animals, talking with each of them as she brought them, one by one, to the car. She lined them up on the back seat next to her car seat, ready for the ride to Williamsburg. She fastened the seat belt around Oscar Mayer because "he worries about getting hurt in a crash." When the animals were all aboard, the back seat was full of toys.

As they were about to leave, Livvy found a box in the back of a closet. She opened it and gasped. "Mommy, look! This box is full of animals and toys. Look. Here's a bear just like my Hamilton. And oh, Mommy! Here are plastic toys that look like Olivia and Thomas!"

Elizabeth came to her daughter and looked over her shoulder. In the box, along with her old pink plastic fairy castle and other toys, were Jefferson and the two tiny fairy figures Papa had made for her. "Ah yes, those were all mine when I was a little girl," Elizabeth said. "I called my bear Jefferson."

"Yes, but Mommy. Look at the Olivia and Thomas toys."

"Yes. Papa made those for me. See the metal wires coming out of their feet? That was so I could stick them in the garden at Grandma and Grandpa's house when I was your age. See the dirt on their feet? That's from our garden." Elizabeth brushed dark crumbs of dry garden soil off the figures.

"Papa made them for you? He must have known about the fairies. They look like Olivia and Thomas. Except my fairy Olivia has blonde hair like me. This doll has brown hair. She looks like you. But it's Olivia. I can tell." Livvy picked up the two figures, knocking more of the black dirt off their feet.

It's odd, Elizabeth thought. *My fairy Olivia had auburn hair the same color as mine. But my little girl, Livvy, is blonde and her fairy Olivia is blonde.*

"I don't think Papa could really see the fairies," said Elizabeth. "He only knew of them from dreams he had about them."

"He had to know. They look like Olivia and Thomas, don't they Mommy?"

"Yes, they do."

"See. You know what they look like, too. You know all about the fairies, don't you, Mommy."

"Yes. But when you grow up, you'll stop seeing them. I'm a grownup so I don't see them anymore."

"I bet you could still see them if you wanted to."

"No. I think it's enough I remember them. I know what they look like and how they act, so I know how it is for you. It's okay if you see them and talk with them. I liked them when I was your age."

"Can we put these fairies out in the garden when we get home to Papa's house? I think Olivia and Thomas would like that."

"Of course. We'll pick a nice spot where we can see them from the terrace."

That was enough talking for Livvy. She tucked the plastic fairies back in the box with Jefferson, and she and Elizabeth carried the box to the car. They locked the townhouse and left, arriving at Papa's house before dinnertime.

They sat at the table on the terrace above the garden sharing a pizza. After the midnight incident when the owl killed the rabbit on the front lawn, Elizabeth felt better about the safety of the garden. She still didn't want to see the fairies, but she enjoyed the security and the quiet of the familiar paths, the shade of the trees, the beauty of the flowers, the dancing statues of children and the armillary.

Part way through the meal, a tri-colored patchwork, rust, black, and white cat softly climbed the steps from the garden and began checking for dropped food beneath the table. Livvy pulled a bit of cheese off her pizza slice and handed it down to the cat.

"Here, Calico. Have some cheese," she said. The cat nipped a dainty bite of the cheese from her fingers and ate it.

Elizabeth watched, puzzled. Except for birds and the animals that worked for the fairies, she had rarely seen any animals in the garden, and certainly not this cat. Even squirrels hesitated to come over the wall, though the garden was full of oak trees and acorns. She remembered how Papa's cat, Lucifer, had stayed in the house most of the time, afraid to go out into the garden. Now here was this cat, seeming to be at home there, and Livvy seemed to be familiar with it.

"You named the cat Calico? Where did you hear the word calico, Livvy?"

"That's the cat's name. Calico. The fairies named her. Calico probably lives over the wall at a neighbor's house, but the fairies like her so they let her come into the garden. And that's what they named her."

"I didn't think the fairies liked cats. I thought they believed cats can't be trusted. They don't like dogs either."

"The fairies don't like dogs, but they don't really worry about them. Loki doesn't see the fairies when he's in the garden. Olivia told me dogs are too dumb to even know about fairies. Even Loki. But Loki's with Daddy so he won't be coming here anymore. But Calico's okay. The fairies have to watch out for most cats and put spells on them to make them behave. But Calico's different. I think Calico is half fairy. She can't fly, but she might be a magic cat. That's what the Queen told me. So the fairies let her play in the garden. But she can't eat the Queen's mice. She's been told not to."

"Does Olivia like Calico?"

"I don't know. I've never seen Olivia with Calico. Only the Queen and Thomas, and some of the other fairies play with Calico. But I think Olivia must like her too. All the fairies like Calico."

Calico came to Elizabeth, purred, rubbed against her legs, and jumped onto her lap. The cat leaned back, stared into Elizabeth's eyes, and purred again.

"Calico likes you, Mommy. You see her, don't you? But you still say you can't see the other fairies?"

"Yes, I can see Calico." Elizabeth scratched the cat's head and stroked her ears. "She's a cat, not a fairy. But no, I don't see the fairies anymore."

"They're still here, so maybe you will, Mommy. Just like Papa saw them in a dream so he could make the toy statues of Olivia and Thomas."

"Maybe." Elizabeth looked into the garden. Dusk had settled and shadows obscured clarity. She saw no fairies, not even fairy lights. That was good. She didn't need them anymore. She didn't want them, but she was more comfortable now with Livvy enjoying them. It was the way she loved them when she was little. Livvy would outgrow the fairies when she was ready.

Calico jumped off Elizabeth's lap and strolled down the steps onto the garden path. The cat paused, looked back at them, then vanished silently into the boxwoods. Once the cat was gone, Elizabeth and Livvy cleaned up from dinner together, putting the leftover pizza in the refrigerator.

Elizabeth tucked Livvy into her bed in the room above the garden. It had been a long two days with the drives to and from Richmond, all the packing and the changes they had made in their lives.

27

Elizabeth – Age Twenty-five

FOR THE FIRST SIX MONTHS after Olivia was born, Elizabeth's mother watched Olivia each day while Elizabeth was at work. Olivia, now nick-named Livvy, slept or played quietly while Elizabeth's mother worked close by in her home office. After those early months, Elizabeth's mother was assigned to a new project and had to return to her regular routine, working from an office downtown. Elizabeth and Lucas began taking Livvy to a child care center near Lucas' office, dropping her at the center first thing in the morning before heading to their jobs: Lucas at the State House or his law office in Richmond, Elizabeth to the nursing home in Williamsburg. One or the other of them would pick up Livvy late in the day. They shared her care in the evening.

Livvy was a quiet, happy baby and Lucas' and Elizabeth's nights were filled with moments of amazement as they watched Livvy grow and pass her first milestones; the first time she rolled over, the first time she slept through the night, her first solid food. Everything changed when Livvy began teething. She cried each night at bedtime and often woke her parents in the middle of the night with her wailing. She was cranky in the morning, and sometimes fussy when they were with her all day on the weekends.

One evening, while Elizabeth was in the kitchen preparing lamb stew for dinner, Lucas shouted from the living room. "I can't take this anymore! Come get your daughter!"

Elizabeth wiped her hands on a dish towel and went to him. Livvy sat on his lap, crying, her nose running, her face a wet, red, tragic mask.

Lucas held their baby girl at arm's length. "She's pooped, she won't stop crying, she won't take her bottle, and I can't get her to sit still. You take her!"

Elizabeth gave an exasperated sigh, hands on her hips. "I'm fixing our dinner. Why don't you get her changed while I finish?"

"You change her. I had a hard day. I don't need all this when I come home."

Lucas stood, thrust Livvy into Elizabeth's arms, grabbed his coat, and slammed out the front door.

"Lucas!" Elizabeth called after him, but he was gone. Livvy screamed, frightened by the slamming door, and for a moment Elizabeth, too, began to cry. Then Elizabeth calmed herself. There was no point in crying. Lucas was gone, and Livvy needed to be tended to.

Elizabeth went into the second bedroom, now Livvy's room, and changed her. She gave her a fresh bottle and sat with her watching a puppet show on television. When the show ended and Livvy had drained the bottle, she tucked Livvy on her shoulder and returned to the kitchen to check on the stew. It was dark, burnt, and stuck to the pan. She took it off the stove, set it aside, and cared for Livvy, holding her on her lap, watching a new show about wild animals. When Livvy fell asleep, Elizabeth put her in her crib and returned to the kitchen. She salvaged what she could of the stew, reheating it in the microwave, and sat down to eat alone in front of the television.

Lucas came home shortly after ten o'clock, a time when they would usually have already been in bed. He came to Elizabeth quietly, contritely, leaned down and kissed her forehead.

"I'm sorry," he said. "I just snapped. I'm under a lot of pressure at work and then I came home and Livvy's such a handful. I couldn't take it. It won't happen again."

Elizabeth shut off the television and turned to him. "It's okay, I understand," she said, though she didn't understand. "Where did you go?"

"There's a pub down near my office where we sometimes go for lunch. I went there and had a burger and a beer for dinner. I just needed time to calm down. I'm so sorry. I should be here for you and Olivia."

"I need your help with her, Lucas," Elizabeth pleaded. "It's hard for me too, for both of us. I'm driving all the way down to Williamsburg each day and when I get back, Livvy takes all our time. We need to help each other. It's exhausting, but it's the only way."

"I know. I shouldn't have let this happen tonight. I'm sorry. I'll be better about taking care of her. I love our little girl. You should quit the job in Williamsburg and get a new job here. That would fix everything."

"I love you too, Lucas. But I've been at that nursing home ever since I was in grad school. I like it there, and they like the way I work. I've been promoted. It's where I'm supposed to be. I don't mind the drive. I just need your help when I get home."

"I know."

"You were at the pub a long time."

"Yeah. I should have come back after I calmed down and ate dinner. But there was a game on TV and I bumped into some folks from work. One thing led to another, and I lost track of the time."

"I saved a bit of dinner for you. It burned while I was tending to Livvy, but it's not too bad."

"No, thanks. I'm full from the pub. Let's go to bed."

"Yes. Tomorrow's a new day."

"Everything will be better tomorrow," he said. He kissed her and they went to bed. They didn't make love, lying back to back in the dark. Neither of them dreamed.

<div align="center">~~~~~</div>

Things were better for a while once Livvy got past the worst of the teething. Then Lucas' work load increased. He began spending more time at his office or at the state house.

"I know I'm never home to help," he once said. "But I'm making great money now. And the best thing I can do for you and Olivia is to keep the money rolling in. I'm more valuable to the family when I'm at work than when I'm home."

Elizabeth nodded. Her income was adequate, but she appreciated that Lucas' income could provide them with a good life. And she could see how fulfilled he was by his work. She loved her job too, and she loved the people at the nursing home. But she was increasingly aware of the distance growing between her and Lucas.

Early on a Saturday morning, even though it was a gray winter day, Elizabeth turned to Lucas. "Let's go to the Outer Banks, just the three of us, for the weekend and maybe a couple of days next week. We can call our jobs and tell them we need some vacation time. They'll understand. I know it's still winter, but it would do us good to get away and spend time alone together. It'll be quiet, and we can walk on the beach and talk."

"That would be great, but it's such short notice. It's unrealistic. My job isn't like yours. I can't just get up and go take a few days off. I'm backed up at work as it is. I have to be there early on Monday for a meeting. I expect they're counting on you at the nursing home too. Maybe another time?"

"Okay. Let's schedule it for next weekend. I'll talk to the people where I work, and you can too. We need to spend time together as a family."

"Maybe. I'll check this week and see if they can spare me for a few days in a week or so."

<center>~~~~~</center>

The next weekend came and went with them still in Richmond. Several nights later, Lucas was late again. Elizabeth fed Livvy, got her ready for bed, read her a story, and put her down for the night. Then, alone in the quiet townhouse, she prepared and ate her dinner. Desperate for contact with an adult human, she called her parents.

"Elizabeth!" Her mother answered the phone. "How nice of you to call. How are you and Lucas? What's up?"

"Nothing really. Lucas is still at his office working, and I'm here with Livvy. She's gone to bed, so I thought I'd give a call."

"Lucas isn't home yet? It's almost eight. What's going on?"

"Nothing. He gets busy and has to stay late some nights. He'll be home soon. How are you and Dad?"

"We're fine. Busy as always. Elizabeth dear, I worry about you and Lucas. You've told us a few times he's late getting out of work. It seems to distress you he's late and misses dinner. You need to be more supportive of him and his job. His work is important. You need to accept that, and you should be more caring of him, more attentive when he comes home."

"Mom, I'm doing everything I can. I'm taking care of Livvy, and I've prepared meals for Lucas when he gets home. The house is clean and well-

200

kept. What more can I do?"

"Take care of Lucas as well as you take care of Olivia. He's a fine young man and a good husband. Be supportive of his career. You should follow the example your father and I set for you. Your father worked long, hard hours with his job. That enabled him to be very good with his sales. There was a bit of travel and a lot of late nights for him, too. But I supported him and his career."

"I remember," Elizabeth said. "He was never home. I hardly saw him sometimes."

"That's true, but he was very successful. He was salesman of the year twice and he made a lot of money. And I was always there to take care of things at home for him. I have my own career in marketing. I worked from home sometimes when there were projects I could work on when you were a child. As much as I could, I was always there for you and Michael, and for your father."

Elizabeth sighed and gave in to years of frustration. "Mom, you weren't there for me. When you were home, you were always working. And then you were at your job, too. I know you and Dad expected Michael and me to do well in school and to get good jobs after college. We've done that. But what does any of this have to do with Lucas and me? We're struggling right now. I need help."

"Oh, Elizabeth, don't be so hard on your father and me. We did the best we could. And I'm trying to help you now. My advice is that you should be there for Lucas. His career is very important. He's doing significant work at the state house. Now I've got to go. Your father and I were sitting down to a late dinner together. It's something you might consider. Save your dinner till Lucas gets home. Put it aside and heat it up and eat with him when he gets there. That way you two can eat together and he can tell you all about his day."

"I try, Mom. But some nights it's ten o'clock by the time he gets home."

"So wait to eat till ten. You need to be there for him. Have candles and wine with dinner if he gets in late."

They ended the call and Elizabeth sat alone, morose, angry at her mother, angry at Lucas. Things weren't right, and her mother's advice wasn't what she'd needed to hear.

Lucas got home at nine. He kissed Elizabeth and crashed onto a chair in the kitchen.

"I'm beat," he said. "It was a long day."

"Would you like me to heat up your dinner?"

"No. I'm all set. Several of us from work grabbed something downtown and then went back to the office to finish up. I'm not hungry. Let me settle in for a few minutes. Then I'll be ready for bed."

They slept, as had become their nightly habit, on their sides, back-to-back in the bed.

28

Elizabeth – Age Twenty-six

ELIZABETH FELT LIKE SHE HADN'T talked to an adult for weeks, except at work, and there, her conversations were mostly with people decades older than her. At the nursing home, it was all business. A few of the elderly men flirted with her when they could. The rest of the men and most of the women saw her simply as a resource; someone who could entertain them, help them with small tasks, check their blood pressure, tend to other medical needs, and ease their days. The staff at the nursing home liked her, but they saw her only as a co-worker and showed minimal interest in her family and her life outside of work.

When she got home to Richmond each evening, it was all about her daughter, and Livvy, though she loved to talk, couldn't yet pronounce most real words. She was a noisy, demanding little creature. Elizabeth loved Livvy desperately, but she craved adult conversation. She needed to talk with a grownup about her struggles. Lucas was too busy, and though he also loved Livvy, his career mattered most to him.

Elizabeth remembered her call to her mother that one night not so long ago, but their talk had been disturbing. She hadn't heard from her father. She thought about calling Papa. Every day she considered stopping at his house to visit. Instead, she felt compelled to rush home, past his house to get back to Richmond, to Lucas and Livvy each evening after work.

There was an unexpected telephone call one evening after dinner.

"Hi, it's Julia," a distant voice said. "Just checking in. I haven't seen you since Olivia was born. How are my girls?"

"One of us is fine. The other one of us can't deal with life because her little baby girl is teething."

"Her teeth will grow in. She'll become a sweetheart again. At least till puberty sets in. That's where both of mine are right now. It'll never be easy being a mother."

Elizabeth sat, one hand holding the phone, her forehead cradled in the other hand. Livvy was asleep down the hall. Lucas was still out. She gave in, sighed and began to unburden to her best friend. "I feel like I'm always running," she said, "like a hamster on a wheel in a cage. I'm dropping Livvy off in the morning. Then I'm dashing to Williamsburg for work. I'm on the go all day at work, and then I dash home again to pick up Livvy and fix dinner for Lucas."

"How's he doing?"

"Fine, I guess. I never see him, what with my schedule and his. We're good."

"Do you want to get together sometime for a drink after work? A couple of days each week my girls stay late at school. One's a cheerleader now and the other's in band. Greg doesn't get home till after six most nights. What time do you get off work?"

"Four. But like I said, I have to get back for Livvy and Lucas. It's an hour drive."

"Well, okay. Let's keep in touch. Maybe we can work something out on a weekend."

"Maybe. Let's try to do that. I'd love to see you and just talk."

They talked a few minutes more. But Livvy cried from her bedroom, and Elizabeth had to end her talk with Julia. After the call ended, Elizabeth sensed Julia was still there for her. But there was no time for them to get together. She wondered if she would ever see her again. She felt very much alone with her baby girl. Where was Lucas? When would he come home?

29
Elizabeth - Age Thirty

LIVVY CAME TO BREAKFAST WEARING her swimming suit. "We're going to the pool," she announced to her mother. "Right after breakfast. We couldn't go a few days ago because we didn't have our swimming suits. And we couldn't go yesterday because we had to pack everything in Richmond. So we're going today. And you can teach me to swim so I can be a mermaid."

"Of course," Elizabeth replied. "Today I'll teach you how to swim."

With breakfast done and the kitchen clean, Elizabeth drove to the pool, taking the route through the neighborhood she had always followed on her bicycle when she was on the swim team with Zach. She and Livvy set their towels on white plastic chairs by a table in the shade and went to the shallow end of the pool. Livvy splashed down the stairs, waded straight in and began frantic dog paddling, struggling, her head craned tensely back, her eyes squinted closed, lips pursed. Elizabeth caught her and began to instruct, holding her little girl, her arms beneath Livvy's torso. Livvy lay cradled in the water, her head still held tense, anxious and scared but trusting her mother.

"Take a deep breath, Livvy. Then put your face in the water and look down. Blow bubbles out and then lift and turn your head for another breath. Watch. Like this." Elizabeth set Livvy standing in shallow water. Then she demonstrated, leaning down, putting her face in the water and blowing bubbles. Livvy copied her, her face breaking the surface, her eyes squeezed shut, practicing blowing bubbles. Elizabeth scooped up Livvy again, holding her prone in the water.

"Now you do it. Blow bubbles! That's good, Livvy. Now reach with your arms. Swing them forward and reach, then pull. Now kick. Kick hard! That's wonderful!" She released Livvy and watched her swim away, splashing and kicking fiercely. Elizabeth waded along beside her, catching her when Livvy ran out of breath. Thrashing, they were suddenly at the far edge of the pool.

Livvy stood next to the pool wall, wiping water out of her eyes, grinning and panting.

"Mommy! I swam all the way across the pool and only stopped once. I'm really swimming!"

Within half an hour, Livvy was able to swim from one side of the pool to the other without stopping. When Livvy got tired and they came out of the water, one of the lifeguards, a young woman with a silky tan, approached them.

"We still have three weeks of swimming lessons left this summer. Would you like your daughter to join the class?" she asked Elizabeth.

"Mommy! Can I? Please?"

"No, Honey Bunny. We've got you signed up at the child care center starting on Monday when I have to go back to work. Maybe next summer. But we can come to the pool every afternoon when I get home from work. You can practice swimming with me."

"The class is half over. If money's a problem, we could let her in the class for free."

"Money's not a problem. Time is. I have to be at work every day, and I'm a single parent."

The lifeguard nodded and walked away.

Elizabeth reflected on what she had just said. "I'm a single parent." It was frightening to admit it, but it released a lot of her anxiety to put it out there. It felt like as much of a positive step forward as had clearing her belongings out of the Richmond townhouse.

Livvy sat on her towel on the pool deck. For a moment, she began to sulk, moody about not being able to take swimming lessons. Then she rolled to her belly and peered through the chain-link fence surrounding the pool.

Beyond the fence was a landscaped border next to a mulched flower bed. Elizabeth watched her, noting how intently Livvy stared into the greenery. Then, she too, looked into the hedge and the garden trying to see what had attracted Livvy's attention. She saw only boxwood and flowers.

"I know it's hot," Livvy said, talking to the flowers. "That's why I went swimming."

There was a pause, Livvy listening. Elizabeth heard nothing. Then Livvy spoke again. "The water-nymphs don't like the pool because of the chemicals? So that's why they only live in the river and the ponds?"

Elizabeth looked again but still saw nothing but the garden. "Who are you talking to?"

"There are fairies who live in this garden. They say they're an outpost of the Queen's realm. And they say it's too hot to be outside. They came to see me, but they usually stay inside their houses during the day when it's hot like this."

"Do you know what 'realm' means?" Elizabeth asked.

"I think it's like the Queen's kingdom. But these fairies live here, not in the garden at Papa's house."

"Can you see their houses?"

"Most of them. They have houses made of mud and pebbles for all year. But in the summer they live inside mushrooms because mushrooms are cooler than mud houses."

"Livvy, I know the fairies don't want you talking about them. Didn't Olivia or the Queen or Thomas tell you not to say anything about them?"

"Yes, they all said that. They want me to keep them a secret. But you already know about them, so if I say something to you, you already know the secret."

"I don't think they want you talking about them even to me. They told me not to talk about them with Papa, even though he knew. Besides, if someone heard you, they would start to wonder. You need to keep quiet about them. Remember when Julia heard you and didn't understand?"

"Okay, but I wasn't really telling you about them. I was just talking with them and you heard me."

"Yes, but what if someone else heard you talking to the flowers? What would they think?"

Elizabeth's telephone rang, ending the conversation. She pulled the phone out of her bag and looked at it. It was Lucas.

"Hello?" she answered.

"Hi. Where are you?"

"Back in Williamsburg. We're at the pool in Papa's neighborhood."

"Oh. Nice and cool, I expect. I'm at work at the state house right now. At least it's air conditioned."

"Yes. It's nice here in the shade, and Livvy's learning to swim."

"Oh. Good. Listen, I'm coming down there tonight. I've got the last couple of papers for you to sign for the divorce settlement. And you left me a message you're thinking of selling our townhouse? We need to talk about that."

"Okay. We're staying at Papa's house. Come by after dinner. Maybe you can tuck Livvy in her new bed."

"Yeah. Maybe. I'll come by a bit after seven. Keep her up till then so I can see her."

<div style="text-align:center">~~~~~</div>

It was long past eight and Livvy was already in bed. Elizabeth sat beside her, reading her a story about bears. The doorbell rang. Elizabeth put the book beside Livvy on the bed and went downstairs to let Lucas in.

"Hi," he said, resting a hand on her arm for a moment. "Where's Livvy?"

"Upstairs. She's just now going to bed."

"I told you to keep her up," he said as he pounded up the stairs.

Elizabeth called after him. "You said you'd be here at seven. I couldn't keep her up while we waited for you. She was tired, and we didn't know how late you would be."

Lucas said nothing, but looked back from the top of the stairs, shaking his head. Elizabeth blew out a slow breath. She needed to stay calm. She went to the kitchen and prepared a cup of tea.

Lucas sat on the edge of Livvy's bed, leaned down and kissed her. "How are you, princess?"

"I'm good. I can swim. Mommy taught me how today."

"That's good. Do you like living here?"

"Yes. I'm going to go to kindergarten here when school starts. And there's a place for me after school while Mommy's at work too."

"That's nice. Do you think you'll like living here more than living in our old house in Richmond? You have friends there."

"I want to move here. I'll make friends here too."

Lucas noticed her stuffed animals lined up on a table next to the window. Oscar Mayer sat on the window sill.

"What's with all your animals? Why are they all over there? Don't you want them on your bed?"

"They're not all over there. Hamilton's here in bed with me."

"Yes, but all the others are there on the table. And the pig is on the window sill."

"Yes. They like to sit there because they can look out the window. And Oscar Mayer thinks he's their leader, so that's why he's on the window sill right by the window. They like to sit there so they can watch the fair—I mean, so they can watch the birds."

Lucas paused. He noticed how Livvy became quiet when she almost said "fairies". He saw her shrink down in her bed now, avoiding his eyes. "Did you almost say fairies? Do you believe there are fairies out there in the garden?"

"No. I said birds. They like to watch the birds."

"Listen, Olivia. Your Mommy believes fairies live in the garden. She's crazy like that sometimes. There are no fairies out there. Don't believe her if she tells you about them."

"Okay, Daddy. That's right. There aren't any fairies."

"No. I'm serious. I don't want you getting crazy ideas about fairies like Mommy."

"Mommy's not crazy. Mommy knows." Livvy said defiantly, becoming stubborn, crossing her arms as she sat on the bed, frowning at her daddy.

"Okay, Livvy. I love you. Sleep tight." He kissed her, moved her book to the table beside Oscar Mayer and the other animals, turned off her light, closed her door, and went back downstairs.

Elizabeth sat with her cup of tea by the window.

"What have you been telling our daughter? She's up there with all her stuffed animals looking out the window watching for fairies."

"Did she tell you that?"

"She almost did. Then she said they were watching the birds."

"Okay. So her animals are watching the birds."

"Look. It's enough you believe in fairies. It's that kind of craziness that has us here getting divorced. Don't steer my daughter into believing that nonsense."

Elizabeth's voice rose. Anger from the past months took charge. "What do you mean that's why we're getting divorced? You think we're getting divorced because I used to believe in fairies? No, we're getting divorced because you had an affair and walked out on us."

"Keep Samantha out of this. We're getting divorced because you're always down here. You're never home. And it's crazy you see fairies everywhere. I can't be married to all that."

Elizabeth lashed back, striving to keep her voice low again, controlled so she wouldn't wake Livvy. Even so, she couldn't stop her anger from showing. "I was home every night for you. I'm the one raising Livvy, not you. And I had dinner ready for you every night. But you were always late coming home, and then it turns out you were spending every evening with your girlfriend."

"Sure. Believe what you want to believe. Just sign these last two papers and we'll be done. It'll be final in a few months." He handed two sets of legal papers to her. They were marked with fluorescent sticky notes where she should sign. She complied.

"Now, about our townhouse. Yes, I left it to you in the settlement. I thought you and Livvy would live there and I could see Livvy whenever I wanted to because she would still be in Richmond. But now you want to sell it and move down here to Williamsburg? It should be the other way. You should quit your job here, sell this house, and move to Richmond. You can get a new job there and raise my daughter in Richmond."

"I work here. It doesn't make sense for me to live in Richmond when my job is here. And I own this house. Papa left it to me when he died."

"I don't care about this house. You should get a job in Richmond. I've told you that. The townhouse is in both our names. I'll need to sign off *if* you sell it."

"Yes, both our names are listed as owners. But you left it to me in the settlement. *When* I sell it, I expect you to sign," Elizabeth said, stressing the "when." "You don't want the word to get out you're shaking down your ex-wife for money in a divorce or anything. It wouldn't be good for your political career or your boss's."

"What about all our furniture and belongings? What do you plan to do with all our stuff?"

"You've still got your key? Go take what you want. I've got most of what's mine, the things I want. Livvy has her things too. The realtor will help me get rid of the rest, whatever's left. Maybe I'll sell some of it, once we have a buyer for the townhouse.

"Don't do this, Elizabeth."

"Does your state rep even know you're getting a divorce because you had an affair?"

"I don't think he knew I was married at first. I told him we were married when Livvy was born. And now he knows we're divorced. Or at least he knows we're getting divorced. He may not know it's not final yet. He doesn't need to. He knows Samantha and I are together. That's all he needs to know."

"So, when I sell the townhouse… and the realtor says it should sell quickly… You will sign off on the sale." It was a command. Elizabeth watched Lucas coldly, waiting for his response.

"I could sue for custody," he stated. "No court would ever let you keep my daughter if they knew how crazy you are with your fairies and all."

"Oh, come on, Lucas. You've got the dog. Isn't Loki enough? You want to be responsible for Livvy? For getting her ready in the morning? For picking her up at five every afternoon? For preparing all her meals and tending to her when she's sick? You've never done any of that."

"It's wrong you have her and now you're moving her here to Williamsburg and my job is at the statehouse. If I take you to court, you'll lose. I'm a lawyer, and I know my way around these things. You don't. Stay in Richmond so I can visit Livvy whenever I want to or I'll take you to court."

"So, sue me for custody. I'll hire a lawyer. And you're not really a lawyer anyway. You got the job with the state rep and dropped out of law school. You never took the bar exam."

"I know my way around a courtroom, and I've got friends who are the best child custody lawyers. You'll lose."

"Fine. Do whatever you want. Livvy and I are staying here and she's starting school next week."

For the moment, Lucas gave up. He shook his head, gathered the papers, and stood. "I don't know why you have to make everything so difficult," he said. "See you in court." He walked to the front door and let himself out.

Elizabeth sat alone in her chair by the window with her tea. Outside it was dusk. She could see two sparrows, nothing but shadows in the growing darkness, hopping on the terrace, flying in the branches, restless, but settling in for the night. She saw no fairies. Only Calico the cat, sitting under a boxwood, calmly contemplating the sparrows but not stalking them. Calico looked up at Elizabeth. Then the cat stood, turned, and walked slowly away, ambling sinuously toward the back of the garden.

Elizabeth took a sip of tea and relaxed. Livvy had almost told Lucas about the fairies, but she caught herself and told him her animals were bird watching. That was what Lucas had told her. Livvy was becoming cautious when talking about the fairies. *That's good*, Elizabeth reflected. She knew the people who were aware of her belief in fairies must have believed she was crazy all these years. Derek, Lucas, her family, maybe even Julia and Papa thought she was insane. She didn't want people to think Livvy was crazy too.

30

Elizabeth – Age Thirty

AFTER LUCAS LEFT, ELIZABETH TOOK a deep breath and sought to find calmness. As she sat by the window finishing her tea, Elizabeth felt very alone. She reflected on the infrequent calls she had gotten from her parents over the past few months while her marriage fell apart. She understood they were disappointed in her for letting the marriage fail, for losing Lucas, for putting an end to their dreams for her.

In the final days before Papa died, she had made it a point to see him at least once a week; quick drop-in visits before hustling off to Richmond to pick up Livvy. Papa always called her in the evening if it was more than a few days between her visits. He had understood what was happening with Lucas. He had tried to warn her, and had offered support, but little advice. His own marriage never experienced that kind of trouble, and he didn't know what to say to her. Mostly he just listened when Elizabeth vented her frustration, her concerns and fears, her loneliness.

Michael had called too, but his calls were casual, cordial, brother-sister calls. He talked with zeal about antiques and about the small successes of the business. He shared news about Eve and their life together. He bragged about the childhood exploits of Solomon. He never asked about Lucas, and Elizabeth didn't want to confide to her brother how they were struggling.

After hearing how good things were for Michael, it would have felt like she was admitting failure.

There had been the disturbing advice from Elizabeth's mother several years ago, telling her to put everything aside to aid Lucas' career. Since the night of that call, her mother hadn't called, and they never spoke about her struggles when they saw each other.

Her father never called. With Papa gone, she felt like she was completely alone dealing with the collapse of her life. At least she had reconnected with Julia. They had rarely been able to get together in the past years because of their schedules. Maybe, now she was living in Williamsburg…

Feeling abandoned in the quiet house, Elizabeth stood and took her empty cup into the kitchen, putting it in the sink. As she was about to head upstairs to bed her telephone rang. She was stunned to see it was her father. She sat back in her chair, hoping it wasn't more bad news. His last call had been to tell her Papa was in the hospital.

"Hi, it's Dad. How are you doing?"

"I'm fine. I'm at Papa's house with Livvy. Lucas dropped by tonight, but he left a while ago. He came to have me sign the last divorce papers."

"Oh. I guess I should say I'm sorry, but maybe that's good news. Divorce is never a pleasant thing to go through, but maybe things are coming to a close with him. Good riddance, I say. You're in Williamsburg? I heard you put the townhouse up for sale."

Elizabeth sat stunned. This was the first time her father had shown anger at Lucas, or any emotion for that matter. He always maintained his composure, particularly with family issues. She took a deep breath and replied.

"Yes, the townhouse is for sale. Livvy and I are going to live here. I've got Livvy all set with kindergarten and childcare. How did you hear I put the townhouse on the market?"

"Lucas called this afternoon. He'd found out you were going to sell the townhouse, and he wanted me to talk you out of it."

"Yeah, he asked me not to sell it when he was here. He said it'll make it harder for him to see Livvy if we live here. He's threatening to take me to court to get custody of Livvy. What do you think I should do?"

Dad's voice edged louder, his anger showing. "He had an affair. You two are getting divorced. The settlement gives you the townhouse. Lucas is a son of a bitch. Sell the townhouse. Screw him.”

Elizabeth was shocked again. She had never heard her father swear, but she agreed with him. She paused, considering her words. “I'm not screwing him over with this. I just have a good place to live here. And this is where I want to be, here at Papa's, near my job, so the townhouse will be sold.”

“You'll get the money from the sale?”

“Yes, but it won't be a lot after I pay off the mortgage. I'm okay anyway. I have Papa's house and I'll have alimony and child support from Lucas, and I have a good job. I can support myself.”

As she said it, Elizabeth could feel herself turning another corner, seeing a clear path ahead. Yes, she was a single parent, and that would be a challenge. But she was in control of her life, and she had Livvy. Things were going to be all right.

“That's good. You'll be fine. I wish I'd known what a son of a bitch Lucas was before you married him. We all thought he was such a fine man, so successful, a lawyer, such a good husband. I thought he was great, back when you two were first together. I mean, your mother and I didn't approve of you two living together, but we knew you were in love. Now that we know what he did to you…”

Elizabeth broke down, giving in to everything she had been feeling in the past months as the divorce proceeded. She gasped and began to sob. “Oh Daddy. It's so hard sometimes when I try to talk to him. I don't know…” Her voice faded.

Dad lifted her up as best he could from miles away. “I've got you. We'll get through all this together”

Dad's voice trailed off, and they sat in silence for a moment. Elizabeth picked up the conversation. “What do I do if he actually sues me for custody?”

“You fight back. You go to court. He had an affair and you're getting a divorce. You're Livvy's mother. He won't win. Do you want me to find a lawyer for you?”

“No. Thanks, Dad. I think I can get one. But I'll let you know if I'm having trouble with that.”

“I can help pay for the lawyer if you'd like. Hang in there, Elizabeth. Your mom and I are behind you all the way with this. We'll do anything you need us to do. How's my little Olivia?”

"She's amazing. She likes the idea of living here. And I taught her to swim today which, she told me, is important because she wants to grow up to be a mermaid."

Dad laughed. "It's never too early to have a career goal. And you have her signed up for kindergarten in Williamsburg?"

"Yes. That's all set. We brought all her animals and most of our clothes yesterday. I figure one more car-load of things and we'll be settled in."

"That's good. Do you need anything from your mom or me?"

"No." Elizabeth smiled. "It's very good knowing you offered. I'll call if I think of anything."

"You do that. I know I haven't always been there for you. But Dad's passing and his funeral made me think about a lot of things. I'm rethinking my priorities. We all have to help each other over the rough spots."

"That we do."

"Okay, little girl. Your daddy loves you. Good night."

"I love you too, Daddy."

<div style="text-align:center">~~~~~</div>

Elizabeth ended the call and started up the stairs. Livvy sat on the top step, her bare feet sticking out beneath her nightgown, her bony knees pulled up in front of her under the thin, flowered fabric.

"I couldn't sleep, Mommy. I heard you and Daddy arguing. I hate him. I was going to come downstairs and yell at him, but you took care of that. Then I was going to come down to talk to you after Daddy left. I don't want you to be sad, Mommy. And I heard you on the telephone. Who were you talking to?"

"It was Granddaddy. He called to tell me he would help us if we needed anything."

"You see. Everybody will help you if you're sad about Papa dying, or about Daddy leaving us. There's Grandma and Granddaddy, and Uncle Michael and Auntie Eve. And there's your friend Julia. And you've got me. I can make you happy, Mommy."

"Oh, Honey Bunny. You make me very happy." Elizabeth sat on the top step next to Livvy and hugged her. "I want to make sure you're not sad."

"I'm not sad. I miss Papa. And Loki. And I was missing Daddy till I heard him being mean to you tonight. Now I hate him."

216

"Don't say that. Daddy made some mistakes, but he's still your Daddy."

"I know. But he shouldn't have said those things to you tonight. He was mean to you."

"Yes. But I'm okay now. We're going to be okay, Livvy." Elizabeth tried to appear sure of herself to make Livvy feel at ease. But the possibility of a custody fight loomed in her mind.

"Yes, we will." Livvy was adamant. "I told you. Everyone will make things good for us."

"Everyone wasn't always there for me. They are now."

"Why don't you ask the fairies for help?" asked Livvy.

"Oh, sweetheart. The fairies helped me a lot when I was little, like you. I'm a grownup now. I can handle things without them. And they can't stop bad things from happening."

"Like when Daddy left us and when Papa died?"

"Exactly."

"But when those bad things happen, they can help you feel better about everything."

"You're a smart little girl. Now go back to bed so you can get some sleep and be ready for the pool tomorrow."

They stood and turned down the hall. There was a quick hug, Elizabeth lifting Livvy off the floor, leaving her feet dangling.

Livvy squealed. "Mommy, don't drop me! I can't fly."

Elizabeth eased her back to the floor, leaned down, and hugged her again. "Go back to bed, Honey Bunny. Tomorrow you'll be a mermaid."

Livvy ran into her room and jumped onto the bed. Elizabeth followed and tucked her in.

"Good night, Mommy. Sweet dreams."

"Good night, Honey Bunny. I love you."

Elizabeth blew her a kiss and went into her room across the hall. She paused for a moment at the window, pushing the curtain aside, surveying the lawn. It was still. There was no sign of the owl. She slid into the bed and slept deeply, without dreaming.

~~~~~

Six months passed. The divorce was final, and the townhouse had sold weeks ago. Lucas agreed to be responsible for child support payments. All
~~~~~

that remained to be settled was the matter of child custody. Meetings with their lawyers and social services failed to resolve the questions of physical and legal custody of Livvy. Lucas was adamant he wanted full custody. Elizabeth fought back. At last, their case went to court for a final resolution.

The courtroom in Richmond might have been a warm, inviting place with its blond maple wood paneling, and cream-colored walls. Tall windows gave it an airy ambiance. But the room was the home of blind justice. Life-changing decisions were made here every day. The comfort that could have been found here had been traded for a harsh austerity.

Elizabeth sat with Edward Smith, her lawyer, a bland, middle-aged man with a dark crew cut and wire-rimmed glasses. He had been recommended to her by the managers at her nursing home as a solid, no-nonsense lawyer with a hardened approach to family law and custody cases in spite of his mild appearance. So far in the proceedings, he had shown himself to be relentless in his preparation and dogged in his handling of the discussions with Lucas and his lawyer.

Lucas sat across the aisle from Elizabeth with his lawyer, a man Lucas referred to only as Jim, a perfectly groomed young man with a finely tailored, blue pin-striped suit and a wide silk tie. Gold cufflinks set in stiff, white French cuffs peeked out from his jacket sleeves. Everything about Lucas' lawyer spoke of money. Elizabeth wondered how much Lucas was paying him. Edward Smith had promised to accommodate her with a reasonable rate because she was a newly divorced single parent. His fee was something she could manage with the proceeds from the sale of the townhouse.

Behind them, Elizabeth's parents sat unsmiling, holding hands. Livvy was settled for the day at her old childcare center across town in Richmond. Michael and Eve sat next to Mom and Dad, uncomfortable in the formal setting of the court room. Julia was with them, watching the judge, seeking a sign, any hint of what his decision might be. All of them were deeply invested in his decision about Elizabeth's custody of Livvy and had given statements to the judge.

Lucas' parents, though they lived in Richmond, were not there. Lucas had told them he and Jim had the case under control so they weren't needed. He promised to let them know as soon as the judge ruled in his favor. Samantha was also not there. She had provided a written deposition in support of Lucas' case, but she had not come to testify in person. Lucas and his lawyer had explained to the judge that her time in the state house was more important.

The judge surveyed the room over the top of his glasses, allowing his silence to convey the importance of the words he was about to deliver. Finally, he picked up his notes, tapped the stack of paper briefly on end on his desk, and began.

"I see that the divorce itself is settled. Custody is the only issue open for debate at this time. I have heard from both sides in this case. Decisions in these matters are never easy. I always consider the welfare of the child first and, whatever I decide, there is always a degree of loss for both parents."

The judge paused, took a deep breath and continued. "Custody can be awarded to whichever parent is deemed best able to care for the child. Elizabeth, you and your family, your friend and others from where you work and from the childcare center have all made clear statements of your fitness to raise Olivia in a good home, to provide for her, to care for her and to love her. Lucas, you too, have shown that you can give Olivia a good home. You have made the case that your income is greater than Elizabeth's and so you are able to offer Olivia things Elizabeth can't, even though you have agreed to pay child support to Elizabeth if she is awarded custody."

The judge checked his notes and, for a brief moment, gave in to a small smile. "You have also stated that Elizabeth is an unfit mother because she is crazy and believes in fairies. Aside from this assertion about Elizabeth's belief in fairies, I have every reason to believe that either of you can raise Olivia well. You both have steady jobs with sufficient incomes, and it would appear you can both provide good homes in which to raise Olivia."

The judge consulted his notes again, no longer smiling. He looked from Elizabeth to Lucas, again letting his silence fill the courtroom. Then he began. "Before I make my decision, I would like to review again what both sides have testified regarding the custody of Olivia. I will ask both of you, Elizabeth and Lucas, a few final clarifying questions. Let me begin with Elizabeth."

"Elizabeth, you have stated that you have been assuming most of the duties of raising Olivia. Is that correct?"

"Yes, your honor."

"Was this the case before the divorce proceedings began?"

"Yes, it was."

"What sorts of things have you been doing for Olivia?"

"I prepare her breakfast every morning and pack a lunch for her to have at the childcare center. When I lived in Richmond, I dropped her off before I went to my job in Williamsburg. Now I drop her at her new school in Williamsburg, near where I live and work. I pick her up in the late afternoon. We're expected to pick her up before five every day. Then I fix her dinner and read with her and play with her. Finally, I make sure she's bathed and I put her to bed."

The judge turned to Lucas. "How about you? Have you been involved with these same things with Olivia?"

"Of course. Before Elizabeth took her away to Williamsburg. I would say we both helped get her ready in the morning, preparing her breakfast and lunch. I picked her up from day care whenever I could and I helped with her at night as well. We were both involved with those obligations."

The judge checked his notes again, allowing more silence to dominate the room. "Lucas, about these 'obligations' as you called them. Would you say you and Elizabeth have shared them equally?"

"As much as I'm able to be, I'm involved with Olivia. My work demands a bit of time, but I think we split the duty about fifty-fifty. Now because she's moved, I've lost even that contact with Olivia."

"Really. The director of the childcare center here in Richmond testified that Elizabeth dropped Olivia off most mornings"

"That could be the case. I have to get in early some days."

"She also testified she couldn't remember a time when you picked Olivia up at the end of the day."

"Again, Livvy's supposed to be picked up by five. They charge extra if we get there after six. And you know how things go in court. We're both lawyers." Lucas hesitated, hoping he could strike up some camaraderie, some understanding with the judge. "The job doesn't end at five o'clock every day, right?"

"Right. But are you now changing your statement and saying that Elizabeth was primarily responsible for getting Olivia to and from childcare each day?"

"Yes. But we both shared the other duties. Raising a child is a partnership."

"What is Olivia's favorite lunch?"

"Peanut butter and jelly sandwiches."

"And her favorite dinner?"

"I think she likes spaghetti. Or a hamburger."

The judge turned to Elizabeth. "How about you, Elizabeth? I've seen your testimony and that of your family, your friends, your co-workers at the nursing home and the director of the childcare center. What can you add to my understanding of this case that isn't in their testimony? Do you have the primary responsibility for dropping off and picking up Olivia at child care?"

"Yes, sir. I did when we were still living in Richmond and I do now in Williamsburg at her kindergarten and new childcare center."

"And you say you prepare most of her meals?"

"Yes. Probably all of them. Maybe Lucas prepared her a pop tart for breakfast once in a while. But most meals I made for her."

"What's her favorite lunch?"

"Lucas might have been right about that one. Peanut butter and jelly, but some days she'll ask for just peanut butter. And she likes an apple juice box and gold fish crackers as snacks."

"What about dinner?"

"Chicken nuggets. Macaroni and cheese, but it's got to be out of the blue box, not home-made. She'll eat spaghetti when she has to, but the sauce can't have meat in it. And pizza, of course. Sausage and black olives on top. She'll pull off any pepperoni slices if she finds them."

"Very good. I won't decide custody based on who knows Olivia's tastes in food. But this is helpful information for me to have. One or two more questions for you, Lucas. Tell me about the day Olivia was born. Elizabeth, her friends and family have testified you were not present at Olivia's birth. Is that accurate?"

"Yes, your honor. I was involved in some very important legislative work that day. Honestly, Elizabeth was responsible for my absence. She went into labor a couple of weeks earlier than I had planned."

"Really? She's to blame because she went into labor early?"

"Yes."

"Was she induced?"

"No. It just happened that way."

"Did she call you to tell you she was in labor and going to the hospital?"

"Yes, but I assumed it would take a while for her to give birth. I had something important I was dealing with at work."

"So you left her alone to give birth to your daughter?"

"She had a friend with her. She was okay."

The judge shook his head and consulted his notes again.

"Let me ask about two other matters. Lucas, you state that Elizabeth is an unfit mother because she is insane and believes her grandfather's garden is, as you put it, 'infested with fairies.' Is that correct?"

"Yes, your honor. That's why she's moved to Williamsburg, so she can spread that craziness to our daughter. I can't let her have custody and live there and do that to Livvy."

"Elizabeth, do you believe the garden at your house in Williamsburg is infested with fairies?"

"Not now, your honor. I did believe in fairies when I was younger, when I was a child growing up and visiting there. It took me years to stop believing in them. Livvy believes in them now, but that's how it is with little girls."

"But you don't believe in them now? That's not why you and Olivia moved there?"

"No. My job is in Williamsburg, and I inherited the house when my grandfather passed away. I live there for free and have a short drive to work."

"Lucas, you attest that Elizabeth is insane. Has a psychiatrist or any medical or psychological professional seen her and validated your assertion?"

"No, your honor, but I'm sure they would agree with me."

The judge interrupted, his voice a trace louder. "Is there any other reason for me to believe Elizabeth lacks the mental or psychological capacity to raise Olivia aside from your statement?"

Lucas looked at the table and shook his head. Quietly he said, "No."

The judge turned to Elizabeth. "Now Elizabeth, you have said that the reason for the divorce is Lucas' infidelity, his adultery with a woman from his work."

"Yes, sir. Samantha. I've never met her but he left us for her."

"Lucas, unlike your assertion of Elizabeth's belief in fairies, adultery is something that bears heavily on my decision in these cases. You left Elizabeth for Samantha?"

"I have many reasons for leaving Elizabeth. The fairy thing might not matter to you, but it's important to me."

"About Samantha, were you involved with her before you filed for divorce?"

"Yes, but that's because of Elizabeth."

"Elizabeth is the reason you got involved with Samantha?" The judge leaned back in his tall chair, eyebrows raised.

"Yes, your honor."

"Are you living with Samantha now?"

"Yes. Elizabeth sold the townhouse. I needed somewhere to live."

"Were you living with Samantha before the townhouse was sold?"

"Yes."

"Were you spending time with her and still going home most nights to Elizabeth and Olivia before the divorce proceedings began?"

"Yes."

"Has Olivia met Samantha?"

"No."

"Is Samantha here with you today to support you in this case?"

"No, your honor. She had to work on some important legislation at the state house. She needed to attend to that today. She would have been here if she could have been."

Lucas' lawyer leaned to Lucas and whispered, his voice an audible hiss. "I told you she needed to be here."

The judged ignored the interruption and continued. "That legislation is more important than the matter of custody for Olivia?"

"No. Of course not, but it is critical we take care of business for our boss who is a representative in the state house. One of us had to stay there to work with him today."

The judge nodded, his face stern. He paused, looking at Lucas over the top of his glasses, assessing. Then he continued. "Would Olivia live with you and Samantha if you are awarded custody?"

"Yes, your honor."

"You have a private bedroom for her?"

"Yes. It's our home office right now, but we could convert it when I get custody. We could buy bedroom furniture and maybe establish a home office somewhere else."

"Who will be responsible for picking up Olivia from school or child care?"

"Me, or maybe Samantha, or maybe Elizabeth's parents could do it if Samantha and I were both busy."

The judge looked across the room to Elizabeth's parents. He saw their looks of shock and disbelief. It was obvious this was the first they knew they would be responsible for picking up Livvy if Lucas was awarded custody.

"I think I've heard enough to make my decision," the judge said. He tapped his papers again, gathering them into a tidy sheaf.

"I still believe the two of you should have been able to work out custody amicably. I believe you both should be able to sort things out together without my involvement regarding visitation after I award custody, but I will intervene if necessary. I see little need to take that step unless either of you is unwilling to accept the decision I am about to give. Lucas, simply stating that your wife is insane with no proof of a medical diagnosis is not enough for me to decide to take Olivia away from Elizabeth. It seems harmless enough that, when she was younger, Elizabeth believed in fairies. And frankly, you have failed to offer psychological testimony to substantiate your claim that she is insane. It is disturbing to me that you would bring such an accusation before me in order to gain sole custody of your little girl.

"I am also disturbed that you really haven't a good plan in place to provide a home for Olivia. You want to bring her home with you and Samantha, but Olivia has never met Samantha and you don't have a bedroom available for her. Honestly, I don't see much evidence that you have been greatly involved in Olivia's life from the day she was born up to today.

"Olivia appears to be a happy child who loves being with her mother. Elizabeth has been the primary caregiver for Olivia ever since she was born. Olivia is settled into the house in Williamsburg with Elizabeth and attending kindergarten there.

"Therefore, I rule that Olivia should remain primarily with Elizabeth who will have sole legal and physical custody. Elizabeth, you will continue to be responsible for her regular, day-to-day upbringing, schooling and healthcare. Lucas, you are her biological father and you do have an interest in Olivia. You are already in agreement from the divorce settlement to provide child support payments to Elizabeth. My decision is that you will have one weekend visitation rights each month with Olivia as well as holiday visitation rights. If you two are unable to agree on a visitation plan, I will have an arbitrator work out the details of visitation, about when and where it will take place. Olivia can stay with Lucas on whatever weekend you both agree to. You will also need to work out a plan for additional visitation days over holidays. Otherwise, Elizabeth has sole physical and legal custody."

The judge closed the case, banged his gavel once, stood and left the room. It was done. Elizabeth sagged in her chair and wept with relief for a moment. Then she hugged first her father, then Julia, Michael and Eve, and finally, her mother. Mr. Smith, her lawyer, stood aside, smiling with satisfaction. Elizabeth hugged him too. "Thank you for everything you did for me. I'm so grateful," she said.

"Not at all. It was an obvious decision for the judge to make. I mean, really? Your ex-husband's approach was to claim you're insane because you believed in fairies? That's all he had? He's a lawyer, and he really thought that was a realistic courtroom strategy?" Smith laughed.

Across the courtroom Lucas and his lawyer talked quietly, gathering their papers, sliding them into Jim's briefcase. As they were leaving, Lucas paused and spoke briefly to Elizabeth. "I'll have to be okay with one weekend a month, I guess. I can spoil my little girl once a month, and you'll have to manage all the other daily details of raising her by yourself."

"So, it'll be no different than it's been over the past years," Elizabeth replied. "I've done fine raising Livvy with little help from you so far, and now the court says I can continue to do it without having to worry about where you are or when you're coming home. Livvy and I will be okay."

Then Lucas was gone, pulled out the door and down the hall by his lawyer.

Elizabeth's father came to her and rested his hands gently on her shoulders. "You've done well," he said, looking into her eyes. "Is there anything you need from me? Can I help with your legal expenses?"

Smith intervened. "I believe we're all set. She's paid me everything she owes up to today. And I won't charge her much for today. It's been a pleasure to work with her and help her through this."

"I've got it, Dad," Elizabeth said. "It feels good to take care of everything on my own. But thank you again for offering."

31

THE DREAM: ELIZABETH – AGE THIRTY

WITH THE DIVORCE MONTHS BEHIND them, Elizabeth and Livvy had established a routine at their home in Williamsburg. Livvy was happily settled in her kindergarten. Elizabeth's days were consistently comfortable, divided between her work and her dedication to caring for Livvy.

One night in springtime, Elizabeth dreamed she was flying, floating above Papa's garden. It took no effort, though she was unassisted this time by Olivia or any of the fairies. She drifted like a falling leaf, pushed by warm, springtime breezes, settling slowly onto the lush grass next to the armillary. She looked around. There were no fairies. She was alone.

Calico appeared, emerging from beneath a hedge, looking straight at Elizabeth and ambling nearer with her rolling cat gait. Standing in front of Elizabeth, Calico meowed. Elizabeth understood what Calico was saying; the same way she had comprehended the tinkling voices of the fairies in the days when she could still see them.

"Get on my back, Elizabeth. I will take you where you should go."

Elizabeth found she had become small. Calico was now, to her, the same size as a small horse. Though Elizabeth had never ridden a horse, she discovered she knew how to mount and ride the cat. Wrapping her arms around Calico's neck, she swung her leg up and rolled, straddling the cat's back, holding onto the patchwork orange, black, and white fur.

The cat walked with no haste along the garden paths toward the back wall of the garden. Elizabeth noticed that wherever she remembered there being buildings in the old fairy town, the cat sidestepped; detouring around buildings Elizabeth could no longer see. When they were near the back of the garden, the place where Elizabeth remembered there were fortified walls and the palace courtyard, Calico stopped, settled to the ground and half rolled to one side so that Elizabeth was compelled to dismount.

"The Queen and Thomas will see you now," the cat meowed. Calico moved aside and lay down, Sphinx-like, tucking her paws beneath her. She purred. Elizabeth waited.

The Queen and Thomas materialized, their shapes forming from a silent flash of light. The Queen was dressed in one of her most luminous, shining gowns. Her crown seemed to be made of white light. She held a glowing scepter. Thomas was at her side, serious as always, dressed in his finest blue coat, the plumed hat and his long red cloak. He held a golden staff.

The Queen spoke. "Elizabeth, welcome again to my garden. When you no longer felt the need to see us, I took your awareness of us from you. I understood that you became angry with all of us; with me, with Thomas and even with your special fairy friend Olivia. This behavior is something I had expected from you for many years. You believed we should have warned you or we could have saved you from some of the terrible things that happened. That is not what I or any of the fairies do. Humans do what they will. We can advise you, and we can do things to assist you in times of trouble. But we cannot stop other humans from doing what they choose to do."

Elizabeth shook her head. She wanted to argue with the Queen, to tell her she should have warned her about Lucas or made Lucas not love Samantha. The Queen could have made sure Papa got to the hospital sooner and maybe the doctors would have saved him. Elizabeth could think of so many ways the Queen might have helped. But instead of shouting, screaming, venting her anger at the Queen, Elizabeth waited to hear what else the Queen had to say.

The Queen continued. "From these past months you have learned much about yourself. You now know that you are able to meet challenges such as these without our help. You are able to take care of yourself. You can make sound decisions about your life without our guidance. You can even take Lucas to court and win without our involvement. At last, you are becoming able to live on your own, capable to choose the right things to do the way adult humans should. You will not always decide to do the best things, but it is now possible for you to build a new life without your fairy friends."

"I agree," said Elizabeth. A trace of leftover anger still edged into her tone. "I like making my own decisions. I don't need you and I don't want you in my life anymore. But I still believe you could have done something to prevent a lot of the awful things that happened recently."

"Everything must die, Elizabeth. It was your Papa's time. I do not control the passage of a human's life. As for Lucas? He did things he should not have done. We could not stop him from doing those things and neither could you. It would have been wrong for Olivia to tell you what Lucas was doing, even though I knew and I shared that information with Olivia. You had to discover for yourself what he was doing, just as you had to discern the activities of that boy Zach so long ago, just as you had to manage the actions of your other boyfriend Derek with only a little assistance from my fairies."

"Where is Olivia?" Elizabeth looked all around the garden, past the Queen and Thomas. "Where are all the other fairies?"

Elizabeth saw none of the other fairies, none of the buildings, not even the Queen's palace or the town. She couldn't see Olivia anywhere. She was alone in the garden with only the Queen, Thomas, and Calico, the cat.

"Olivia is near. She will always be near to you, even if you do not see her. You and she share a rare bond. But you do not need her help anymore, so you will no longer see her. For you to see her, or any of my fairies, would be to tempt you with falling back into your ways of dependence on her, and on me and Thomas, and the rest of the fairies."

"Oh. I will miss her. Tell her for me that I miss her."

"She knows. She misses you as well."

Elizabeth smiled. "So what about my little girl, Livvy?"

"Livvy is starting to become a part of my kingdom, just as you did when you were her age. It is enough for us to look after her without having to be concerned also with your well-being. One human is plenty for us to tend to. Livvy is a lovely little girl, and Olivia is already becoming a fine fairy friend of hers. We will be with Livvy as long as she needs us, just as we were with you as long as you were in need."

"Will she be involved with you and your kingdom as many years as I was?"

"That is unlikely. I can see some things that will happen in the future. I knew that you and Lucas would live for a time in Richmond, and I knew what he would do to you. I knew what was coming for your Papa. But I can only see a small way into the future. I cannot tell if Livvy will remain involved with the fairies as many years as it took for you to become independent. It will most likely take less time."

"What will become of me?"

"I should not tell you everything I know. If you knew what is to come, you would act in a different way than you would naturally. I cannot let that happen. I will tell you only this: you will discover something important in your Papa's house this coming morning. It will require you to do some work, but it will be a special token, a gift to you from your Papa and from me, and Olivia, and the rest of the fairies. You will share this gift with Livvy and she will enjoy it with you."

"How will I know when I discover this special token? Papa's house is big, and there are so many things in the house, so many places to look."

"You will not have to look for it," the Queen answered enigmatically. "It will become apparent. You will know when you find it."

The Queen paused and took a brief breath. "Second, perhaps I should not say this, but there is more. You have lived through a difficult, perhaps a painful time in your life. But when you are ready, you will find happiness and live a life with Livvy filled with joy and love. You will also share your life and love with a new, good man. Be patient, Elizabeth. Things will become better for you and Olivia."

"How will I know this good man when I meet him?"

"You will know. As surely as you will know when you find the treasure in the house tomorrow, you will know when you meet this man."

Elizabeth thought about everything the Queen had said. "Is there anything else you can tell me? Are there any other secrets? Is there anything more you can do for me, Your Highness?"

"No, Elizabeth. I know many secrets. They are not for you to know. We have done what we needed to do for you. Remember always that you are special. Goodbye, Elizabeth."

As suddenly as they had appeared, the Queen and Thomas blinked out. With a small flare, they were gone.

Calico sidled up to Elizabeth, purring. She meowed, "Go Elizabeth. You need your rest. Go back to the house and go to bed. I have made sure the terrace door was left unlocked for you. Morning is coming, and you will have much work to do when the sun rises."

Elizabeth discovered she was her usual size again, standing at the back of the garden, next to the ivy-covered wall. She looked around, but there were no fairies, no animals or birds or fireflies. Calico, too, had vanished. Alone, Elizabeth walked back to the terrace, let herself in the house, locked the door again, and went to bed. She was asleep in a second.

~~~~~

At sunrise, Elizabeth was woken by Livvy, standing beside the bed, giggling. "Mommy! Guess what?"

"I don't know Livvy, what?"

"Guess, Mommy. Don't you like guessing games? The fairies play guessing games all the time." Livvy pulled herself onto the bed, hugging, snug against Elizabeth.

"Oh, I don't know Livvy. I'm not good at guessing. It's Saturday, and the pool is open for the first time since last summer. You want to go back to the pool today for more mermaid practice?"

"Yes, I want to go for mermaid practice. But you know what?"

Elizabeth sighed with exasperation at her excited little daughter. "I don't know, Livvy. What?"

"Calico was waiting at the door to the garden when I got up. So I let her in. She's come upstairs to tell you good morning."

"Oh Livvy! You shouldn't have let her in. Calico is an outdoor cat who stays in the garden."

"Well, she's in now."

Calico jumped onto the bed, purring. The bed was suddenly crowded with Elizabeth, Livvy, and the cat.

Elizabeth pushed the blankets aside, tumbling Livvy and Calico in the covers. She pulled herself past them and stood. The cat sprang off the bed and ran from the room. Looking back at Elizabeth and Livvy, Calico trotted
~~~~~

down the stairs.

"I think she wants us to feed her," Livvy said.

"We don't have any cat food," Elizabeth answered as she and Livvy chased down the stairs after the cat.

But Calico wasn't looking for food. She dodged through the kitchen to the door to the garage, nudged it open with a paw, and looked again at Elizabeth and Livvy. The cat meowed and went down the short set of stairs into the garage. Elizabeth and Livvy followed. Elizabeth turned on the garage lights and watched as Calico jumped up on Papa's old, cluttered work bench. There, among the tools, the shavings of wood and plastic, old rags and paint brushes was a small plastic figure. Calico purred again, a sound almost like a satisfied growl. She rested a paw on the tiny statue.

Elizabeth picked it up, noticing that it, like the old fairy figures of Thomas and Olivia, had a wire sticking out of one foot. It was almost ready to be placed in the garden with the first two statues, but this figure was plain, bare white. Though it was unpainted white polymer, it was unmistakably a figure of the Queen.

Livvy recognized it. "Mommy! It's the Queen! And it belongs with the Olivia and Thomas toys we found in the box at our old house. We can put it in the garden when we put Olivia and Thomas out there. But the Queen's statue is white plastic. Her dress should be many colors. That's what the Queen wears. And her hair should be golden."

Calico meowed. Next to the cat were small jars of paint in assorted colors, including gold. There was also a selection of narrow paint brushes. Calico purred and walked across the worktable, jostling the paint jars.

Elizabeth laughed. "Livvy, look. We have paint and brushes right here. I think we can paint the Queen. We can make her look just the way she really does."

"I knew it Mommy. You *do* know what the Queen looks like. I want you to paint her because you're better at doing things like that. You won't make a mess. And I'll watch to make sure you get it right."

"When should we paint the Queen?" asked Elizabeth.

"Right after breakfast. That way her paint can dry while we go to the pool. This afternoon we can put all the fairies in the garden where they belong."

Calico jumped off the table and trotted up the steps to the kitchen. Her morning duty was finished. She meowed once and ran to the French doors, eager to return to her garden. Livvy ran after her and opened the door to let Calico out.

"I have to open the door for her," said Livvy. "She's not a fairy so she can't fly through the wall."

Elizabeth smiled. "She might not be a fairy, but she does appear to know everything about the fairies."

Calico faded into the greenery of the garden. She knew there was still Livvy for her to consider, but Calico's work with Elizabeth was finally complete.

Acknowledgements

Writing *The Fairy Garden* was fun! It was also a difficult book to write, requiring years of research. What made it so difficult was my decision to write the story from the perspective and in the voice of a girl/woman. My belief is that women go through more dramatic changes than men as they mature, both physically and emotionally. I wanted to display those changes in this story. I needed to get inside the mind of a woman. I needed Elizabeth to speak in the voice of a girl and a woman. And, of course I am a man. That's where the years of research came in.

I am indebted to countless women and girls I have known and observed at different stages of their lives. After all that research I still won't claim to understand women, but I did the best I could to speak from their viewpoint for Elizabeth at different ages. If the story seems unrealistic from a female viewpoint, forgive me. I tried.

The fairies were easier to research. I was able to consult with my young granddaughter Ginny who was five years old when I was writing this book. She knows about fairies, she told me during one long discussion. She knows about the Queen. She knows where the fairies live and agrees with me that they favor gardens. She knows about their houses and about the Queen's castle. She is aware of the Queen's soldiers. Much of the fairy lore in this story is based on her social anthropological studies. We discussed fairies many times, and she stayed after me to finish "her fairy book." The authenticity of the fairy lifestyle is due in great part to what Ginny taught me about fairies.

All books depend on the work of many more people than the author. First, I am always thankful to have an editor and publisher like Narielle Living of Blue Fortune Enterprises. Without her support and encouragement, none of my writing would reach anyone other than a few close friends. I also want to thank her staff, her proofreader Ashley Smith and her graphic designer Wesley Miller.

Before I submitted my manuscript to Narielle, I shared it with two groups of fellow writers here in Williamsburg. Their discussions of this book have been an adventure, rarely sticking to literary, structural or grammatical suggestions. I would listen in amazement as they held what seemed at times to be theological debates about the real or imagined existence of fairies. These sometimes heated debates rarely changed any of their grownup minds. It seems that people either accept the reality of fairies, tolerate others' beliefs, or flatly reject the existence of fairies. They would try to draw me in, asking, "What do you believe? Are fairies real?" I never responded with a firm answer, usually saying things like, "Does it appear that I do from the story?"

These two critique group members include Tim Holland, Cynthia Fridgen, Cindy Freeman, Elizabeth Brown, Mary Shipko, Bob Archibald and Susan Williamson in one group and Dave Pistorese, Caterina Novelliere, Sharon Dillon, Barbara McLennan, Chris Pascale and Pattie Procopi in the other.

I also value the suggestions from my beta readers who reviewed the book in its entirety. They are Ellen Smith and Jocelyn Callister. The final touches to assure that it all worked together are due to them.

Do I believe in fairies? You read my story—what do you think?

About the Author

Peter Stipe enjoyed a long career that included time in education as well as work in Human Resource Development and Training for a variety of businesses. He has a Bachelor's degree in History from Boston University and a Master's in Education from Tufts. In addition to his writing, Peter is an accomplished artist, working with photography and in watercolor. He has photographs on display at the On The Hill Gallery in Yorktown, Virginia.

A competitive long distance runner for many years, Peter has completed numerous marathons with six finishes in the top fifty places in the Boston Marathon and participation in the 1972 U.S. Olympic Trials. A New Englander for most of his life, he now lives and writes in Williamsburg, Virginia.

www.ingramcontent.com/pod-product-compliance
Lightning Source LLC
Chambersburg PA
CBHW070930190726

48292CB00004B/1184